# From the
# Shadows

# MCKENZIE BURNS

This is a work of fiction. Names, characters, places, and incidents either are the product of the author's imagination or used fictitiously. Any resemblance to real persons, living or dead, events, or locales is purely coincidental.

Text copyright © 2021 by McKenzie Burns

All rights reserved. No part of this publication may be reproduced, distributed, or transmitted in any form or by any means, including photocopying, recording, or other electronic or mechanical methods, without prior written permission of the author, except in the case of brief quotations embodied in critical reviews and certain other noncommercial uses permitted by copyright law.

Cover image copyright © Ervin Usman via Getty Images
Licensed on August 18, 2020
www.ervinusman.co.uk

Cover design copyright © McKenzie Burns

Edited by: Ashley Taylor Clark
Proofread by: Camilla McCann and Emma O'Connell

ISBN: 9798670063845

*For anyone who has ever felt left behind.
Know that there is always light after the darkness.*

# From the Shadows

# CHAPTER 1

THE SWORD CAME crashing down upon Valora's weapon with more force than she had anticipated.

She stumbled back one, two steps before regaining her balance and righting her own weapon in retaliation. She didn't enjoy using man-made weapons, per se, but Valora knew she required one in this particular fight.

Her opponent was quick and took Valora's small misstep to her advantage, charging forwards and swinging her sword with all the skill Valora expected. The strength behind it was another thing. Such strength didn't often find itself in such a small body.

Ducking low wasn't really an option when fighting short opponents, so Valora feinted left, then dodged right, making sure to stay on the nondominant side of her rival. She, on the other hand, favored her right side, and was able to use her new position to her advantage, striking her foe with a series of swift strikes.

The girl blocked them all, leaving Valora no option. Time was running out and she'd yet to even come close to a victory. Something needed to happen, and it needed to happen soon. All eyes were on her….

Valora knew the moment they obeyed her—her abilities. The shadows crept along the ground, pulled from sources around her, conjured from anywhere the sunlight couldn't reach, to join with those she'd created of her own will. Valora wrapped them around herself and her opponent, and what should have been complete darkness was not. Not for her. The other girl trapped in the shadows, though, could not say the same.

Valora watched with clarity through the pitch black now surrounding them as her opponent's head turned every which way, trying to find an escape from the trap she found herself enclosed within. Valora smiled.

All it took was one quick jab of her sword's pommel into her opponent's stomach, only hard enough to knock the wind out of her. Then Valora hooked her leg behind the other girl's ankle and pulled.

Her opponent landed on the ground with a satisfying *thump*.

Valora released her hold on the shadows as soon as she knew the tip of her sword's blade was pointed at the girl's neck. It took the sunlight seeping back in for Valora's opponent to realize she'd been bested.

"Victory. Valora."

Valora drew her weapon back and replaced it in the sheath at her hip. A few of the watching warriors clapped, though less enthusiastically than when Valora had first started being used as a demonstrative sparrer.

"Shocker," Juno said from her spot on the ground, a faint smile upon her lips.

Valora returned it as she extended her hand to help her friend from the ground.

"Sorry," she said. "I didn't want to use the shadows."

"Why?" Juno questioned. "If I'd been paired off with any other person with abilities, they wouldn't have held back using them. You shouldn't either."

"I just feel bad since—"

"Since I don't have any special powers?" Juno chuckled. "Val, it's fine. I knew what I signed up for when I joined the ranks."

"Yeah, that you'd become the weakest link."

Valora and Juno turned to where the rest of their friends approached. The comment had come from Myrcella. Her twin, Mona, laughed alongside her while Aurelia ambled behind, a small curl at the corner of her lips.

"For the record," Juno defended with a playful smile, "Val's the only one with *real* powers."

"Whatever," Mona dismissed. "Elementals always get all the credit. Everyone knows the Master favors them."

Valora, knowing better, kept her mouth shut. The twins liked to use their abilities to their advantage anyways. They'd sneak into her mind and see what she was too much of a coward to say out loud.

Aurelia moved from the back of the group to stand beside Juno, a hand placed on her shorter friend's shoulder.

"Good job out there, Val," she said.

Valora gave her friend a soft smile. "Thanks, Aurelia."

"Very good, indeed, Miss Bellemore."

The girls stopped their chatter and stood at attention as the

Master approached them, clad in all black, his hands clasped behind his back. A grey goatee surrounded lips that offered Valora a small, proud smile. She returned it, seeing a bit of truth in Mona's recent comment within it. She'd been improving for months, going from shy recruit to confident warrior, and Valora knew the Master had noticed.

Not that Valora could call herself—or any of her friends, for that matter—recruits anymore. They'd been a part of the Norlynian warrior ranks for just about three years, spending their days training for the off-chance that Norlyn might actually be attacked. So far, Valora hadn't seen any action outside of training. She was still a tad too young at eighteen to join the patrolling ranks that kept the village safe from internal crime. At twenty-one she'd come of age and be able to join the patrol.

Or, better yet, she'd be able to become the Master's apprentice. All training warriors knew he was searching for someone to replace his last prospect—a fire bender who'd just…gone missing. There at training one day and gone the next.

It wasn't abnormal for people in Norlyn to go missing. In fact, it happened all the time, and Valora knew why.

She'd never understood the people that willingly ventured into the forest. Everyone in Norlyn had been told the haunting tales of what happened to those who got too close, let alone those who dared to enter the dense expanse of trees. Valora, for one, knew she never wanted to go anywhere near it, out of pure superstitious fright.

"Do you mind if I have a word, Valora?" the Master asked when he stopped before the girls.

Valora nodded eagerly, caught a bit off guard at the request, before her eyes fell on her friends.

"I'll, um, catch up with you guys later?"

The twins smirked, their eyes settled sidelong on the Master. Aurelia nodded, while Juno offered the only true smile out of the bunch.

"We'll meet you at the tavern?" she suggested. "I could eat an entire cow right now."

Valora nodded as the girls walked away, leaving her alone with the Master. He waited until they'd traveled a far enough distance away before speaking.

"Your friends do enjoy using their gifts, don't they?"

Since Juno and Aurelia had both been born without abilities, Valora knew the Master referred to Mona and Myrcella.

"I thought they couldn't use their powers on you?"

The Master chuckled. "A small blessing, being born a negator, but it does not stop people from trying. I feel the small nag of their abilities trying to press in. Like a fly that won't stop buzzing around your head."

Valora smiled. "That sounds awful."

"It could be worse," the Master said. He dropped his hands to his sides. "I could be one of your recent opponents. You've been improving, Miss Bellemore."

Valora blushed. "Thank you, sir."

"Do you feel your abilities growing stronger?"

Valora shrugged, paused, then nodded. She had, and as much had been evident in her recent sparring during training. For so long she'd paired herself up with her friends, knowing she could succeed against them if she tried hard enough. Only recently had the Master started forcing Valora against different opponents—everyone from strongmen to speedsters to various types of benders, like her. They'd been challenges, but, as shown that afternoon, Valora's powers had strengthened, as well as her knowledge of how to use them. Juno, though Valora hated to say so being her friend, had been the easiest opponent in weeks.

"There was a correct answer to that question, Miss Bellemore." The Master grinned, his head tilted. "I'm glad to see you've passed my pop quiz."

"They're stronger, sir, but they aren't perfect." And Valora needed them to be perfect if she ever wished to become the Master's apprentice—then one day the Master.

The Master's brows rose. "Did you beat the time I set for you today, Miss Bellemore?"

"Yes, sir, but—"

"Have you beaten the time even when facing off against opponents with abilities?" he interjected, as if he'd suddenly developed telepathy like Mona and Myrcella. Valora nodded. "Then you don't need perfect, Miss Bellemore. All that heeds a warrior's success is victory, no matter the enemy. Unfortunately, losing in our line of work is often synonymous with dying."

A shiver crawled up Valora's spine. She knew the path she had chosen when she'd joined the warrior ranks, but she'd also done so knowing Norlyn hadn't seen conflict from any neighboring villages since the peace treaty had been signed decades before she'd been born.

The only true enemies anyone from Norlyn faced were other Norlynians.

"I just wanted to make sure you knew I've noticed your improvement," the Master finished. He nodded in the direction Valora's friends had just disappeared. "You deserve a bit of fun after that display today. Go join your friends and have a nice weekend."

"So, what did the Master want with you?" Mona asked before taking a massive bite out of her burger.

"Did he shower you with praise, per usual?" Myrcella added.

Valora shrugged. She knew the twins already knew what the Master had told her. She'd been thinking about it when she entered the tavern, and spotted her friends when their heads turned in her direction. The immediate attention clued Valora in on them slipping into her head. They could sometimes use their abilities with subtlety, but not often.

On the non-mind-reading side of things, Aurelia and Juno lifted their eyes from their food to Valora, indicating their interest in the answer to the question. A shrug wasn't an acceptable answer, no matter how badly Valora wanted it to be. It didn't feel right talking about what the Master had told her, not only because he'd told her in private—likely meaning he wanted it to stay that way—but because it felt like bragging. Her friends trained just as hard as her—okay, *almost* as hard as her; Valora knew her friends sometimes slacked off during training—and she had seen their improvements as well. Juno and Aurelia had improved in physical combat, and Mona and Myrcella had learned to use their telepathy to anticipate an opponent's next move.

Those developments should have been worthy of praise from the Master, too, but he'd chosen to specifically focus his attention on Valora.

"He just…complimented me," Valora said, trying to keep things as vague as possible. "Said he noticed my advancements.

Nothing super important or exciting."

"That sounds important and exciting to me," Aurelia commented before she lifted her spoon to slurp some soup into her mouth, her eyes never leaving Valora's.

Valora offered a one-shoulder shrug in response, turning her attention to the drink one of her friends must have ordered for her before she arrived.

Her eyes lifted again when she heard another pointed slurp.

"Think it's enough to be named his apprentice?" Aurelia continued.

"The Master hasn't shown any interest in another apprentice in nearly three years," Mona said. "You think it's going to be Val? No offense, Val."

Of course, Valora took much offense but kept her mouth shut.

"I don't see why it couldn't be," Aurelia countered. "You said it yourself, Mona, that elementals get the favor."

"I'm not, technically, an elemental," Valora argued.

Aurelia rolled her eyes. "Fine—*benders* get all the favor."

Valora's eyes fell back to her drink, and she lifted it to take a sip, saving her from needing to respond.

"Wouldn't it be fun if someone without abilities got named his apprentice?" Juno offered. "That would be a first, and it might encourage more Norlynians without powers to join the ranks."

"You sick of being the weak link?" Myrcella teased, and Juno threw a pea from her slice of pot pie at the telepath.

"Might I remind you that Aurelia and I are on even ground with the whole no-abilities thing?" Juno defended herself.

"Yeah, fair," Myrcella agreed, and her twin nodded along.

"But at least Aurelia almost beat Val when they got paired up."

"Aurelia almost beat me too," Mona added. Her eyes slid to the mentioned party. "It's almost like you could read *my* mind or something, A. You guessed every single move."

"Wouldn't that be nice?" Aurelia mused before she took another slurp of her soup.

Valora was about to respond when she noticed something catch Mona's eye—or mind. Sometimes the twins would know someone was approaching before they even appeared just by picking up on their thoughts.

"Brother incoming," Mona warned. "Three, two…."

Valora heard the doors to the tavern open before she managed to turn around. Had it been her and Myrcella's brother, Mona might have groaned before announcing who was coming. That was the only reason why Valora turned and knew exactly who had entered the tavern.

Her little brother, Bo, scanned the room in search of his sister before his eyes finally landed on her. He sighed with relief, then made his way over to the table.

"Bo!" Juno squealed, happy as ever to see her little buddy—or that's what he'd been before he hit his growth spurt a few years ago. He'd shot past Juno's height in a matter of weeks.

Bo smiled at Juno before leaning down to give her a one-armed hugged.

"Come to join the party?" Aurelia asked, offering a smile too, and knowing full well that Bo couldn't join any sort of party at the tavern for a few more years when he passed the legal drinking age.

Not that Valora and her friends were partaking in any crazy activities. After she finished her ale, Valora had every intention of going home and sleeping off her exhaustion from training.

"I need to steal my sister," Bo announced, and Valora raised a brow. "Mom and Dad need help at the shop."

Valora groaned and turned in her bench seat, her drink in hand. "Can't they wait until I at least finish here? I just got off training."

"We had a rush about an hour ago, and the stock on the shelves is completely wiped out. Well, *almost* wiped out," he amended when Valora challenged him with that same brow.

"Can you help them for a little bit?"

Bo shook his head. "It's almost time for my shift at the stables. Mom asked me to come get you on my way there."

Valora had completely forgotten it was her brother's night to handle the end-of-day work at the village stables. He'd been doing the job for a few years now with his friends, but the schedule tended to change based on when the stable master needed the extra hands. It was easy, part-time work for some of the Norlynian boys born without abilities.

The eyes of her friends bored into her while Valora contemplated what to do. While she'd had every intention of going home after one drink, she also wanted to stay just long enough to prove a point to her friends. She'd been so tired lately, wanting nothing more than to go home after long days, the constant use of her powers among the other physical activity during training draining her energy. As a result, Valora had missed more than her fair share of social gatherings lately.

Her friends hadn't failed to point it out to her.

An obligation to her parents was different though—or at least Valora thought so. Her friends knew Imogen and Jeffrey Bellemore ran a successful candle shop within the village, and as the only true employees, they often sought the help of their children.

Valora sighed and slid her drink to Myrcella, who she knew would have no objections to finishing it for her.

"I'll see you guys tomorrow," she said as she stood from the bench. She hadn't even gotten to order any food, and her stomach reminded her as she left the tavern with Bo.

He pushed the door open and held it, allowing his sister to pass through beforehand. Bo had always been generous like that. Annoying at times, as all little brothers were, but at the end of the day Valora knew he held her best intentions at heart. He'd looked out for her since they were little, always rushing to Valora's defense, picking fights with the bigger and stronger kids when he thought they were bothering her.

No matter how annoyed his appearance at the tavern made her, Valora knew she'd always have her brother's back too—starting with taking over at their parents' shop so he could go to his shift at the stables.

Still….

She glanced back over her shoulder as she passed through the door to the tavern. Her friends hadn't moved—and Myrcella had finished off a lot more of Valora's drink than she'd managed while she possessed it. But instead of the laughing Valora expected, they were listening, all four of them leaning forward on the table, intent on whatever Aurelia was saying.

"I think I'm going to head to Cash's place after our shift, by the way," Bo announced, earning Valora's full attention. Her friends were probably just discussing training, nothing more.

"Oh, *that's* convenient," Valora teased, elbowing her brother in the side. "Do Mom and Dad know that's part of the reason you're not helping them stock the shop?"

Bo smirked and shook his head. "I was hoping you would tell them."

"Even better."

Bo chuckled as he returned his sister's gesture. "You can join if you want. Cash's older brother trains with you. He can regenerate."

Valora knew just whom Bo spoke of. She'd faced off against Cash's brother—Rhett, if her memory served her—a few times. She'd won each time no thanks to Rhett's severe fear of the dark.

Still, even with the mention of a familiar face, Valora shrugged at the idea of a party. Such events had lost their thrill for her. Once upon a time, Valora had relished in the idea of shouting over others to hold a conversation while a group of local musicians, usually hired and stuck in the corner, played something to dance to. She had loved the burn as drink after drink made their way down her throat, and she had stumbled home on wobbling legs, she and her friends laughing at the absurdity of the night—or sometimes just laughing for no reason at all.

The novelty of being allowed to drink legally in Norlyn had soon worn off, though, and Valora decided to dedicate herself to more important things, like her training—or like helping her parents when they needed it. That wasn't to say she had stopped attending all social gatherings; just the majority.

"I might pass," Valora told her brother. "Training was rough today."

"Well, if you change your mind, I can warn Cash you might show up," Bo offered. "I think it'd be fun. We don't party enough together."

Valora smiled. She could only imagine the antics her little brother got up to when he went out with his friends and truly would have loved to see it. Maybe she would find out what her friends were doing after she finished at the shop. They might appreciate her finding a party for them to attend, seeing as they were always looking for something to do with their nights on the weekend. Plus, it might make up for Valora declining most offers to join lately.

"I'll see how I'm feeling after I help Mom and Dad," she told Bo, and he smiled. "Just promise me you'll actually go to work and not straight to the party."

"Of course I'm going to go to work, Val," Bo said, rolling his eyes. "I have to earn money to give to Rhett when he buys us booze."

Valora scoffed and hit her brother's shoulder, knowing full well he participated in underage activities, but still wanting to appear like a responsible older sister.

"Be safe," she said.

"I always am," Bo assured. "I wouldn't want you to worry."

Little did Bo know, Valora would always worry about him. She offered a soft smile.

"Enjoy your shift," she said. "Maybe I'll see you later."

THE JINGLING BELL above the door to the candle shop announced Juno and Aurelia's arrival before Valora saw them. She smiled, mid-reach to restock a honeydew-scented candle, when she turned over her shoulder and spotted them.

"Working hard?" Aurelia asked. She positioned herself by the checkout counter, resting an elbow on it, a picture of ease and comfort. Aurelia tended to be comfortable in just about any setting, and having known Valora for so long, might've very well considered the candle shop an extension of the Bellemore household.

"I should be just about finished," Valora replied. With the end of the day drawing near, she wouldn't have to stick around much longer. "I was going to find you guys actually. Bo told me that one of his friends is throwing a party. Well, his brother is.

He's the warrior who—"

"Eh, you've been to one party around here, and you've been to them all," Aurelia said dismissively with a wave.

Valora placed the last honeydew candle on the shelf and lowered herself from her tip-toes. Her brow furrowed as her eyes landed on Juno, hoping her other friend might offer some sort of explanation. Aurelia never turned down the opportunity to go to a party.

"Did something change since last week?" Valora joked.

Aurelia offered a smile, but it was Juno who said, "We had a lot to drink at the tavern after you left. Mona and Myrcella got called home too. Something about needing to take care of their dog."

Juno shrugged off the reasoning for the twins' absence as Valora worked on closing up the rest of the boxes of candles. The shelves were nearly full after her two hours of work around the shop, even with her parents having gone home. Her mom had left shortly after she arrived to start working on dinner, her dad a little bit after that, not wanting to leave all the work to Valora alone. She'd assured him she could lock up the shop, though, if he wanted to go home and relax a little bit.

Valora had been so intent on trying to find her friends—on proving to them that she wasn't all that boring and would go to a party—that she'd given up on resting herself. Aurelia's sudden claim put a damper on that really fast.

"We wanted to do something different when we're all together," Juno continued. "Something exciting!"

"Parties are pretty exciting, aren't they?" Valora tried.

"Not as exciting as going into the forest."

Valora paused on her way to stash the box behind the

checkout counter, nearly tripping over her own two feet in the process. She managed to set the box down normally, though, before she rose and met Aurelia's waiting stare.

"You're kidding," Valora accused.

Aurelia pointed to her very serious face. "Do I look like I'm kidding?"

"We talked about it after you left," Juno explained. "We thought it might be…fun."

"Oh yeah, real fun," Valora replied. "Nothing says *fun* to me like getting torn apart by wolves."

"There's probably bears too," Aurelia added.

"Oh, now I'm sold."

Valora weaved around her friends as she continued to prepare the store for closing. She knew her friends came up with some pretty stupid ideas sometimes—and she'd been a participant in a fair amount of them—but this wasn't one that she intended to join in on.

The forest bordered the village on the western side, and though it towered, dark and ominous, a fair distance from Norlyn, it was still close enough to send a shiver down Valora's spine each time she paid it close attention.

Pure darkness resided in the thick of the trees—hiding the wolves and bears and whatever other creatures lurked there. She should've been more than intrigued to venture there. She'd find nothing but shadows, the canopy of the trees preventing any sunlight from getting through.

Yet, the forest terrified Valora. It always had—as it should terrify any Norlynian. There were some stories that she knew were just that, but she'd heard other tales too over the years. People went missing in the forest, either after they ventured in by themselves or became the unlucky one out of the groups that thought it would be *fun* to see what all the fuss was about.

Valora could survive the forest, and she knew it. As a master of shadows—well, almost, with a bit more training—she knew within the darkness she would find the most strength. Training in the daylight always proved a challenge, her powers shying away from the light, even when Valora dug deep inside herself to the darkness that resided beyond the physical. The kind that lived in some of her thoughts and feelings.

She could survive.

Her friends might not, and Valora would never agree to something that would put them in danger.

"Oh, c'mon, Val," Aurelia pleaded. "Aren't you the one who's always asking us if we can do different stuff?"

It was true. Valora did try to convince her friends to partake in activities other than visiting the tavern or yet another house party, but….

"Going into the forest wasn't exactly what I was talking about," Valora clarified. "I was talking more along the lines of shopping in the village shops or going on a hike."

"Visiting the forest could be considered a hike," Aurelia countered, a proud smile on her lips. Valora hated how her friend was technically correct.

Her eyes slid to Juno, who was obviously slightly less thrilled by the idea but was likely going along to please Aurelia. That tended to be how things worked out—no matter what Juno might confide in private to Valora when Aurelia wasn't around to hear.

Aurelia groaned and rolled her eyes when no one continued the conversation further. She stomped over to the front door of the shop and flipped the open sign to closed, making sure the three of them would be the only ones in the room.

"Look, we all know the stories," Aurelia said. "That didn't stop any of us from agreeing to go into the forest," she added, motioning to herself and Juno, then pointing out the door, trying to include the absent Mona and Myrcella in the conversation.

"We're doing this for you, Val," Juno added. "We thought you would like it."

Valora's eyes widened at her friend's claim. If they thought she'd willingly venture into the forest without any sort of fear, they must not know her very well at all.

"Think of it as a chance to improve your skills even further," Aurelia said, echoing Valora's thoughts from only moments before. "After today's display, I'd say you're on the fast-track to becoming the Master's apprentice."

The comment made Valora freeze. Given her lacking enthusiasm at training, then subsequent display at the tavern, Valora thought for sure Aurelia's jealousy was at a high that afternoon. It was no secret that her friend took pride in her success at becoming one of the first few warriors without abilities and even less of a secret that Aurelia excelled at most of the training exercises. She always fell just a little short, though—as if she lost all momentum the moment the Master came around to evaluate.

Aurelia's success came at the price of Valora's failure, however. Valora knew she was one of the few warriors who stood in Aurelia's way of becoming a stronger trainee. She'd likely never become the Master's apprentice without any abilities, but she could find a promising future within the warrior ranks. Valora would have been stupid to deny her friend that much credit.

Still, it didn't stop the small, friendly rivalry that had been in place since Valora and her friends had joined the ranks of training warriors three years prior.

That Aurelia had so openly admitted she believed Valora would become the Master's apprentice....

"Not everyone who goes into the forest is harmed," Juno reminded her.

"Just a lot of them," Valora countered.

Aurelia chuckled as she placed a hand on Valora's shoulder. "Between all of us, I think there's a high chance of survival," she said. Then, with a soft smile, "Don't you trust us, Val?"

Of course she trusted her friends. They'd been through a lot in the years they'd known each other—everything from bad breakups to mornings spent piecing together hazy nights out to helping each other train.

The only problem was that Valora didn't know if she trusted her abilities to save them all should they run into trouble, no matter how strong and promising they were becoming.

It was as Aurelia said, though, she supposed. There was strength in numbers, and Valora wasn't the only training warrior in the bunch. They'd be able to handle anything if they faced it together.

"No one is going to know about this, right?" Valora questioned. The last thing she needed was for her parents to find out that she'd decided to tempt death and venture into the forest for frivolity's sake. Imogen Bellemore had put a ban on her children going near the forest—let alone in it—when Valora had been a child. Something told her the ban still stood, no matter that she neared nineteen-years-of-age.

Aurelia shook her head. "No," she assured Valora. "It's our

secret."

Valora's eyes slid to Juno, who plastered an encouraging smile on her face as soon as she realized the attention had fallen to her. If Juno felt comfortable enough to go into the forest….

Valora sighed. She definitely wouldn't be going to the party now—not knowing what lay ahead of her the next day.

"Fine," she agreed. "I'm in."

# CHAPTER 3

THE FOREST SEEMED even more daunting up close.

Valora stared into the dark depths before her, unable to shake the tales of countless disappearances and deaths from her head. In all her years of training as a warrior, she'd never imagined she would come so close to the place known for swallowing the people of Norlyn and never spitting them back out.

She jumped when a hand clapped her on the shoulder. Turning, she found Aurelia standing there, a confident grin on her lips.

"Ready?" Aurelia asked.

Valora scanned the others who had joined them. Juno, Myrcella, and Mona didn't appear as afraid of Aurelia's idea to venture into the woods. Perhaps her continued hesitance came of her tendency to err on the side of caution. The others never thought twice about anything, which ultimately led to more trouble than good.

But she'd promised herself she would remain open-minded to the adventure, and Aurelia's suggested trip into the forest had come at just the right time to put that resolution into action. A time to prove not everything was doom and gloom in her world of shadows.

She nodded her reply, trying her best to smile back at Aurelia. Of course she was ready to venture into the darkness. Surely the forest couldn't take *all* of them as its victims….

"You sure about that, Val?" Myrcella taunted.

"Doesn't sound like it to me," Mona added while she tapped her index finger to her temple.

Valora's attention cut to the twins that stood nearby, knowing grins on their faces, their hands on their hips near the plethora of weapons strapped to their belts.

She narrowed her eyes at her friends. "I would really appreciate it if you stayed out of my mind."

Mona shrugged as Myrcella's body shook with silent laughter. "Can't help it sometimes."

Valora must have grown noticeably irritated by the invasion of privacy because Juno jumped forward.

"You know they mean it, Val," she said encouragingly. "You understand how hard it is to control sometimes."

No—Valora didn't know. She had never had any issues controlling her ability. But hers was easy, she supposed; if she had been born with the ability to dig into other people's minds, she might not show as much restraint, especially when enticed by emotions as obvious as Valora's present fear.

Aurelia's hand, still on her shoulder, progressively squeezed harder into her skin, forcing Valora to remove it. Aurelia shot her friend an apologetic look before striding away. Valora couldn't blame her for her jealousy—Aurelia took her lack of powers far harder than Juno did.

"Let's go, before Val starts telling us why we shouldn't do this anymore," Myrcella joked and went to catch up to Aurelia. She and her twin each patted Valora on the back as they strode past.

Valora watched them journey into the forest, not wanting to let them get too far ahead but also not wanting to join quite yet. It seemed Juno held the same apprehensions as she ambled up beside her. She wore an expression Valora couldn't quite place.

"You nervous too?" Valora asked. Juno peered up at her, a half-foot separating their heights. "It's okay if you are. I can bend shadows, and the darkness *still* scares me."

Valora watched her friend's throat bob as she swallowed her evident fear. Juno looked almost as if she wanted to say something but refrained. She had never been one for confrontation, and Valora accepted that. She never enjoyed confrontation either, though she knew that Juno would often go out of her way to avoid it. She was kinder than the rest of them, but Valora wondered how much of that kindness was genuine and how much came from fear of rocking the boat.

"Are you two coming or what?" Myrcella called out, walking backward to talk to her straggling friends. The telepath smiled from where she, Mona, and Aurelia waited just within the trees. When she turned back around, Mona jumped out at her twin, causing a brief fright and a subsequent round of laughter from the three girls.

Valora looked back to Juno. The short blonde ran her fingers back through her hair and sighed. She smiled up at her friend, albeit faintly.

"We should go," Juno said, almost too quietly for Valora to hear. Then to the others, "You bitches sure you can handle it?"

She smiled as she jogged to catch up with the rest of the group, leaving Valora standing alone at the edge of the trees. It wasn't the first time Juno's innocence had disappeared at the expense of impressing Aurelia. It always came down to remaining in her favor, no matter what Juno had to say or do to achieve it.

Juno walked right under Aurelia's protective arm and wrapped one around her friend in return. Neither they nor Myrcella and Mona displayed any nerves, despite standing well within the confines of the forest.

Valora watched the darkness of the forest consume them as they left the bright outskirts of the trees before she jogged in after her friends.

Every rustle of the leaves in the autumn air, every crack of a twig, every chilling breeze that tickled the back of her neck made Valora tense. The others noticed. They tried to pull her under their arms and assure her that everything was all right, laughing and joking casually even as they ventured further and further away from the village of Norlyn. Still, Valora couldn't help but fall victim to her nerves. The forest set her on edge. It had since she had been a little girl. Now that she stood within it, the darkness seemed too extreme for even her to control.

Valora squinted to keep her friends in her vision. She adjusted her scarf, pulling it tighter around her. The only other cover she had were cotton leggings, a white t-shirt, and a leather jacket. Out in the sun, they had kept her warm, but during their walk even her wool socks and knee-high boots failed her. Any longer and Valora feared her toes might fall off. Better them than her fingers, she supposed. What good would she be wielding a weapon with her feet?

Mona and Myrcella howled, mimicking the wolves that lurked nearby, watching and waiting for the perfect time to strike. The sound of the surrounding brush rustling had all the girls jumping, then screaming, then laughing.

"Not so scary, right?" Aurelia asked. She stood beside Valora and draped a casual arm around her companion's shoulders. "See, Val? Nothing to be scared of."

"No, I guess not," Valora replied, though she wasn't sure she believed herself.

Aurelia must have noticed her hesitance because she pulled Valora in closer, hugging her from the side. "Oh, come on. A brave warrior like you afraid of the forest? Who would think the Master's favorite would be so shaken up?"

"I'm not his favorite," Valora argued softly. She didn't enjoy the bite in Aurelia's tone. She recognized it from the other arguments they had gotten into over the years, and the last thing she wanted to do was fight in the middle of the forest.

"No?" Aurelia challenged. She nodded towards the twins. "That's not what I've heard."

Valora peered sidelong at Myrcella and Mona. They stood nearby, grinning like they always did in that devilish kind of way. Juno watched them. Only when her eyes cut to the twins' hands on the hilts of their weapons did Valora's follow suit.

Aurelia removed her hold on Valora and moved to stand in front of her, also placing a hand on her weapon. The twins moved behind Valora, Juno taking the spot they'd vacated. Valora couldn't see their shadows, but every step that crunched against the forest floor alerted her to their position. It was a strange formation for them to take—if they'd heard wolves, shouldn't they be on the defensive? Unless….

Forget the wolves. Valora had fallen victim to a different pack of predators.

Valora instinctively tried to pull the shadows toward her, to use the darkness as a weapon the same way she did during training, but they wouldn't come. The forest remained indifferent to her quick, desperate attempts—perhaps she'd been wrong in thinking that it would be easy to control, or perhaps her fear was causing her power to fail.

She channeled every bit of training the Master had ever shown her—every bit she'd learned on her own growing up. No matter what Valora did, she couldn't find the strength to control the shadows. She could hardly even feel them, as though they refused to fall under her control.

Perhaps the forest was the true master of darkness, just as all the stories claimed. Perhaps not even she, the one person in all Norlyn who might be able to offer a challenge, could find success against the evils and terrors that lurked within the trees.

Whatever the reason for her sudden failure, she was left exposed. Defenseless. Surrounded.

"What's going on?" she asked, her voice tinged with nerves.

Aurelia's head cocked to the side, and she grinned. "Do you think you deserve it, Val? Being the Master's apprentice?"

"I work hard. I-I—"

"*I-I-I,*" Aurelia mocked. "Sweet little Valora—always getting the special privileges and attention because she's in the Master's favor. There are a lot of people who want to be in your position, Val. You know that, don't you?" Valora did know, but she also knew better than to answer the rhetorical question. "It's a dog-eat-dog world, Val. It's no secret becoming the Master is the greatest achievement a training warrior can receive, but what about the rest of us, huh? What happens to those who don't get chosen?"

"We get tossed on the patrols or tossed aside," Myrcella said. The bite had edged itself into her voice as well. "When we grow too old for patrol, we're forced to find some other profession to feed our families. All that hard work put in for no return."

"You all have a chance at being picked by the Master," Valora said defensively. "You all have enough skill."

Aurelia shook her head, her grin fading into a stone-cold glare. The angry fire burned so brightly in her brown eyes that not even the darkness could shroud it.

"That isn't good enough," she spat. "It's not good enough for any of us."

A blood-curdling scream erupted from Valora's throat as a knife pierced her back. Another followed soon after, and when it was pulled out, Valora fell to the ground, the pain too much to handle, as warmth spread across her back and blood pooled out of the fresh wound. The twins stood above her, the same wolfish grins they had worn before spreading wider, their daggers glistening with the crimson sheen of her blood in the dim glow of light allowed through the canopy of the trees.

She tried to remain on her knees, staring into Aurelia's eyes as she too removed her dagger from its sheath. Valora's breaths hissed out through her gritted teeth while she fought the pain shooting through her veins. The blood poured out fast and Valora wobbled on her knees, her head growing light.

Aurelia stalked behind her only when Valora could no longer hold herself up. She fell forwards, catching herself on her palms before her face hit the ground. She tried to turn her head as she heard Aurelia command Juno to draw her weapon. Her friend's voice faded in and out with Valora's spotting vision.

She heard Juno's shaking breath as the girl moved beside the twins. Valora pleaded with silver-rimmed eyes, desperate for some sort of escape. Juno wouldn't do it. Out of all of them, Juno wouldn't betray her....

"What are you waiting for?" Mona encouraged.

"Do it!" Myrcella added. "Let's finish this."

Juno's eyes slid to the twins, her dagger still raised and ready to strike should she choose.

"I...I think that's enough," she said. "She'll bleed out from those wounds."

Then, her eyes slid to Aurelia, and Valora knew her friend would fall victim to the waiting stare—the disappointment she so desperately sought to avoid.

Aurelia shook her head, her eyes narrowed.

"Always the weak link."

Juno's throat bobbed as she stared at Aurelia. Valora continued to struggle on the ground, using the moments the small squabble allowed her. If only she could get to a weapon. If only the shadows would obey her....

Juno returned her attention to Valora and took a step forwards.

Valora waited for it—knew it was coming—and still the sharp, piercing pain of the dagger in her back made her scream.

Her arms wobbled as she tried to push herself back onto her feet, fighting the lightheadedness and ignoring the warmth of the blood spilling from her wounds. Even if she managed to grab her weapon, she couldn't fight. Not in her condition. She stood no chance of escaping the forest, of seeing her family again. Their faces swam in her vision as she realized the moment the girls left her, she would become food for the creatures drawn by the copper scent of her blood.

Aurelia crouched next to her, fisting Valora's long, black hair and pulling her up just enough to hear Aurelia whisper, "If you by some miracle survive this, no hard feelings, right?"

Valora gritted her teeth and tried to reach for her weapon while Aurelia's hold remained, unrelenting. But her shaking hands couldn't grip the handle before another knife found its mark in her back. Twice. Three times. It seemed Aurelia would go to any length to make sure Valora couldn't escape her demise.

Her hair was released and a foot connected with her back. She fell forwards onto the ground and tried to claw her way back up to no avail. Her breathing came out ragged. Her blood seeped into the ground. She could no longer do anything but stare into the forest, watching and listening as the voices of the girls she had once considered her friends faded into the distance while she waited for death to take her.

# CHAPTER 4
## THREE MONTHS LATER

**LIFE IN THE** village went on as usual. Day after day—month after month—the people of Norlyn went on working and training and educating. They went on *living*. The more time passed, the more they forgot that, once, Valora had been a part of that same day-to-day living.

She watched the bustle of the village in the mid-afternoon as warriors continued their training and citizens went about their last-minute errands, trying to beat the clock before the shops closed for the day. Children ran from the schoolhouse, slates and chalk pouches clutched in their hands as they headed home to their waiting parents. Those who were old enough left school to attend their after-school job, just as she knew her brother would be doing. On the other side of the village, her parents would be one hand down when dealing with the shop because of Bo's impending shift at the stables.

Valora loosened her control on the shadows she'd bent around herself. She sat perched on the same tree branch she'd viewed the village from for the past month since her healing had improved. At first, she'd stayed on the ground at the outskirts of the forest, but the distance between her and the village had been too great to get a good look at what was happening. When her strength had improved enough that she could climb trees, she had done so in order to enjoy an aerial view of Norlyn. The Master had always told her those on higher ground possessed the advantage. Horses, hills, or—even better—mountains gave Norlynian warriors an edge on their enemies.

He'd never considered trees in that lesson, the ones in Norlyn being too few and far between to bother with, or certain warriors' abilities to bend shadows to keep hidden beyond what cover the leaves provided.

The cool winter had shifted to an equally chilly spring. Valora adjusted her leather-boot-clad feet on the thick branch she sat on and subsequently pulled her jacket tighter around her. Norlyn never grew warm until the middle of summer—the only, very brief time of year when the villagers enjoyed a break from their daily routines and went to visit the nearby lake. Her brother had always loved visiting the lake, jumping in, swimming around, trying to catch the small fish with his bare hands when he was younger and the bigger fish when he grew older. Three years her junior, Bo had always been the much freer spirit of the two.

The always stoic Valora let her vision drift to where Bo worked with his friends in the village stables. The group of them tossed hay at each other and laughed until the stable marshal came and put them in their place. But seeing her brother's smile…. As much as it hurt to be forgotten, watching Bo slowly heal from her disappearance made her smile. Just a little.

Valora quickly took hold of the shadows again when Bo turned towards the forest. Her obsidian hair and monochrome clothing gave her some semblance of camouflage, but her pale skin stood out against the dark backdrop of the forest in which she hid. Being seen by anyone, even her brother, would ruin her plan. Valora would never put that at risk.

Soon enough, Bo looked away and went back to laughing with his friends. With the stable marshal gone again, nothing stopped the fun from ensuing. She watched them for a moment more before climbing down from her perch, shadows wrapped around her tighter than her jacket until she hit the hard ground.

Valora stalked through the forest, nocking an arrow from the quiver on her back. She held it more for comfort than defense. In her time spent in the forest, she'd learned a lot about the true dangers that lurked. Yes, the darkness sometimes seemed to go on forever without any promise of light breaking through, but it wasn't the creatures Valora had learned she needed to fear.

It was the people those chose as their company when they ventured into the forest to begin with.

Valora pushed aside some brush and lowered her weapon, replacing the arrow in the quiver. Hidden in the middle of the densest part of the forest was a clearing containing a small log cabin. Smoke billowed out of the flue cut out from the roof.

She scowled at it. Maybe her housemate no longer cared about giving away their position, but she certainly didn't want to be found until she completed her self-assigned mission. Smoke would do just that. He could have at least waited for her to return home and put a shadow shield around the home to hide the smoke like she had requested. Repeatedly.

Valora marched through the front door, slamming it behind her with a bang.

Ryker peered up from their kitchen table. Everything within the small, one-bedroom home was made of the same drab, grey lumber. Had it not been for Ryker's brown hair and amber eyes, Valora would have believed all color had drained from the world upon entering the structure. *She* certainly didn't bring about any brightness.

"And how were the adventures today?" Ryker asked in the same cheery tone he always used when she came home.

Valora stared at him, straight-faced, before she stalked through the kitchen to the shared bedroom and slammed that door shut as well.

On the other side of the door, Valora removed her quiver and dropped it and her bow onto the ground by her bed. Like everything else in the house, the frame was made of grey wood and housed matching grey wolf pelts for covers. They were nothing like the down feather mattress at Valora's home in the village, but they did well enough. She figured she would've been in pain no matter what she slept on while her injuries healed.

Making her way over to the shard of broken mirror glass Ryker had collected from who-knew-where, Valora removed her leather jacket. She watched herself, the darkness curling around her legs and up her body like tendrils of smoke, and angled herself to see her back in the reflection. Valora hissed, having used just enough motion to elicit a stinging pain in her back. After so many months spent healing, she thought such simple movements should no longer be such an issue.

She lifted her shirt ever-so-slightly so she could see the scars left behind by the attack.

The wounds remained raised and red. She bent her free hand back to run her fingers over them. They no longer hurt to the touch, but the feel of the puckered skin under her fingers made her blood boil.

Valora gritted her teeth and stared at the wounds in the mirror, trying to hold back the tears she never let Ryker see. Each brush of her fingertips caused her to relive the pain, the weakness, the betrayal—

She jumped when a knock sounded on the door. Quickly, Valora dropped her shirt. Seconds later, the door creaked open, and Ryker appeared without any further warning. She supposed he had every right. He slept in the next bed over.

In his hands, Ryker held a bucket with three damp rags hanging over the rim. That was what they had learned it took to cover the area the wounds spread across. Valora stared at them then moved her eyes to her housemate's face.

"Are you ready for your treatment?" he asked.

*No.* "Yes."

Valora sat down atop the wolf pelts and grabbed her shirt at the back, lifting it for Ryker. She heard the bed he'd constructed for her groan as he sat on the space behind her and placed the bucket on the ground. It would come in handy later. For the time being, Ryker only needed himself to help heal the wounds on Valora's back.

She hissed when she felt his heated hands on her back—the same hands that had tended to her for three months. Just as Valora had imagined the wounds would be able to withstand simple motions, she also thought the healing should have gotten easier to withstand. Still, each time Ryker came in with his ointment, she dreaded knowing what came next. The sharp burn of his palms from the heat, the sting of the ointment, the tension at being touched by a near stranger.

She tried to catch sight of her companion in her peripheral vision but failed. After the first few sessions, Ryker had learned how to keep out of view. The fire had scared her when she had regained consciousness. It had taken them multiple sessions to learn the happy medium of heat.

She'd never met a fire bender before. A whole range of citizens with abilities existed in Norlyn, but elementals didn't appear so often as those with mental or physical abilities. Similar powers tended to pass down within families, so one of Ryker's parents had likely possessed some sort of elemental ability too. Or, perhaps, Ryker was like Valora and the ability gene had come to pass after years of dormancy.

However, while Valora had not personally known any fire benders before Ryker, she knew the rumors surrounding them—the anger, the spontaneity, the chaos that followed.

So far, Valora couldn't see it. Despite their lack of proper conversation, Ryker always seemed eager to interact, greeting her with smiles and cheesy jokes. Since he'd lived alone until he found her, Valora had assumed Ryker would kick her out once she could stand without too much pain. Clearly, he preferred to be alone if he chose a solitary life in the middle of a forest—she never inquired as to why one would prefer such a lifestyle, knowing full well she wouldn't have wanted her personal life to be invaded. But there was nothing yet, and Valora intended to take advantage of the small kindness shown. The last thing she wanted was to return to Norlyn—at least until her self-assigned mission was complete.

"They look a lot better," Ryker said as he moved his hands to other wounds. "I'm not sure how much longer we'll need to keep this up. It might be time to let nature take its course."

"It's been three months," Valora replied flatly. "I think this could have stopped once the bandages came off."

"But would you have taken care of yourself?" Valora stayed silent. Ryker moved his hands again. "I didn't think so."

They remained quiet for the duration of the session. The heat helped the blood flow, making the wound heal faster.

Many would have considered themselves lucky to be found at the brink of death by a man who controlled fire. Valora wasn't one of them. She found it more of a nuisance than anything else, especially considering the man was Ryker of all people.

She remembered his face vaguely from before he had disappeared from the village years ago. He'd been at warrior training—the last person anyone would've ever considered a contender for the Master's apprenticeship. That had been just as Valora and her friends first started training, so she hadn't gotten the chance to face off against him before—nothing. One day Ryker had been at training, then the next he wasn't.

People gave their reasons, and gossip swirled among the warriors, but Valora paid very little mind to it. She didn't attend training to spread rumors about a person who had been missing for three years.

Missing, until he stumbled upon the severely injured Valora during one of his hunts.

In the three months since he'd discovered her, abandoned and bleeding out on the forest floor, Ryker had proved to be…a decent housemate. Valora could've had it worse, she supposed, when it came to who—or what—found her there that day.

She also could have died.

Instead, Ryker had worked on healing her, day after day, using his heat to speed up what surely would have been a very tedious natural process. He'd fed her and even given Valora her own bed to sleep in.

Still, his generosity didn't mean they needed to be friends. Nor did it mean Valora intended to stick around in the forest any longer than necessary.

Ryker nudged Valora's shoulders with the heels of his hands. She shifted on the bed, her back still hot to the touch, and lay on her stomach. Her breath hitched when the cool rags touched her skin. The sensation made her sweat more than the heat had.

"I'll come back for them when I'm done with the hide I'm working on." Ryker stood and grabbed the bucket off the ground. "Will you need anything in the meantime, sunshine?"

Valora wouldn't have given him any attention had it not been for use of the nickname. Ryker had started using it once he found out what abilities she possessed.

"Sleep," Valora responded. She crossed her arms on the bed and placed her chin in them. "I need sleep."

Ryker extended his hand in a sweeping motion and bowed at the hip. "As she wishes," he said while he backed out of the room, closing the door with him. Valora waited for the click, but it never came.

"When is the plan being put into action?"

So, he hadn't left. Valora shut her eyes and sighed. "Soon, Ryker. Very soon."

The door clicked shut.

## CHAPTER 5

**WOODEN SPOONS SCRAPED** against stone bowls as Valora and Ryker sat at the table, eating their breakfast. The low fire filled the room with a bit of extra warmth. Valora found she often didn't need any more than the wolf pelt blankets to keep her comfortable during the night. When she woke and caught sight of Ryker in the middle of the night, she found him with nothing covering his half-clothed body. She wondered if his abilities created a higher body temperature than the average human.

Valora kept waiting for any of the signs of a typical fire bender, but none had shown themselves in their three months together. So far, Ryker had done a brilliant job of proving every rumor wrong—no temper tantrums, no sudden outbursts, certainly no burning anything down. Valora might not have known any other fire benders, but she'd taught herself about their tendencies, just as she had for all benders. Being one herself, Valora assumed she'd be able to learn from the techniques of others.

Aside from his amber eyes, Ryker didn't match the textbook description of fire benders—*at all.*

He'd truly been nothing but a companionable housemate, no matter if Valora didn't always wish to participate in the conversation he tried to start with her.

Valora felt Ryker's eyes on her every so often, but she refused to give him the satisfaction of acknowledging him. She continued to eat spoonfuls of her bland rabbit soup, as did her breakfast companion. The attention made her increasingly uncomfortable. Only when Ryker slurped his soup out of his spoon in a very obnoxious manner did Valora drop her own utensil into her bowl and look up at him, annoyed.

Ryker grinned while he slurped another spoonful of broth then placed his spoon in his bowl. Valora narrowed her eyes at him.

"Do you mind?" she asked coldly.

"Apologies." Ryker continued grinning while he took his empty bowl and moved it over to the wash bucket to clean. "My male ego couldn't handle being ignored for so long."

Valora rolled her eyes and shook her head. She finished up the last few spoonfuls of her soup and sat back in her chair, her arms crossed over her chest. The remainder of the soup sat inside the stone cauldron hanging above the last burning embers of the fire. She could look forwards to eating it for lunch and dinner for the next couple of days, unless either one of them managed to have a more successful hunt.

A small flame shot towards the residual logs in the fireplace.

Valora jumped, watching the black smoke rise up and out the flue, then turned to stare at Ryker, who seemed oblivious to what he had done. At least she had her shield around the house this time.

"Do you mind?" Valora repeated. "Or was that little trick your male ego speaking again?"

"Just trying to make sure you're nice and warm, Val," Ryker responded without looking up from cleaning his bowl. "With all that darkness surrounding you, we don't want your heart to ice over. Would make all my hard work healing you pretty pointless."

Valora felt a low growl rumble in her throat. But sure enough, shadows swirled around her. She quickly released the hold her temper had created, and the light from the fire instantly swallowed the shadows.

Her chair screeched on the floor as she stood and took her bowl to where Ryker sat crouched by the washing bucket. "Don't call me Val."

She dropped her bowl into the bucket. Ryker jumped back when the dirty water splashed up at him.

Valora didn't look back as she grabbed her quiver and bow and headed out the door.

THE WARRIORS HAD improved since she had left them. Not by much, but Valora noticed some changes.

She still didn't believe they would be enough for the Master to name anyone else his apprentice. Not yet. Not so soon after she'd disappeared, and not before Valora had the chance to make it back to Norlyn.

Becoming the Master was the greatest honor a Norlynian warrior could achieve. If he named Valora as his successor...she could hardly imagine what would happen. She'd be revered as the current Master was—a hero of Norlyn. Their village's great protector, responsible for training the next great ranks of warriors should any major conflict arise.

Valora could only receive that honor if she returned to Norlyn.

In her usual perch, Valora felt her shadows growing darker, more powerful, as she watched the girls she had once called friends fight against each other. Much like Bo had taken his duties lightheartedly the day before, it seemed her old crew didn't feel like trying very hard either. Juno and Mona jabbed at each other as though they fought with fencing sabers rather than full blades, often taking their eyes from each other to laugh. Myrcella sat by idly, making jokes about the very clear height difference between her six-foot twin and five-foot friend.

Aurelia fought a male warrior nearby—a metal manipulator, if Valora remembered him correctly. He'd been a newer recruit, and it was clear that he was giving Aurelia some trouble, his ability putting a twisted end to the blade of her weapon. New warriors always proved an issue for the seasoned warriors. Valora had struggled with them too, needing to learn the best way to use her shadows against the new selection of abilities.

Without any abilities of her own, Aurelia must have—

Valora sat up straighter in the tree. She'd been following Aurelia's movements the whole time, yet somehow her friend had ended up behind the metal manipulator, a new weapon pointed at his back.

"Aurelia."

Valora's eyes found the Master at the same time Aurelia's did. His were narrowed in disappointment, despite the accused having just won her match.

"Go take a break," the Master instructed, nodding off to the side.

Aurelia smirked as she said, "Yes, Master," then followed orders.

Valora rolled her eyes and sat back again on her tree branch. Life truly hadn't changed much since Valora had been removed from it.

From what she had witnessed, it didn't seem like her old friends had gone through any period of grieving. It made sense, really, considering they'd orchestrated the assassination attempt. Still, something deep inside Valora had hoped that maybe—just maybe—the four girls would show some kind of guilt.

Nothing. Ever. Not even a tear. Not in the time since she'd grown strong enough to climb the tree and watch over Norlyn, at least.

The shadows spread as her anger grew, and Valora quickly reined them in before she lost control. In the recent months since her injury, it had been difficult to control herself. She knew she had had a temper in the past, but each time she saw her betrayers her blood boiled, her limbs grew jittery, and she wanted to hop right out of the tree and put her plan into action in plain sight, consequences be damned.

She pulled the darkness back inside herself, concealing it rather than letting it spread with her abilities. At the end of it all, Valora wanted to return home. She wanted to see her mom and dad and comfort her hurting brother. As much as she wanted revenge, she wanted to see her family more. Until then, she could—*would*—learn how to control her abilities.

The Master called for the end of training, and Valora's attention shot back to reality. He stroked his goatee as he examined his warriors—with and without abilities—and gave instructions for the next day. Each one, no matter how distracted they might have been before, responded with the classic *Yes, Master* before they fell into their cliques and left the training ground.

Sometimes Valora wondered what the girls had said—how they'd explained to their friends outside the main group, to the Master, to her family, why they'd all survived and she had been lost forever. She couldn't imagine her mother, who read people as easily as she read books, would fall for any lie they gave. She couldn't imagine her dad—who had never been particularly fond of her choice of friends and had so kindly given Valora her temper—would sit back and listen quietly. And she couldn't imagine her brother, who always tried so hard to see the kindness in others, would miss the evil flowing in their veins.

The group disappeared through the door to the tavern. Valora waited. Her stomach growled, and she wished she had Ryker's abilities each time a squirrel ran past her. She could stick it with an arrow, hold out her palm full of fire and—

Her daydreams of food disappeared when laughter echoed from the village. She moved to stand on the branch in order to get a better view of the cheerful group exiting the tavern. Aurelia had found a companion. Juno had picked one up as well. Myrcella's chatter—or perhaps the better word would be shouting—could be heard clearly even at Valora's distance, cluing her into what she and Mona were talking about.

Valora watched the twins as they separated from the group, waving goodbye to their two friends and the new nighttime companions. She craned her neck as the twins ventured further and further into the village, the various shops and lodgings restricting her view. But Valora knew enough to locate Mona and Myrcella's family home. She had ventured there plenty.

She waited another few hours until the light faded completely from the grey sky, to make sure the twins stayed indoors once they returned home. Only when they needed to use the outhouse did they leave. The rest of the time, Mona and Myrcella remained hidden by their house.

The twins had been the first to shove their knives into her back. One of them had kicked her to the ground while she tried to find her strength.

Likewise, they would be the first to go.

# CHAPTER 6

When Valora returned to Ryker's home well after dark, he all but jumped out of his chair at the kitchen table. She startled, shock transforming to confusion as she stood in the doorway.

"Where have you been?" he demanded, doing little to mask his concern.

Valora's brow furrowed. She glanced at the table, where her plate of roast rabbit had grown cold. Next to it sat the normal wooden utensils and stone cup filled with water. Ryker's plate had been cleared already.

"What are you? My mother?" Valora challenged.

She hiked the strap of her quiver further on her shoulder and strode towards the bedroom. She hoped that would settle the discussion. She needed to spend the evening planning her first attack. With her wounds healed almost entirely, Valora was itching to start her mission. She'd thought of nothing but revenge for the past three months, and the last thing she wanted at that moment was for Ryker to bother her with some stupid—

"So, now that you've been going into the forest all by yourself in the day, you think you can handle it at night?"

Ryker burst through the door before it finished shutting behind Valora. She closed her eyes and sighed. Oh, how she wished the house had just one more room. But it wasn't as though Ryker could have predicted he would rescue a dying girl from the forest when he had constructed it. Valora couldn't just kick the man out of his own bedroom, whether she shared it with him or not.

"I think I can fend off a few small dangers, yes," she countered as she removed her weapons and jacket.

"'A few small dangers?'" Ryker let out a huffed laugh. "Do you know how many months it took me to get used to this forest? It's not just backstabbing friends that kill people here, Valora. There are creatures out there that will kill you. And they won't stop even if you plead until your last breath."

Valora turned to him. As she pulled off her boots, she said, "That doesn't sound much different than what I already experienced."

"You won't feel that way when a mountain lion has you in its maw."

She tossed one boot to the side of the room where it landed with a thud. "Then it's a good thing I have no intention of going into the mountains, isn't it?"

The other boot followed, and Valora stood up straighter, her nose slightly in the air. Ryker remained in the doorway, his arms crossed over his chest, his stare just as leveled and cold.

She heard him exhale through his nose. "You should eat your dinner."

Valora ignored the hunger, which dared to betray her by making her stomach rumble, as she said, "I will eventually."

Ryker continued to watch her, taking in her stance, her stare, her *everything* with great scrutiny. Valora hated it. She could only hold her confidence for so long before she shrank away. As an excuse, Valora hung up her coat on her bed's headboard. Ryker was quite the craftsman.

Much to her surprise, her roommate left without another word and shut the door behind him. She glanced back over her shoulder hoping for…what? She didn't want the distractions of pointless arguments while she needed to train for her first plan of attack.

The twins had never been the strongest fighters. Aggressive? Yes. Easily angered? Most definitely. But even after years of training, they tended to fall just shy of mastery when it came to using weapons.

Their ability to wield weapons was not what made them difficult targets, but rather their abilities to read minds. Telepaths caused a lot of trouble for warriors. Their abilities always kept them one step ahead of their opponents—able to sneak into minds and foresee any plans.

Shields and negators were lucky. Their capabilities to render all others powerless made them immune to the twins' mental invasions. Even Valora's shadows couldn't work against a shield or negator. And they most certainly did nothing to stop Mona and Myrcella from sneaking into her head.

That was where she would use their abilities to *her* advantage.

Valora sat cross-legged on her bed thinking repetitive

thoughts until she could no longer keep her eyes open. She let their rhythm lull her into a deep sleep.

Ryker didn't return to the room, even for the nightly treatment of her back, until well into the night.

**T**HE NEXT MORNING, Valora woke and found Ryker's bed empty. She couldn't tell if he'd slept in it at all or if he'd simply made it straight away. Ryker was a naturally tidy person, so she assumed the latter until she stepped into the kitchen for breakfast. There was no rabbit-anything prepared. There weren't even embers left over in the fireplace. As grateful as she should have been for the lack of smoke rising into the sky from their hidden clearing, Valora found it slightly disconcerting, especially after Ryker's grand speech about forest creatures eating people alive.

After what felt like hours of impatient waiting at the kitchen table, Ryker strode through the door, his shirt in his hand and his skin glistening with sweat.

He started when he saw his companion in the room, but Valora didn't cease her examination. Despite the sweat, his face showed clear signs of being exposed to the outside chill—the tip of his nose, his cheeks, and ears were all red. With the door still open, the early morning cold of the transitioning winter made each exhalation of his breath visible.

"Where have you been?" she asked him when he hesitated.

Ryker kicked the door shut and began to unwrap worn straps of black leather from around his wrists. "What are you? My mother?" he sassed.

Valora supposed she deserved that particular comeback but still narrowed her eyes at him. Ryker didn't seem to care and ignored her as he tossed his discarded shirt on the table. Valora watched his muscled back after he strode past her.

Ryker crouched down by the fresh, untouched logs in the fireplace, then turned to her over his shoulder. She quickly moved her eyes from his muscles. If he caught her staring, he didn't let on.

"Did you think of cooking something? Especially after leaving your dinner sitting uneaten."

Valora had forgotten food altogether the night before, and guilt briefly overcame her. Ryker was the kind of person to sit up all night, waiting for her to eat if only so she didn't have to eat alone, heating the food every so often in the meantime.

"I can't start a fire," she admitted.

Ryker stared at her a moment longer before he turned back to the fireplace. He faced both his palms towards the logs and seconds later, small flames bloomed from them. They caught on the firewood and soon the fireplace housed dancing orange and yellow and red.

He stood and rubbed his palms together while Valora watched the flames. When Ryker moved away, she allowed her attention to wander elsewhere.

"That venison I have hanging in the shed should have aged nicely by now," Ryker said as he pulled out a large knife and some wooden skewers. "Would you be alright eating something other than rabbit for a change?"

Seeing as he did all the hunting while she healed, Valora didn't want to seem unappreciative of the rabbit. But she nodded excitedly while she confirmed, "Most definitely."

Ryker smiled softly and disappeared outside again. He reentered not too long after with two large cuts of meat on the skewers. Even before they were cooked, they made Valora's mouth water. Her stomach responded to the sight of food by rumbling nice and loud. She clutched her gut, trying to make it stop in vain. Ryker chuckled.

"That's what you get for leaving that fine-cooked rabbit sitting out with no one to eat it."

Valora rolled her eyes and sat down at the table. She crossed one leg over the other while she watched Ryker crouch down by the fire again. He held the skewers with one hand and used the other to control the flames so each cut got cooked evenly, Valora's a bit more than his, just how she liked it.

Over time, his sweat subsided, despite sitting next to the roaring flames he created. His face went back to its normal coloring—for the most part, anyways. The heat still caused a slight flush.

Valora wondered what it was like—the ability to manipulate fire. She couldn't imagine being in control of such a powerful element. She'd trained with other warriors in Norlyn that controlled air or water, but Ryker was the only person she knew capable of working with such a deadly natural force.

He seemed to have enough control, though, and soon the smell of cooked meat filled her nose. Valora's stomach grumbled its thanks just as Ryker placed the well-cooked cut on a plate in front of her.

"Don't," she warned when she heard him laugh again.

Ryker kept grinning like a fool when he took the seat across from her and cut into his venison. Valora shook her head and looked down at her meal. It smelled delicious.

"Were you up long before I got back?" Ryker asked with a mouthful of half-chewed venison, attempting to make idle small talk.

Valora hated idle small talk. She found it awkward.

Still, she shrugged. "Not terribly." Just long enough to watch the sun rise halfway into the sky. When she could no longer contain her curiosity, Valora asked, "Where did you go?"

Ryker kept his head down, brows raised, and watched her from under his eyelashes. Not often did Valora ask questions. Not even during the first few days—which should have been filled with them—had she bothered much. Ryker hadn't seemed to care, though. He probably attributed the silence and stunted conversations to sadness.

Little did he know she had only silently cried once while he slept. The rest of the days were filled with unrelenting anger.

He swallowed his bite of meat and set down his fork. Valora instantly regretted asking the question.

"I go out sometimes in the mornings to run—just as the sun starts to rise." He shrugged, then added with a grin, "You aren't the only one who enjoys getting out of the clearing every now and then."

Valora worked on cutting another bite of her venison while she asked, "What happened to those nighttime monsters you were telling me about?"

"I didn't say *monsters*, I said *creatures*. As in wolves and mountain lions and bears," he retorted before taking another bite. "And besides," he said between chewing, "I went out at dawn, not night."

"Manners, Ryker," Valora reprimanded. She emphasized her point by finishing chewing and swallowing her bite before speaking again.

He blushed before swallowing.

"Sorry." Ryker stabbed another piece of his dinner before adding, "So, now you know what I do during the day. What about you? Where are you always off to? And don't say avoiding me, because I already know that."

Valora took another bite of her meal to disguise her grin. Ryker knew her very well after only a few months.

"What I do during the day is very important," she replied without meeting his eyes.

"For the top-secret mission?"

"Uh-huh."

Valora took the last bite of her meat and got up to dump her dirty plate and utensils in the wash bucket. When she turned, she jumped. Ryker's hand was on her upper arm. She felt the heat on it increasing and pulled away to avoid being burned—and because she didn't appreciate being manhandled.

"Want to tell me about this mission yet?" he suggested kindly.

"Not really."

Ryker grinned. "You say that like you don't trust me." He nudged her with his hip. "I *did* save your life, remember."

"I remember," Valora assured him. "I'm not telling you as a favor."

As she stared into his amber eyes, Valora couldn't imagine what the truth of her self-assigned mission would do to dim them. Knowing what she planned, Ryker might very well kick her out of his house sooner than planned, and Valora couldn't risk that happening. She needed somewhere to return to between each of her tasks.

No, Ryker couldn't know. Not yet. Perhaps not ever.

Much to her surprise, Ryker replied by shrugging one shoulder.

"Alright," he said. "But sooner or later you'll warm up to me—no pun intended, of course."

Ryker left her to go retrieve his shirt off the kitchen table.

"You know where to find me when that time finally comes."

## CHAPTER 7

**VALORA LOUNGED BACK** against the trunk of the tree she frequently occupied on her daily watch of Norlyn. Her leg dangled off, swinging lightly, the other stretched out straight in front of her along the sturdy branch. She wiggled her fingers, bending them up towards her palm in a wave, making the shadows at least a hundred feet below rise up, up, up to spiral around her dangling limb.

Normally, Valora didn't need to use physical motions to control the shadows. Before the assassination attempt, she had made them do her bidding with nothing more than a quick thought. She still held the ability to do so when it came to shielding herself but to spread them out or bring them up from such a great distance....

If she intended to succeed in her mission, full mental control of the darkness would be necessary. Otherwise, she might end up the same way she had been left in the depths of the forest. And Ryker wouldn't be there to save her the second time around.

Valora continued to swirl the shadows through her fingers until something out of the ordinary came from the village. She moved towards the sound, doing her best to stay out of sight as she crawled and sidled along the thick branches. She leaned forward to get a closer view and squinted, trying to bring clarity to her barely-out-of-focus eyes.

While her sight was not the strongest, Valora took great pride in hearing even the faintest noises. It had often prompted her brother to grow increasingly annoyed with her, especially when she picked up on the shenanigans he and his friends partook in.

But at that moment, she was very glad she had picked up on Bo and his friends, for they were standing not too far from her old group.

"Did you expect my respect or something?" Bo asked. Even from her distance, Valora could hear the anger—the pain—in her brother's voice. "I don't *have* to talk to you."

"We haven't seen you, and we wanted to say hi." Aurelia shrugged. "What's so terrible about that?"

Bo laughed. His friends flanked around him. He had never been the tallest of his group, but he was one of the boldest. But where Bo lacked height, a few of the boys in his group certainly made up for it.

Her brother moved to the front of the group, mere steps from Aurelia, who was acting as though nothing were wrong.

"This village is big, but it's not that big, Aurelia," he said. "We see each other nearly every day, and you've hardly said anything to me. Only small talk—oh, and that my sister died while you all miraculously survived." Bo squinted his eyes at her. "Bit strange, don't you think?"

"We've been giving you time to grieve." Valora wanted to gag at the false sympathy dripping from Aurelia's voice. "We are just as torn up as you about the loss of Valora."

"Sure haven't shown it."

Aurelia crossed her arms over her chest and tilted her head ever-so-slightly. "People grieve differently." Myrcella and Mona moved to her sides. Juno moved forward too, though Valora suspected it was more to help her see beyond her taller friends. "We happen to grieve by honoring Valora's love of her craft."

"You mean by taking her spot as the Master's favorite?"

Aurelia didn't reply. The small smirk growing on her lips fell into a straight line. Juno shifted uncomfortably and turned away from Bo. Whatever small friendship they'd formed over the years must have dissipated since Valora had been lost to the forest.

The talking grew too hushed for even Valora's sensitive hearing to pick up on. She tested the branch she held onto, leaning forward even more, but heard a crack. She quickly leaned back and dropped into a squat. She clung to the branch she stood on while she watched her little brother step closer to Aurelia. Mona and Myrcella wouldn't do anything to him. Juno most definitely wouldn't harm him. But Aurelia… Valora couldn't be sure about her anymore.

Mission be damned. Valora drew an arrow from the quiver on her back and nocked it loosely in her lowered bow. She wouldn't fire unless Aurelia showed clear intentions of harming Bo, but preparation never hurt. She could get revenge in other ways if she gave herself away. No one would harm her little brother if she could prevent it.

But moments later, Bo took a step back, still glaring at Aurelia. He spoke at too low a volume for Valora to pick up on it, but whatever he said made Aurelia, Mona, and Myrcella narrow their eyes at him. Even Juno stared at him with worry. Whatever her little brother said had stirred some kind of emotion in her old friends and clearly not a positive one.

"It's only a matter of time," Bo called as he turned on his heels and ushered his friends away, "before you're exposed for what you are, you two-faced bitches."

Valora let her bow hang at her side. The corners of her lips curled up into a small smile. For the weeks she had watched him from her treetop perch, Valora had seen her brother do nothing but grieve in private. It was reassuring to see him beginning to climb out of the abyss his sorrow had driven him into.

Valora felt a fierce rush of pride for her brother. She watched him stalk away with his friends, leaving the four girls in his wake. They stared after him with some of the coldest looks Valora had ever seen them give. She had only seen them once before, on the day they'd shoved their knives through her back.

Whatever Bo had said to them caused them to look at him the same way they'd looked at her.

Bo wasn't stupid. He most likely accused them of causing her disappearance and death, and that worried Valora. She knew the girls wouldn't take lightly to being blamed for murder, and knowing how they dealt with those who got in their way….

That night. She would begin her mission that night, if only to protect her little brother.

"Valora?"

She startled and nearly fell sideways off the tree when she heard her name. With her free hand, Valora grabbed hold of a branch above her head and looked down to see who could have possibly found her.

Standing on the ground under the tree, a dead wolf slung around his shoulders, was Ryker.

Valora cursed under her breath and wrapped her shadows back around herself.

"Valora, I *saw* you," Ryker called up. "Your shadows don't erase memories, I'm afraid."

Slowly, the shadows uncurled from around her, and when Valora peered back down at forest ground, Ryker was still standing there. He even had the audacity to smile and wave up at her.

Valora rolled her eyes before she started her careful descent.

"What the hell were you doing up there?" Ryker demanded when Valora had successfully navigated most of her way down the tree.

Valora hopped down the small distance to the ground and let out a relieved sigh when her feet landed on solid, non-shaking ground.

She adjusted the strap of her quiver on her shoulder and met Ryker directly in the eyes. "Sightseeing," said Valora. "It's a lovely day out, don't you think?"

She brushed past him, nudging his shoulder with hers while she passed, but Ryker didn't seem to care much. He was far too preoccupied trying to figure out what Valora might have meant, his brows furrowed and his mouth moving, repeating what she had said until he could decipher it.

Suddenly, his eyes popped open, and he jogged, wolf still on his back, to catch up with Valora's brisk pace. He fell into step beside her, but Valora didn't look anywhere but directly ahead.

She kept an arrow nocked loosely in her bow like always while walking in the forest, but there was something additionally comforting about having Ryker at her side.

"Were you watching the village?" he demanded. Valora remained silent. "You were, weren't you? Why would you watch over the village? If anyone in Norlyn sees you—"

"They won't see me because they *can't* see me." Valora pulled a shadow up and around her, casting herself into greater darkness than the thick canopy of the forest provided. "Shadow bender, remember? If I don't want them to know I'm there, they won't."

Ryker didn't seem convinced, but he changed the subject anyways. "Why do you want to watch it? Doesn't it…stir up memories?"

"Not all my memories of Norlyn are terrible," Valora muttered, thinking of Bo, her parents, and the random others she had been friends with.

"Is that what you do all day? Sit in that tree and watch everyone continuing their lives without you?"

"I'm sure you did something similar when you got stuck here."

"No. I didn't."

Valora moved her eyes to Ryker. Not once in the three months since she had started living with him had she asked anything about why or how he had ended up in the forest. Ryker knew her whole story—he'd seen the attack happen and had run to Valora after the others disappeared—yet she knew nothing of his. If he felt no desire to return to his home, it couldn't have been positive.

For a man of so many words, she'd expected him to have told her outright, if only for an excuse to hold one of the many conversations he yearned to have with her. But when she thought back on it, none of the conversations ever seemed to fall onto him. Ryker tried to learn every little thing about Valora, but she never reciprocated by asking him about *his* past life—the life before seclusion in the forest.

His empty eyes found her and softened. "Another time," he whispered, answering Valora's unspoken question. "First, I would very much like to say that, despite your abilities, you should no longer spy on the people of Norlyn."

Valora's eyes narrowed. "And who are you to make the rules?"

Ryker shrugged, the dead wolf rising and falling with the action. "I *do* have a little more experience hiding in the forest."

"You're the only one who's hiding, Ryker. I intend to return to Norlyn at some point."

"Yes, that's why you wrap your shadows around you every time you're in the trees or when you hear a twig snap," he retorted. "You're not hiding. You're trying to be rescued. Though, from experience, it's much easier to be found when you're not shrouded in darkness."

"I'm not trying to return *now*." Valora glared stubbornly at the ground, watching each of her steps. "I'll return when I'm finished here."

"When you're finished? Finished with what? Your secret mission? And then what, Valora? You're just going to traipse into the village all 'Surprise! I'm alive!' and expect *not* to be attacked by those bitches again?"

Right. Left. Right. Left. Right. Valora stayed silent, staring at her feet. She pulled the shadows from around them and swirled them around her legs, wanting desperately to hide in them if only so Ryker didn't figure out why she *could* traipse into the village like nothing had happened. Out of sight, out of mind, right?

"For the love of—" Ryker jogged ahead and stopped in front of Valora. She peered up at him and his wolf. "Your mission. You're—are you planning on killing them all, Valora?" Her continued silence allowed him to piece more of the puzzle together. "You go out to spy on the village…but you're actually spying on *them*. You want to know their routines so you know the best time to strike."

Ryker shook his head and looked off to the side, his mouth hanging open in disbelief. Valora could not and would not willingly give Ryker credit for much, but she couldn't deny he was quite bright. He would have done well as a warrior should he have stayed in Norlyn.

"Did you ever think how that might look? All of your old friends mysteriously dropping dead at the same time?" Ryker continued. "Did you think this through, or did you let your anger consume you like your shadows?"

"I've thought about it, yes. I'm not as stupid as you think."

"I never once thought you were stupid," Ryker admitted. "Not until you told me you were planning a quadruple murder."

"It's not a quadruple murder." Valora rolled her eyes then stared sheepishly at her feet again. "It's four murders occurring at separate times."

Ryker tilted his head to the side. "Valora." He sounded like her mother when she calmly reprimanded Valora for doing something foolish.

He raised a brow at her, and Valora looked up again. The stare he leveled at her made Valora's blood boil. Ryker was treating her like a child. At twenty-one, he was only three years older than her. That small an age gap didn't justify his superior attitude. Valora could very well make her own decisions without any guidance from his end.

"I have a little brother. I have parents that I miss very much," Valora began. "And just because you're deciding to stay hidden in this dark, depressing forest for whatever forsaken reason, doesn't mean I have to follow suit."

"I have no choice but to stay here, Valora."

"Oh, bullshit," Valora spat. "We all have a choice, Ryker. You're just choosing the coward's path."

Warmth radiated from him. Valora could feel it even with the distance between them. Her comment had angered Ryker enough that he lost some control of his abilities. Heat flowed in his veins just as greatly as darkness flowed in hers.

They stood there, staring at each other through narrowed eyes, until Ryker took a courageous step forward. The maw of the wolf on his shoulders hung open, revealing sharp teeth to Valora. Her eyes darted between them and the—quite literally—fiery young man in front of her.

"You know nothing about me," Ryker said through gritted teeth. "Don't call me a coward until you know even half of what I've been through."

Valora took the same step forwards, putting herself within inches of Ryker. If she had been just a little taller, they would have stood nose to nose, but instead, she had to tilt her head up to continue their unrelenting stare down.

"And *you* don't know *me*. As much as you like to think you've got me figured out, Ryker, you've still only scratched the first layer." She dared a quick glance at the wolf's teeth. "I was left to die in this forest. Left for that beast on your shoulders to devour with no remorse from those who betrayed me. They took from me the only life I've ever known, and until they are gone, I can't return to it. Judge me—*hate* me—all you want, but I'm going to exact revenge, starting—"

Both Valora and Ryker jumped, a small gasp escaping her lips, at the sound of a twig cracking. The bushes beside them rattled. Valora raised her bow in the direction of the potential threat. Ryker remained at her side, the wolf still on his shoulders but his body radiating even more heat than before. Valora hadn't noticed how few weapons he carried. She supposed he didn't have to wield any if his greatest strength lie in his ability to manipulate flames. Valora had burned herself on a campfire once when she was little. It had hurt far more and put her out of action for far longer than any injury ever sustained during weapons training.

She glanced quickly at her companion, realizing, for the first time, the true power Ryker held. Whatever waited for them on the other side of the bushes would be less of a threat with him there.

Valora got her answer as to what it was when a low growl and a pair of glowing yellow eyes came from the darkness.

# CHAPTER 8

THE WOLF WAS not alone. It came with four prowling friends, making the battle odds a very uneven five on two.

The leader's lips curled back, revealing sharp, yellowed fangs, long enough to rival the pierce of a knife should they find their way into Valora's flesh. The others were no better, their fur raised, eyes glowing in the dark of the forest.

They stalked around Valora and Ryker, tails whipping, walking on the toes of their padded feet as if anticipating the proper moment to strike. At least one's fur was tinted crimson around the maw.

Valora could only hope whatever poor creature had died that evening filled the predator's stomach—and those of all his friends too.

Her aim darted back and forth between the animals.

Whichever wolf decided to show the most of its teeth or growl the most threateningly would receive the pleasure of being Valora's target. She had to pick wisely, seeing as Ryker had yet to drop the dead wolf wrapped around his shoulders to help her.

"Maybe if you ditched their friend, they would leave us alone," Valora whispered, hardly moving her lips.

Ryker moved to stand behind Valora, his back to hers. The wolves circled them. Three remained within Valora's potential aim while two were in Ryker's. Bastard always got it easy.

"Maybe if you weren't so cold all the time, I wouldn't need their friend to make another blanket."

Valora's head whipped to him but quickly returned to the predators when one let loose another intimidating growl. She pulled her arrow back in response, letting the animal know its fate should it choose to jump.

Each time she moved her aim to a different predator, another inched closer. The pattern repeated, causing Valora to lose her wits and panic.

"Drop the damn animal, Ryker," she hissed while the wolves continued to prowl forward. "I won't need a blanket if I'm dead."

"I'm told that's when you're the coldest," he replied casually.

It was Valora's turn to growl.

"Alright, listen," Ryker whispered. "I'm going to need you to trust me. When I say jump, you jump, got it?"

Valora nodded. Her legs shook so terribly she wasn't entirely sure how successful she would be, but she would certainly try to jump if it meant living to see another day. She refused to die knowing those girls still breathed. Knowing her family had no idea how hard she was willing to fight to get back to them.

The wolves were only a few feet away. If she released an

arrow on one, the others would be on her in one small pounce, tearing her limb from limb in a desperate attempt to get some source of food.

"Ready?" Ryker asked. Valora nodded once. "Jump!"

He crouched, arm extended, palm out with flames shooting in a stream from it. He spun in a circle, trying to hit each of the predators with just a little bit of fire. Valora landed back on the ground just after the blaze passed under her raised feet to find the wolves stumbling backwards, whimpering in fear of Ryker's power. They had lost their organization in the commotion, providing a large gap for their prey to escape through.

Ryker noticed it too. He grabbed Valora's arm and pulled her with him, shouting, "Run! Run!"

She didn't need to think twice about it.

The two set off at their greatest speed, not taking for granted the still-frazzled wolves' hesitation. Even with the head start, Valora knew the wolves would catch up within moments.

She knew she shouldn't have, but Valora turned over her shoulder. Sure enough, the wolves were approaching, gaining on them a tad too quickly for comfort. Valora tried to pick up her pace. Ryker was ahead of her, and he had the wolf still slung over his shoulders. If he could carry extra weight on his back and still manage to outrun the oncoming danger, certainly Valora could do better.

But she hadn't run in a long time. Her one other encounter with the predators had been easy—a quick one-on-one battle involving one arrow through the skull. And her back hurt. Apparently, the deep wounds weren't as well healed as she'd thought.

Valora turned back around and willed herself forward, faster, stronger. She heard the wolves panting, howling, barking. The sound of her breathing became so heavy it nearly blocked out that of the animals. Her legs felt ready to give out at any moment if she didn't stop to calm herself. Her chest was ready to burst as her lungs fought to suck in whatever air possible.

Valora threw her head back and screamed in agony before falling to the ground, the agonizing tear of the wolf's claws suddenly digging into her back too much to bear. She quickly turned onto her back, ignoring the searing pain coming from the fresh wounds, and held up her bow to defend against the chomping maw of the predator. The fangs came centimeters from catching her nose.

Struggling against the sharp, strong mouth of the animal, Valora thrashed on the ground. The others had arrived, or were close to it, based solely off what she could hear. One bow wouldn't defend her against five wolves.

Thinking quickly, Valora lifted her knee into the wolf's stomach. It whimpered in pain and fell to the side, temporarily distracted. Another took its turn, but Valora was ready.

She grabbed an arrow from her quiver and stuck it through the pouncing wolf's neck. It fell to the side, not moving, but the first attacker was back on his feet and especially angry with her. The other three had joined the fight as well.

Valora tried to reach for another arrow while using her bow as a shield, but struggled against the onslaught. She kicked, she swung the bow, she did anything in her power to keep the animals at bay long enough for her to draw another weapon.

But she didn't need to.

Bursts of fire knocked one, two, three wolves away from her, giving Valora a few seconds to catch her breath before she had to fight again. The one unlucky wolf that hadn't been caught by Ryker's power got an arrow through the skull. It fell, immediately dead.

The remaining wolves, burned and angry from Ryker's attack, turned to him. Valora might as well have no longer existed. He stood in a defensive stance, legs bent, ready to move and palms out, ready to fire.

Valora watched in awe as the three wolves advanced towards Ryker, her body still shaking with so much fear she was unable to go to his aid. From the looks of it, he needed no one's help.

Ryker threw his arms down and flames surrounded his hands like torches. The fire crawled up his arms, making light and shadow dance in his amber eyes as though they'd caught fire themselves.

The sweat that coated his skin glistened in the light of the flames, making it appear as though Ryker himself were glowing. Perhaps he was. Valora had never seen him produce flames outside of heating their food or lighting the logs in the fireplace.

She'd never seen anything like the vision before her—the pure power flowing out of every part of Ryker.

It was he who took the first step towards his enemies.

A wolf pounced immediately, but Ryker shot it down with another burst of roaring flames from his palm. Valora covered her mouth, hiding her gasp as she watched the animal struggle then eventually fall still like its two defeated brethren. It took Ryker seconds to kill it.

Another dared to challenge Ryker, followed quickly by its last living companion. Ryker shot down the first attacker like he had the previous, but the second caught him slightly off guard. Valora did nothing to hide her gasp that time as she watched, moving onto her hands and knees to crawl forwards, while Ryker wrestled with the ravenous, angry animal.

The wolf didn't seem to care about the flames at first, repeatedly braving them in effort to get to Ryker's unprotected flesh. But Ryker had lived in the forest. He had battled the predators many times.

Now, Valora understood how he lived to tell the tale.

His arms wrapped around the animal, and it whimpered as the fire burned its fur and the flesh hidden beneath. The wolf squirmed, but Ryker kept his hold—not without difficulty, if his facial expressions were any indication, but a hold nonetheless—until the wolf had no choice but to succumb to its inevitable death.

Ryker kept it in his arms for a few moments after it stopped moving before he rolled it to the side. The flames on his arms disappeared, and Ryker was left lying on his back, chest heaving, staring up at the forest canopy.

Valora fell off her hands and knees, her legs bent out to the side and her weight resting on one palm. The position stretched her back, though, and caused a hiss of pain to escape her. Ryker sat and focused on her instantly.

She reached for her back and, sure enough, when she brought her palm back in front of her, she saw crimson. Valora hardly had time to process what had happened beyond the adrenaline and the defense and the shock before Ryker took her hand and examined the blood on it. His hands didn't burn her as she had expected, but they certainly weren't a normal temperature.

"Did I…?"

Valora quickly shook her head when she saw the worry in his eyes. "It's what caused me to go down initially." She looked down at her bloodied palm. "I'm sorry. I should have been faster. I should have—"

"Don't worry about what you should have done. You're alive. I'm alive. That's all that matters." Ryker peered around her to see the damage on her back. "We should go home. This needs to be cleaned. There's dirt in it from when you were lying on your back, and the last thing we need is an infection."

Before she could say anything, Ryker scooped Valora into his arms. She noticed how careful he was not to place too much pressure on her new wounds and wondered if he had taken the same kind of care when he'd first found her in the forest, suffering from similar injuries.

Out of an irrational fear of falling, she wrapped her arms around his neck. Only then did she notice he no longer carried a dead wolf there. She looked around at the mess of carcasses they left behind and then ahead to where she found his first kill of the day.

"Don't you want your wolf?" she asked, desperately searching for anything that would get him to put her down. Valora knew he wouldn't do so with just her asking, and any struggling on her part would make her back hurt more, tear the wounds open further.

Ryker let out a small huff and grinned. It faltered slightly as his eyes turned down to her. "You're more important right now. And besides," he began, his eyes sparkling, "you said you didn't need *one* extra blanket, let alone six."

Valora rolled her eyes. "Asshole."

She felt his chuckle rumble in his chest and tried not to glance up at his soft smile for the rest of their walk home.

# CHAPTER 9

**VALORA HADN'T REALIZED** it—seeing as she had been in and out of consciousness—but passing out from intense blood loss after being betrayed had actually been a blessing in disguise.

She bit down on a scream, her back arching while Ryker applied a homemade ointment. She had watched him rush around the kitchen, throwing previously collected materials into a stone mortar, crushing them, heating them, stirring them, crushing them some more, and heating them again before returning to the bedroom where Valora remained in pain.

The shallow cuts stung without showing any signs of stopping. She couldn't imagine the pain she would have been in with the deep stab wounds. Had Ryker used the same ointment or did he have another trick up his sleeve to deal with the more severe wounds? Her leather jacket had done a much better job protecting against the claws of the wolf versus the knives of her friends.

Valora shifted uncomfortably on the bed, trying to shake the stinging from her back. She wanted desperately to groan but didn't dare do so with Ryker there. Not that he would have noticed. Each time Valora glanced back over her shoulder, she found him in a state of unrelenting concentration.

She continued to hold her shirt up her back, refusing to take it off no matter how much easier having a bare back would've made Ryker's job. He understood, though his cheeks did flush. Again, Valora's thoughts wandered back to the first time she had been healed, unsure of exactly what had gone on during her fits of unconsciousness. All she knew was that when she finally woke and stayed that way, her clothes were on, all blood stains washed as best they could be from the fabric of her shirt.

If it had not been for that, Valora wasn't sure she would have trusted Ryker as quickly as she initially had. Injured or not, Valora knew the way the male mind worked when presented with any kind of dominant opportunity—as disturbing as it was to consider.

But Ryker had not touched her except for her healing. She didn't need to ask him to know the truth. The way he touched her now, trying but failing to press gently on the fresh gashes if only to make the cleaning process less painful, told Valora enough about his intentions.

Heal her.

Train her.

Release her.

Valora understood solitary life enough to know Ryker would likely want her gone as soon as possible. His kindness came from sympathy and he would offer her shelter until she could go back to the village. But after she completed her mission, Valora held no doubts Ryker would send her on her way. He'd stayed in the forest for a reason after he ran away from Norlyn. Her presence, no matter how much he claimed outwardly it did not bother him, probably hadn't done much to change a three-year mindset of wanting to be alone.

"Do you mind trying to keep still?"

Valora straightened her spine and lifted her shirt in the back just a tad more. She breathed heavily while she waited for the next round of ointment to come. Ryker cleaned three of the five slashes down her back, then came the heat treatment. The beginnings of *that* particular regimen had already started, based on the warmth that occasionally brushed across Valora's otherwise chilled skin. Sometimes, she couldn't tell if she shuddered from the pain or from the drastic change of temperature.

Ryker's hot hand pressed hard on her skin as he smeared ointment across four of the five gashes, and Valora finally screamed. She jumped away, which made the pain worse and yelped again.

"Hold still and that won't happen!"

"I can't hold still if you keep hurting me with your stupid ointment and heat, fire boy!"

Ryker remained still for a moment, then suddenly left with his bowls. Valora only knew when she felt the bedframe shake and heard the floor creak under his steps. She did a quick double-take over her shoulder, dumbfounded he was actually leaving while she still had open wounds on her back.

"Where are you going?" she asked.

Ryker stopped in the doorway, not facing her. "I don't want to hurt you."

She paused for a beat, unsure how to respond. "They're fresh wounds. They're obviously going to hurt no matter how much ointment you use."

Valora turned as much as her body would allow her without the pain becoming too much. She watched Ryker's shoulders rise and fall with his heavy breaths. He acted so strange since they returned. So quiet. It wasn't like Ryker at all.

"It's not the ointment I'm worried about," he whispered. "It's the...."

Valora's eyes shot to the hands that had been aflame only a few hours ago. In a voice quieter than Ryker's, afraid to say anything that might upset him further, she said, "You can't help it. Besides, I moved. You asked me to stay still. If I had, nothing would've happened." When Ryker didn't respond, Valora swallowed and continued, "It didn't hurt *so* bad. I'm just a little sensitive right now. All the nerves reacting and such."

Finally, Ryker turned around. He scrutinized her, trying to catch her in a lie, and Valora willed herself to remain composed, to not show any of the pain from the ointment that remained on the gashes. For whatever reason, she felt she owed him the comfort of knowing he hadn't harmed her.

Actually, she owed him much more. Ryker had saved her life on more than one occasion in the mere three months they had known each other. Therefore, she owed her life to him, by warrior law, twice over.

"It didn't hurt," Valora whispered for affirmation. "Not bad."

Ryker watched her a moment more before he sighed and skulked back over to the bed. She turned away from him and pulled her shirt up at the back again, expecting the ointment application and occasional heating to continue. But all that came was the gentle caress of his fingertips along the injuries.

"You're a mess," he commented.

"I bet you get all the girls with that line," Valora sassed.

Ryker pinched her shoulder lightly and went back to examining her torn-up back. Valora wondered how much could have changed in the past five minutes. Surely he didn't need to run another full assessment?

His hands trailed up her back, pushing up her shirt further than she could hold it up on her own. "You're going to hate me."

"That suggests I don't already." Ryker didn't laugh, and Valora sighed. "What is it?" When he still didn't answer, Valora figured it out. "No. *No.* Under absolutely no circumstances."

"I can't reach the entirety of the gash like this. Seeing as the wolf caught you at the top of your back and dragged down...."

She knew what that meant. The deepest part of the injury was on the top of her back where Ryker couldn't reach—not unless she removed her shirt. Bindings were out of the question. They would create friction on her back that would hurt worse than the blasted disinfectant.

Reluctantly, Valora grabbed for the front of her shirt, her fingers trembling. Her housemate had done nothing but prove he could be trusted during her moments of vulnerability, but there was something about knowing she was half-naked that made the situation different—even if she never did bare herself to him.

Ryker continued to hold it in the back so it didn't fall on top of the already treated parts of the wounds. He said nothing as Valora proceeded to lift the fabric over her head and immediately press it over her uncovered chest. Never before had she felt so exposed, but, as Valora expected, Ryker didn't do anything to acknowledge her nakedness. He simply continued with his work as if it were perfectly ordinary to have a heavily wounded, topless woman in front of him.

"You feel tense," he commented.

"Do I?" Valora retorted. "Wonder why that would be."

"If you didn't want to—"

"I want to be healed. If that means this is how it gets done, then so be it."

Ryker remained silent for a beat. "Lie down on your stomach."

"Why the hell do I have to—?"

"I'm trying to make it more comfortable for you. I can't imagine you're comfortable sitting up so straight it's like you have a rod for a spine."

He was right, of course. Valora desperately wanted to slouch. But more than anything, she wanted to put her arm down. Keeping it raised to protect her chest made her shoulder hurt.

Ryker nudged her with the heel of his palm, and Valora sighed. She leaned forward, careful not to let her shirt slip from where it covered her, and kicked her legs out behind so she lay flat on her stomach. In her new position, the sleep Valora so desperately needed finally caught up with her. She crossed her arms and placed her head in them, promising to shut her eyes for just a moment.

She heard Ryker laugh while he continued to rub the ointment on her wounds. A warm cloth followed shortly after and finally, his heated palms. Valora felt the restraint in his heat. Even so, it was still enough to make her weariness increase.

"I told you you'd be more comfortable." Ryker brushed her

long, black hair off her back, and Valora bristled. "Or maybe not," he chuckled.

"Shhhh," she shushed. "I'm trying to sleep."

"Aren't *you* lucky you can do that."

His hands moved over a particularly tight part of her back, and Valora couldn't help but smile—just a little. "Yes, and I'm so lucky to have had my back torn up by a wolf," Valora remarked, making Ryker chuckle.

The warmth spread across her back as Ryker continued his work healing the fresh wounds. They still stung each time a particularly large glob of ointment was spread over them, but overall, the healing treatment appeared to be working quicker. All the months spent healing her original wounds must have paid off, saving both her and Ryker some time.

It was time Valora needed, she realized.

If the near-loss with the wolf taught her anything, it was that she needed to train, not just with her man-made weapons, but with her abilities as well. It had been too close a call back in the forest proper—one that, upon thinking of it once more, brought the phantom scent of the wolf's musty breath as it snapped at her nose. She caught the coppery tang of blood mixed in with it, and knew, had Ryker not been there to rescue her—again—she might have become the creature's dinner.

Under no circumstances could Valora find herself so close to defeat when she finally ventured into Norlyn to begin her mission. She needed to be ready for anything that might come.

The only way she could ensure that was by starting to train again.

She didn't want to think about how out of shape she would be. Her daily treks to the edge of the forest and subsequent tree-climbing had helped Valora build up some of her strength and endurance, but she would have been crazy to think it was anything like what she had possessed while training with the Master. He had worked them hard, starting the day with basic stretches and cardio exercise before going into full-fledged sparring.

That had been Valora's daily routine for the past three years. All it took was three months for her to lose enough of her skill and strength to nearly fall victim to a wolf.

"So, while I have you here with no chance of escaping, I wanted to say something," Ryker started again after a few minutes of Valora being lost in her thoughts.

"Yes?" she asked, groggily, his heat having lulled her closer to sleep than she had realized.

"You were right earlier when you said I have no power over you. We hardly know each other, really." Ryker slowed his healing. "But would you mind listening to some advice?"

Unfortunately, it appeared Ryker was right. His hands trapped her against the bed, and Valora was far too tired and too topless to sit up and refuse. So, Valora nodded into her crossed arms and shut her eyes again.

"I watched them attack you. I heard what they said, and I can tell that they're spiteful and cruel and far behind you when it comes to maturity. Their reason for doing what they did—" He paused. "It was uncalled for, which might make it harder for you to handle. Maybe that's why you're still so upset about it so many months later. I see the way you tense and your eyes darken when you think about it. You're too kind to do that in return."

Valora let silence consume the room for perhaps too long before she replied, "How do you know? Who's to say I'm not a ruthless killer? As we have now both admitted, we hardly know each other."

His hands roamed over her wounds, warming her skin, her blood, to speed up the healing process. It all felt so intimate—his hands on her bare skin, his steady whisper as he listed his concerns, her *listening* to his concerns and actually taking them into consideration. She hadn't taken advice from anyone but her old friends. Remembering that made it very difficult to continue listening to Ryker, but she did anyway.

"Something tells me you're not, in fact, a ruthless killer. A warrior, yes—and one of the better ones from my understanding—but not a killer by any means."

"I can't go back until they're gone," Valora whispered. She opened her eyes and stared blindly at the wall.

"Is there any other way you can think of…luring them away?"

"Not without angering them further."

Valora had thought long and hard about other options. The only one that made sense was walking straight into the village, alive and healed, and exposing the girls for what they were. She knew some of the villagers would believe her, especially when she showed them the scars on her back. But then what? Her old friends would remain in Norlyn, waiting for their trial, angrier than before? And she would remain in that same village in full susceptibility to their wrathful revenge? If their first attempt at killing her had been so terribly brutal, Valora didn't want to try to live through a second attempt.

Tears silently spilled down her cheeks. He was right. Valora didn't want to kill them. At one point, Juno, Myrcella, Mona, Aurelia—they had all been her friends. She had trusted them with her secrets, her fears, her joys. And they had taken advantage of that trust. She might never live without regret of her actions, but she also couldn't live with anger every day when she thought of how they still wandered around Norlyn as usual, while she hid in a stranger's cabin in the forest.

"Do what you think is best, I guess." Ryker shrugged. "But as someone who's been there, I would ultimately advise against it."

Valora's brow furrowed. "Been there? What do you mean?"

Ryker turned a little too quickly and walked out of the room. From the kitchen he called out, "That's a story for another time. Get that much-needed rest. I'll be back with some dressings for the wounds when you're awake."

# CHAPTER 10

THE THING ABOUT training by herself, Valora quickly learned, was that squirrels didn't react half as well as she wanted them to when she used her shadows. As creatures so accustomed to the dark of the forest, it shouldn't have surprised her.

Valora groaned as her latest opponent scurried up a tree. Then, as her anger overcame her, she brought all the shadows around her hands and waited until the squirrel revealed itself again on a branch.

Her hand lashed out in the direction of the creature when she caught sight of it once more, hopping along unaware of any potential danger. Valora knew her shadows wouldn't physically harm the creature, but she could confuse it—make it react to the darkness the same way any other opponent might.

The shadows followed her command, going out toward the

squirrel in rapid movements, each one just a tad late in Valora's attempts to trap the creature.

All she could think about each time she failed was Ryker's success the previous day when the wolves had attacked. He'd been able to hone his abilities in a way Valora had never witnessed before—a way she wanted to learn how to master herself.

Mere months ago, she'd been able to command her shadows with no more than a thought. To an extent, she still could, primarily putting that skill to use while she sat in her tree perch overlooking Norlyn. But the strength she'd gained when it came to her abilities had faded since she'd been left in the forest. Years of hard work reduced to almost nothing.

She'd always laughed at the Master's preaching that the warriors needed their daily training to keep up their strength. Valora understood that when it came to keeping up physical strength but not the strength of any abilities.

"Your abilities are an extension of yourself," he would tell his ranks. "They need just as much practice in battle as you do."

Valora harrumphed to herself as the squirrel managed to evade her once more by hopping onto a branch thick with leaves. So much for her abilities helping during any sort of battle. She couldn't even use them to catch dinner.

"No spying today?"

Valora turned when she heard Ryker. He emerged from the house, dressed as he always did for his runs in casual, comfortable clothing. She'd dressed similarly that morning, her long, obsidian hair tied up with a leather strap to keep herself cool while training.

"I might later," Valora said. "I wanted to wake up early to

train a little."

"How's your back?"

Valora shrugged, not wanting to admit each movement she made in her attempts to wrangle a squirrel hurt more than she wanted them to. Ryker had given her fresh wrappings before she went to bed, and a fresh coat of ointment to help with the healing overnight while she slept. Still, she'd woken with a sting she hadn't felt in months.

At least this time it came from an expected source. She'd never doubted the wolves would attack her if given the chance. Her friends on the other hand....

"Fine," she replied, nonchalantly. "I'm surviving."

The corners of Ryker's lips curled up. "You're very good at surviving."

Valora ignored that and turned back to the tree. Her squirrel was long gone, and he didn't appear to have any friends for her to practice on either.

Her shoulders sagged on her exhalation.

"What were you doing out here so early?" Ryker asked, never one to let a conversation die.

"What does it look like I'm doing?"

Ryker's brow rose and his gaze flickered past Valora to the tree that towered above them.

"Well, when I first got out here, it looked like you were silently giving that tree a piece of your mind," he said. "Though I'm not sure what it ever did to you, other than offer protection from anything outside this clearing."

Valora rolled her eyes.

"I was training," she said.

"Against a tree?"

"There was a squirrel," Valora informed him. "I wanted to see if I could catch it."

"With…shadows?"

"Within them," she clarified. "I wanted…." Valora sighed. "I don't know. I don't actually know what I wanted to do with them. I think I just wanted to prove I could."

"You know you can use your abilities," Ryker said. "You use them daily when you sit in that tree of yours. If you hadn't had them down yesterday when I passed by, I probably never would have known you were there."

"That's just it, though—I want to do more than disguise myself," Valora admitted. "I want to be able to fight again."

Ryker opened his mouth to respond, but shut it again. Valora knew he was thinking back to the day before, during the attack. She'd tried to fight back, alright—just not with her abilities. She'd opted to use the bow and arrow, as she often had since coming into the forest. Since she'd felt betrayed by her own powers when she needed them the most.

Valora sighed and bit her lower lip, deciding how honest she wanted to be with her housemate, before finally saying, "I was brought into this forest at my strongest and…and I couldn't defend myself then either. Yesterday, when we were attacked, I'd never felt so weak in all my life. I wanted to fight back on my own, but—but I couldn't. My abilities didn't feel strong enough."

"So, you want to be able to use self-defense," Ryker concluded.

Valora nodded. "Yes. Like I used to be able to when I trained in Norlyn."

Ryker took a few steps towards her. "You were a very skilled warrior, weren't you, Valora?"

"Many assumed I would be named the Master's next apprentice."

Valora watched Ryker's eyes flash at that, brighter than normal, as he comprehended what that meant. He had once had the same said about him before he disappeared. That meant, at one point, he and Valora had been on the same skill level—that Valora, should she regain her strength, would be able to hold her own against him. Better yet, she might win.

Of course, Valora didn't foresee herself ever engaging in a heated battle with Ryker. She knew what the Master favoring both of them meant, though....

The power she'd been so in awe over the day before could very well be her own, with her own abilities, if she trained hard enough. Then nothing could stand in her way when she eventually sought her revenge on the girls who had left her in the forest to die.

Ryker's throat bobbed as he swallowed. Then he shrugged.

"I could help you."

Valora's brow rose. "Help me?"

Ryker nodded. "With the self-defense," he clarified. "I've gotten pretty good at it over the years from my training when I still lived in Norlyn, then also—well, you know. From run-ins with wolves and such."

Valora's lips curled upwards slightly. "The creatures you warned me about."

"As much as I was kidding, I wasn't," Ryker said. "There is a lot in this forest that requires the use of self-defense. I've been lucky enough to usually only encounter the wolves, but there's been a time or two where a buck gets defensive when I try to hunt a doe." He shook his head, as if shaking away a bad memory. "Antlers are no joke. But they do make for wonderful kitchen utensils when carved."

Valora's brows furrowed. "Then why do we eat with the wooden spoons?"

"I only bring out the fine cutlery for dinner parties and holidays." Ryker grinned. "You'll have to stick around a little longer to use it."

What should have been an answering grin faltered on Valora's lips, appearing as something more akin to a grimace.

Ryker chuckled. "I know, I know—the idea of spending more time with me is painful. But I'm serious." He ignited his palm so a ball of fire floated in it. "I can help you with some self-defense training. You're going to need it if you're going to stick around a little while longer."

*Stick around.* While she thought of another plan as to how she could go back to Norlyn without committing her quadruple murder.

She knew he'd been serious the previous day in his attempts to stop her from going through with her self-assigned mission, and Valora would have been lying to him if she claimed she hadn't thought about it as she fell asleep. She'd thought about it for months—every option, every angle that might allow her to return to her family without the threat of her old friends looming over her.

Being her friends had been the biggest mistake they'd ever made, though—aside from failing in their mission, of course. It guaranteed that Valora knew them better than she might have even known herself. While she'd opened up to them, the girls had done the same to her. A lot of information had been spilled over the course of five years—secrets and private musings Valora intended to use to her benefit.

But what she'd garnered over the years also gave her no reason to doubt the girls would continue to seek revenge. She couldn't go back to Norlyn and not expect some sort of retaliation or attack.

The only way she could return to Norlyn feeling secure was to make sure she succeeded in the mission her friends failed.

And Ryker couldn't know that. She couldn't risk him kicking her out of his home—yet. Valora would happily leave at the conclusion of her mission, but until that day came, she needed a safe haven to return to.

Ryker was as close as she got to that.

"Do you know anything about shadow benders?" Valora challenged, returning their conversation to his offer.

With a one-shoulder shrug, Ryker replied, "Probably no more than you do about fire benders. This could be a fun learning experience for us, sunshine."

Valora rolled her eyes and shook her head.

"What do you want out of this little deal?" she inquired.

Ryker's brows took their turn to furrow. "What do you mean?"

"Surely, you want something out of this too, right?" Valora pointed to herself. "I'll be the one receiving the training. What do you get in return for your teaching?"

"I'd be training too," Ryker countered. "As much as I'd be helping you learn to defend yourself, I'd be strengthening my own abilities as well. You aren't the only one who's felt desperate enough to train with the rabbits and squirrels."

That sounded reasonable enough to Valora. "Anything else?"

"I'd be getting that companionship I've been craving and

trying to coax out of you." Ryker grinned. He shrugged causally before adding, "And if you agree to this, it must mean you trust me a little bit."

If Valora was not mistaken, she would classify the edge in Ryker's voice as desperation. He truly wanted her to accept his offer for training.

Valora regarded him for a moment, taking in his burning amber eyes, wide and shining with hope. She regarded the tightness of his chiseled, square jaw as he waited for an answer. Valora even noted Ryker's hands, balled into lose fists at his sides.

He always kept his hands tucked away. His fire tucked away—unless absolutely necessary….

Now that Valora had seen a glimpse of it the day before, she wanted to see more of what had made the Master consider Ryker as his apprentice. She wanted him to teach her how to grow strong enough again to be named the apprentice herself. Killing the girls would do her no good if she couldn't go back to Norlyn and continue life as it was, her life as a warrior included.

"Fine," she agreed, then crossed her arms over her chest. "But this doesn't mean we get to hang out all the time. I still want my privacy and my time to go spy."

"We share a one-bedroom-and-one-kitchen cabin in a secluded area of the forest," Ryker reminded her. "Privacy hasn't been a thing since you got here, sunshine. But I can respect your second request."

"Good. It's a deal, then," Valora agreed. "When do we start?"

"How's your back feeling today?"

Valora shrugged. The slight stinging caused by her failed attempts to entrap the squirrel had faded. The wolf had done damage, but Valora had survived much worse—literally.

Ryker grinned. "I'd say we start right now."

Valora fell to the ground in order to dodge the sudden sweep of fire that Ryker sent her way. She cringed from her place among the fallen leaves and twigs, a fresh sting risen in her back, as her eyes managed to find Ryker, his arms ablaze up to his elbows.

He grinned, clearly proud of his ability to get an injured, out-of-shape warrior to drop so easily.

"I wasn't ready!" Valora exclaimed.

"Were you ready for those wolves yesterday?" Ryker retorted.

Unfortunately, he had a point.

"Rule one of self-defense—especially in this forest," her trainer continued. "Always expect the unexpected."

Valora rolled out of the way before another blast of fire hit the spot she'd just occupied. The ground was damp enough with morning dew that the kindling that coated the forest floor sizzled and burned to ash, rather than roaring into a full blaze.

Smoky tendrils of purple-black shadows formed around Valora's hands. When Ryker noticed them, he grinned, her bending abilities having mirrored his own, she realized.

"Cut it out," Valora demanded.

"You wanted to train," Ryker said.

"I thought I'd have more than a few seconds to prepare."

Ryker nodded at Valora's hands. "You know how to control the shadows, now use them to defend yourself."

"I…I don't know how."

It hurt her pride more than she thought it would to admit such a thing, but it was the truth. Valora had always known how to control her shadows and used that skill to her advantage during training. As a shield, as a distraction—but Valora had never honed her abilities as a true weapon. Not as Ryker could—and did.

Valora tried to use her shadows the only way she knew how to then, lashing them out at Ryker and using the benefit of the forest's darkness to do so. They gathered around him in a great opaque shroud in just the same way they had all her sparring partners at training. She knew what would come next, should she hold and keep him trapped long enough. The fear, then the confusion, then the restlessness as he tried to figure out how to escape the dark. By that point, Valora usually had her opponent in a compromising position with her chosen weapon, the fight won.

What Valora didn't expect was the orange light that came from the center of the shadow cloud, first no bigger than the glow of a candle. Then it grew almost to the size of a bonfire before the shadows dissolved, and Ryker emerged, his arms still ignited—up to his shoulders now—and his body glowing with fiery light.

"You ever fought someone whose ability revolved around light?" he asked. When Valora neglected to respond, Ryker chuckled and added, "Training with you will be fun, sunshine."

Ryker lowered his flames back to his elbows, the fire at his palms growing. Two more fireballs flew Valora's way, and she managed, by some small miracle, to dodge them both.

She lashed out with her shadows again, trying to trap Ryker long enough to give her back some reprieve from all the movement. For someone who would need to heal her later, Ryker certainly didn't seem to care about her physical well-being as he continued with his *training*.

Valora should have known better than to think she'd be able to handle him right away or that Ryker would ever go easy on her. He was a fire bender. His kind weren't exactly known for showing mercy, no matter how charming and playful Ryker might be. As soon as his arms lit, he became another one of his ability brethren that Valora had read about.

Ryker was still smiling as he said, "Light beats dark."

"This isn't rock, paper, scissors," Valora shot back, annoyed by the fact that she was losing and by the increasing pain in her back.

But she refused to stand down. She wouldn't quit. She wouldn't fall victim to defeat again.

Valora sent more of her shadows his way, only to have them blocked by a shield of flames. They didn't even get close to entrapping Ryker before he sent more fire her way.

With a small squeal of surprise, Valora mimicked his actions, lifting her arms and dragging the darkness up with them to prevent the fire from reaching her. The shadows did their job, though the flash of heat that warmed Valora's skin made her heart beat at a rapid pace.

That had been too close.

"You almost hit me!" Valora gasped.

The sheer joy that had graced Ryker's face throughout the sudden training session diminished, his voice somber as he said, "I wouldn't hurt you. I know what I'm doing."

"Do you?"

At that, his arms extinguished. Valora's chest rose and fell with heavy breaths as she watched him chew the inside of his cheek, his jaw tense. She'd never seen him so…so offended. And Valora wasn't even sure what she'd said to cause such a reaction.

Their bickering had reached far greater levels than what just took place, and Ryker had never reacted in such a way. In fact, he usually one-upped her with a comeback. He was annoyingly witty that way.

Then it came to her. Valora remembered the night before, when she'd flinched from the sting of the ointment Ryker had used in conjunction with his heating to heal her back. She remembered the fear in his eyes at how he thought he'd been the one to cause her pain.

To hurt her.

Valora released the hold on her shadows and lightened her defensive stance.

"Ryker…" she tried, but he interrupted.

"Maybe you were right," he said. "Maybe it's best if you train by yourself."

"Ryker, I—"

Valora wasn't even sure how she would have finished apologizing, but Ryker once again saved her from having to complete her thought.

"I'd recommend venturing out a little bit—to train with some of the bigger animals. The squirrels won't cooperate. Deer are a better challenge anyway."

With Valora still standing dumbstruck and confused, Ryker retreated for the cabin.

**V**ALORA ENDED UP taking Ryker's advice, and instead of venturing to her usual tree perch to spy on Norlyn that afternoon, she found another clearing. It didn't take long for two does to venture in for some fresh food—some of the only green grass Valora had ever stumbled across in the forest—and they'd proved to be a bit of a bigger challenge than the squirrels.

Training didn't last long, though, as Valora's usual tactics only managed to confuse them for a few minutes before the does ran out of the clearing, too fast for Valora to hope to catch. She might have tried, had her back not hurt so much from the morning's sparring.

When Ryker had first brought up self-defense, Valora thought what she already knew would be enough. She could disorient speedsters, scare the daylight out of regenerators, and even sneak up on strongmen before they got the chance to grab her. Her skills had never failed her before against opponents, but, then again, not many of her opponents had been benders.

Valora had never strengthened her ability as a weapon because, frankly, she'd never needed to. She'd never known how.

She admired the Master a great deal, but his ability of negation would never be able to help her do that either.

Only another bender could help Valora learn that skill.

She huffed a laugh to herself as she trudged back through the forest to the cabin clearing. If the morning's events were any indication, Ryker wouldn't be offering his services again anytime soon. She'd be stuck on her lonesome to train, and as much as she craved time away from her housemate sometimes, the idea that he'd revoked the proposal so quickly bothered Valora.

Fine—if he for whatever reason didn't want to help her anymore, she would learn to live with that. It was probably for the best anyway. He'd have found out sooner or later that the defensive techniques weren't for self-growth but for her mission.

The shadows pulled from the forest floor swirled around Valora's legs in tendrils, their controller completely unaware of their presence, too lost in her thoughts to notice.

This was the reason they'd brought her into the forest, so convinced Valora didn't deserve the favor she'd been shown. Had they seen the weakness Valora hadn't believed she possessed? Did they know the true strength of what her abilities could be and what she hadn't yet mastered?

All this time, Valora had thought she'd been an expert of her powers, but really, she'd perhaps only scratched the surface of what they could do.

No. That wasn't true. That *couldn't* be true.

Her abilities were still strong enough, even without the defensive maneuvers Ryker had tried to show her during their spontaneous training session. They were stronger than the girls had believed when they'd dragged her into the forest.

Valora had become a favorite of the Master for a reason. He knew her abilities were enough to become his apprentice and someday take over his position within Norlyn.

She'd prove it to herself—she'd prove it to anyone who doubted her strength—that she could survive and return to claim that honor just as she was.

Starting that night with the first two who had tried to take that honor away from her.

## CHAPTER 11

**T**HE FRESH WRAPPINGS Ryker had given her that evening during healing hugged her tight but were nothing Valora couldn't handle. They pulled slightly when she sat up in the middle of the night to change from her pajamas into her daily clothes. She tried to move as silently as possible while she fought against her leggings so as not to wake Ryker who slept in the next bed over.

She'd fallen asleep thinking of his reaction that morning. As much as she wanted to have answers, Valora had refrained from asking. She'd refrained at dinner. And she'd refrained as they lay silently in the shared bedroom, waiting for sleep to overtake them. Valora never did find her much-needed rest, but Ryker certainly did. She tried to see through the darkness of the room and lifted the shadows that surrounded him to confirm he slept soundly.

Only when she got that confirmation did Valora grab her weapons—two whetted knives, her bow, and a small quiver with a few arrows—and leave silently and quickly from the cabin in the forest clearing.

Trying to forget her failure earlier in the day, she made her way swiftly through the pitch-dark forest. The pain of the wounds on her back sharpened each time she heard a rustle in a bush or a snap of a twig. More often than not, it was nothing too dangerous—an owl flying down to catch a mouse, a raccoon scurrying past, a doe up past her bedtime—but Valora still kept a steady pace down the memorized path to the forest edge, not wanting to test her luck.

She stopped when she reached the point where the dense collection of trees met the open space separating the forest from the village. Months stood between Valora's last steps outside the confines of the trees and the present. Even when she couldn't yet climb to her perch, she'd never left the outskirts of the forest. The darkness provided the extra shielding she needed, despite the distance between the village and her current position. The open plain allowed for sounds to carry further than she could actually see.

At that moment, she heard only the rustling of the half-dead leaves in the gentle night breeze.

Valora took one timid step outside the shelter of the trees and pulled the darkness they created with her. Normally, she had someone with her to tell her the disguise worked. Alone, Valora needed to trust her skills.

She let loose a deep sigh and shut her eyes. When she opened them again, the darkness tricked her into seeing her old friends. Within a few blinks, they vanished.

She was alone.

Valora sighed again and stepped further out into the open, making sure she kept her hold on the darkness surrounding her. The pitch of the night did its job well enough, but she could never be too safe, especially considering her purpose of being out so late—for traveling back to Norlyn in the first place.

The land outside the forest felt foreign after her time away. Based on the moon's fullness, the fourth month since the attack neared. She had been living with Ryker for four months. She had been away from her brother, her mother, her father, for four months.

A breath shuddered in her throat when Valora first caught sight of the houses and stores that made up Norlyn. Somewhere in one of them, her parents slept after a day of selling their candles. Bo enjoyed a rare few hours of rest at home, away from friends, in his lofted bed. Apparently sleeping on the ground was too boring.

Valora smiled at the thought and fought back the tears threatening to spill over. She swallowed the lump in her throat and dabbed at the corner of her eyes. She couldn't get emotional. If she planned on completing her mission, Valora needed to be unyielding. Unafraid. Undaunted.

She marched into the village, her shadows wrapped as tight as her bandages, shrouding her from the few stragglers still out at such an absurd hour of the night.

A set of voices came too close for her liking, and Valora pressed herself against the side of a village shop. She disappeared in the shadows from the overhanging roof and two young men strolled past, laughing. Given the time and the stench of alcohol coming from them, Valora suspected she could have remained out in the open and still gone unseen.

She watched them disappear around a corner, removing her cover slightly with each step they took. Then she was off in the direction of her desired destination, jumping from shadow to shadow cast by the moonlight on the houses. It covered Norlyn in a bright blue glow that would have given any other intruder some issues. For a shadow bender, the moonlight was never an issue.

Valora crouched below the window at the front of Mona and Myrcella's family house. She tapped into her abilities, making sure her cover would hold, before she rose to peer into the window. She saw everything inside, but if anyone passed by, Valora would look like a spot of darkness, a creature of the night, created by legends, coming to haunt.

No one in the family stirred. Not the parents. Not the older sister or younger brother. Most certainly not Mona and Myrcella. Even malicious assassins needed their rest.

Valora sat on the ground, taking a moment to collect her thoughts. She breathed in, deeply out. She knew exactly where to go—through the window Myrcella and Mona never locked, to the right to slice one neck, then the left to slice the second. She would be in and out in seconds if everything went as planned. That included keeping her thoughts in line, just as she had practiced.

She knew from countless conversations and sleepovers that Myrcella slept like the dead, but Mona woke easily. With that in mind, although Myrcella had inflicted the initial wound, Valora needed to kill Mona first. If she heard anything, she would wake and alert the rest of the house.

As stealthily as possible, Valora snuck around the side of the house. No matter if she had darkness surrounding her, while people couldn't see her, they could still hear her. One misstep and her cover would be blown.

The luck she'd enjoyed so far continued when she noticed that Myrcella had left the window open a crack to let cool air in, likely despite Mona's protestations. She pushed it open slowly to avoid any potential squeaking and hopped onto the ledge as silently as possible.

She was in, but she couldn't dwell on it for long. Valora needed to keep her thoughts controlled, perhaps even more so than her shadows. She lifted the darkness slightly so as not to cloud her concentration.

*Why did you kill her?*

*Was it worth it?*

Myrcella stirred, her face twisting. Valora grinned. It was working. Even in her slumber, the telepath had picked up on Valora's thoughts—the ones she'd trained herself to repeat over and over and over again. In their last moments, she wanted the twins to feel haunted, just as she had felt for the months since their betrayal.

*You hurt her.*

*You left her for dead.*

She crept towards the bed, careful to dodge every creaking floorboard. The amount of time spent in the very same bedroom gossiping about boys and petty drama had taught her well which spots to avoid. Never step to the left of Mona's bed—it would creak every time. Myrcella's mattress had bad springs—move quickly to avoid hitting it. Avoid the bedroom door—the hinges were unoiled.

Valora stood over Mona, on the right side of the bed. Behind her, Myrcella continued to stir, haunted by Valora's repetitive thoughts, but did not wake.

*Why did you do it?*

*What did she do wrong?*

She removed a knife from the sheath at her hip. Once upon a time, Valora had confided in Mona. She had *cried* to Mona when she'd felt she couldn't fulfill the expectations the Master held for her. They had consoled and laughed with and sympathized with each other.

And now Valora stood over her one-time friend with a knife in her hand.

*Why did you kill her?*

*Why did you betray her?*

Before she could let her emotions get the better of her, Valora put a palm on Mona's forehead, pressed her head back, and sliced the knife across her exposed throat. She left no chance for Mona to wake and scream.

Blood gurgled and pooled from the gash. Valora watched it with far less guilt than she liked to admit. In killing Mona, she stood one step closer to returning home—and she hadn't even needed her abilities to accomplish it. She would be another step closer in a few seconds.

Valora tiptoed to Myrcella's side of the room. Myrcella groaned in her sleep and began to stir more violently. Valora found their last moments oddly reminiscent of their personalities—Mona quiet unless given reason to comment and Myrcella thrashing about as if ready to wake and throw a punch.

Valora had given Mona no opportunity to comment, nor would she allow Myrcella the chance to show her violent side. Not this time around, anyway.

*Watch out, Myrcella.*
*You're next.*

Suddenly her victim shot up in bed and turned to where her twin should have been sleeping. Valora moved quickly, still shrouded in shadows. Just before Myrcella could scream at the sight of her dead, bloodied sister, Valora wrapped an arm around her forehead and dragged her knife across Myrcella's throat. Blood bubbling out of her throat and mouth swallowed what would have surely been a spine-chilling scream.

Valora released her hold, and Myrcella fell back onto the mattress. The way she landed caused the blood to spill from her neck onto the floor, rather than neatly onto the mattress like it had with Mona.

Replacing her knife in its sheath, Valora gazed around the room. Blood slowly covered it as it leaked from her victims, but at least, for once, it wasn't coming from her back.

The thoughts of her injuries made her skin tingle. She needed to get home and lie down. The activity was not good for wounds so fresh, especially after the day she'd already endured.

Valora turned to head back out the window, her shadows released in what might as well have been an otherwise unoccupied room, when she heard the unoiled door open and reeled back round.

Two eyes met hers—ones attached to a furry, growling body with bared teeth—before she could pull her shadows back into place.

She'd forgotten about the dog.

Valora slowly backed away, her palm extended in an attempt to keep the growling, black beast calm. Her feet waded through the pool of blood that had collected on the floor, courtesy of

Myrcella's neck. With each bloodied footstep, the dog growled louder, a bark threatening to tear from her throat.

Ash knew Valora. She'd built up a friendly relationship with the gentle giant of a dog over the countless times she'd visited the house. She might have been able to use that to her advantage, had she not been standing in the pools of two of Ash's owners' blood. The dog likely no longer saw Valora as a friend. No—in that moment, Ash saw Valora as a threat to the family, and based off the snarls escaping from behind the bared teeth, the dog might very well be ready to alert them with a bark.

She drew the line at killing the dog. Valora refused to kill two people *and* a dog that night. Ash had done nothing wrong, other than utilize the very irritating trick of opening the door.

"Easy, girl," Valora soothed her in a relatively calm voice. "It's just me. It's Val."

Ash's growls rumbled lower, quieter, and Valora lowered her hand ever so slightly. Had that done the trick? Had that been enough to bide her time to escape out the window?

The shadows would do her no good against Ash. The dog's sense of smell would allow her to keep track of Valora even if she were hidden in plain sight. Valora had figured that out one afternoon not too long before. With the added scent of Mona and Myrcella's blood on her shoes, there was no way the dog wouldn't pick Valora out of any hiding spot.

Valora jumped when Ash barked, loud and angry, for the whole house—probably the whole village—to hear.

She staggered back, grabbing onto one of the posts on Myrcella's bed for support, but ended up tripping over a stray boot. Valora landed with a thud and soft splash in the blood on the floor. She lifted her hands to examine the damage. Crimson ran down her fingers, her palms, her forearm—

Feeling the blood made Valora's anxiety rise. She had committed a double murder, and now she would be caught in the act.

From somewhere else in the house, she heard the twins' father yell for Ash to quiet down. The dog did no such thing as she continued to advance on the scrambling Valora. She felt a horrible sense of déjà vu from the previous day. At least she knew Ash didn't enjoy eating human flesh like the wolves.

Back on her feet and covered in blood, Valora rushed for the window. The quick movement excited Ash, and the dog chased after her, barking and snapping until Valora barely made it out of her only available escape.

She heard the scream not long after, piercing the silent night alongside Ash's echoing barks. Mona and Myrcella had been found, and it was only a matter of time before she was discovered, too—the dead girl returned for revenge.

Valora tried desperately to get hold of the darkness, to wrap it around her like a cloak, but her mind raced too frantically to concentrate on anything but escaping the village without being caught. Her throat stung with the burn of her heavy breathing and welling tears.

She couldn't control them. The shadows wouldn't obey like Valora needed them too. Perhaps…perhaps everyone was right. Perhaps she wasn't as strong as she—and the Master—had thought.

She bolted through Norlyn. Her adrenaline had kept her pain at bay during her escapade thus far, but the sprinting—the movement of her arms propelling her further—pulled at the wounds. Valora felt them tearing under the wrappings, causing blood to soak through her shirt.

Barking and yelling followed behind her. Valora, having not learned her lesson the day before, glanced back and saw Ash advancing. Further behind, two silhouetted figures chased after her as well, both with deep voices—the twins' brother and father.

Valora picked up her pace, running for her life for the second time in two days. Around the village, more windows lit up, the unnatural chaos waking the usually peaceful place. But Valora neared the edge of Norlyn. When she reached it, there would only be the open space between her and the forest left to cover.

That was, if Ash or one of the angry villagers didn't catch her first.

Valora fought against her weakening legs. Her face twisted in pain as she willed herself on, the edge of the forest growing closer and closer with each stride. No one would dare track her there.

She broke through the first thin line of trees and kept going. Bushes and low branches scraped against her exposed skin. Valora panted and gasped each time one caught her, but ignored the pain. A droplet of blood ran down her cheek like a tear.

The barking faded. The yelling stopped, but Valora did not. She kept going and going until she broke into the clearing. Only then did she slow and hunch over, her hands on her knees, trying to catch her breath. When she looked up, Valora saw smoke rising from the chimney.

Suddenly, her worry overpowered her fatigue.

Valora swallowed audibly then began her slow journey into the house. Blood caked her arms up to her elbows. Crimson soaked her clothes, a mixture of her own blood and Myrcella's. She looked like the ruthless killer Ryker had denied her being. In reality, she was nothing more than a clumsy killer who'd gotten spooked by a barking dog.

Valora peeked inside as she slowly opened the front door. Ryker sat at the kitchen table, already watching her. She stepped inside, closing the door behind herself. The click of the lock and the crackling fire were the only sounds in the room. The reflection of the flames made Ryker's amber eyes dance, but not with the anger Valora expected.

They stared at each other, unrelenting, until his gaze scanned her full body twice over. When Ryker's eyes met hers again, Valora stopped breathing, waiting for his nasty remark about how stupid she had been, how reckless her plan was, how she should have—

"Come on," he said calmly. "Let's get you cleaned up."

**VALORA TRIED TO** sleep, but it mostly consisted of her shutting her eyes, coming somewhere near a deep slumber, then opening them again. This went on for a few hours before she finally saw the sun beginning to rise. She sat up, wounds freshly wrapped, and peered at the bed beside her. Valora found it void of Ryker.

He'd stayed up just as late as her, if not later, in order to help her clean and dress the wounds on her back and face. His bed looked as though it hadn't been slept in, but then again, Ryker never failed to make his bed in the morning.

She got up, putting on a pair of loose cotton pants and an oversized wool sweater. She tied her hair up in a bun with a leather strap, and when she caught sight of herself in the broken glass Ryker called a mirror, Valora froze.

Not even a full day had passed, and yet the person that stared back at her in the reflection was significantly different from the person she'd seen the prior morning. Now, the person that stared back could call herself a killer.

She turned away, unable to stare into her dark eyes any longer, and went outside to the kitchen. A plate of food sat on the table. Roast rabbit. Valora averted her eyes and crossed her arms over her chest.

Outside, she found Ryker squaring off against a slab of iron. Fire flew from his palms, his fists, and his bare feet, hitting the giant metal wall and leaving nothing but a black mark behind. Valora watched him, bare except for his wrist wrappings and a pair of cotton trousers rolled up to his knees, as he went about his routine. He didn't seem to notice her.

Soon enough, the fire stopped. Ryker stood still, panting and sweating, staring at the iron in front of him. He ran his hand over the marks he'd left, touching them as gingerly as he had Valora's open wounds the day before.

She cleared her throat and his head turned slowly towards her. Ryker met her eyes for only a moment before he went to work untying the wrappings from his wrists.

"Did you eat?" he asked.

"Did you sleep?" she countered.

One side-eye later, Valora had her answer.

"I'll go today," he volunteered, and Valora lifted a questioning brow. "I don't want you too close to the village after what happened last night."

"You won't be able to shield yourself."

"I've done well enough on my own for the past few years,

thanks."

He finished unwrapping his wrists and clutched the worn fabric in his fist.

"I don't know why I ever thought you would only want to train as self-defense," he muttered. "I thought, well—I thought you might have listened to my advice."

"It's what needs to be done, Ryker," Valora returned, her face and voice somber. "I can't go back with them still in Norlyn."

"But killing them in return? You're better than that, Valora," her housemate challenged. "You're different than them, and I know if you succeed—and you will succeed, given your stubborn determination—you won't be able to live with yourself afterwards."

Valora didn't respond, only wrapping her arms tighter around herself, her eyes shifting from Ryker to the ground.

Twigs and dried leaves crunched under his steps as he moved closer to her.

"I'll go watch what happens today and report back, alright?" He stopped in front of her and placed a hand on her shoulder. "In the meantime, you get some rest. I know you didn't sleep last night. And please eat. I feel bad killing those cute little bunnies if you're not going to benefit from it."

Valora scoffed. "If I didn't want to eat before, now I definitely don't. You can't go around telling people to eat cute little bunnies!"

Ryker chuckled and ran his hand up and down Valora's upper arm. The chill in the morning air made both their breath visible. The sweater she'd chosen to wear was warm, but nothing compared to the heat of Ryker's hand. She missed it when it dropped back to his side, and her skin felt colder than before beneath the wool.

"Eat. Sleep. I'll be back, and we can work on healing all your nice new battle scars, yeah?"

Valora rolled her eyes and Ryker chuckled.

"Looks like you were right," he said. "Nothing has changed. You're still as stubborn as you were before your mission began."

Ryker smiled at her and disappeared into the house. But he was wrong. Everything had changed in one night. And Valora still had two more to go.

## CHAPTER 12

**RYKER RETURNED AT** sundown. Valora, who had waited very impatiently and without sleep all afternoon, hopped up from her bed and ran out to meet him in the kitchen as soon as she heard the door open. He met her eyes, looking first at the still-untouched food on the table. He wore an unamused expression.

As it turned out, it wasn't her lack of eating that had upset him. What he'd learned while out watching the village did.

Even though they rose before or with the sun, the village went into action long before then. Ryker told her that when he got to the top of the tree Valora usually utilized as her lookout— "You found quite the perch. How do you not fear for your life every time you climb up there?"—the villagers were already in a frenzy.

Finding two girls murdered in cold blood, in the middle of

the night, in a locked house was cause for concern that went beyond the standards of the forest.

When Ryker revealed he'd seen the bodies, Valora shuddered. But instead of making her feel guilty about her decision, Ryker actually complimented her. Based on what he'd overheard, they wouldn't have been found until morning had the dog not been brought into it. A quick, quiet kill. One belonging to an expert warrior.

"No wonder they dragged you in here to be rid of you," he said. "I have to admit I'm somewhat afraid to sleep next to you. The family said they didn't hear a peep."

Valora rolled her eyes and stuck the points of a fork into the kitchen tabletop. As reassuring as the comment should have been, especially after their issues the day before, Valora couldn't help thinking about all the mistakes she'd made—how her control over her abilities had been so weak in her panic. It could have been better, no matter how cleanly and quietly Valora had performed the actual murders. If her shadow-bending skills were stronger, she wouldn't have run into any issues at all.

"Who's Bo?"

Valora's head shot up. The fork remained stuck so far into the table that she couldn't pull it out without struggling.

"What?" she breathed in disbelief. She had never mentioned her little brother before, not wanting to give Ryker too much information about herself without gaining anything about him in return.

"Who. Is. Bo?" Ryker repeated. He looked more curious after her reaction. "The small one who attacked you—the blonde one—she was crying, but the ringleader kept mentioning someone named Bo."

"What did they say about him?" Valora leaned in, scooting her chair closer to Ryker's. "I need to know what they said about him."

"They blamed him." Valora's face paled. "They…they said there was some kind of altercation a few days ago? They thought he killed the twins because of it."

Valora leaned back in her chair. Her determination to kill Mona and Myrcella had made her forget that potential obstacle. She'd been so desperate to prove herself and the others wrong that she hadn't thought of any other repercussions.

Valora cursed to herself. She should have remembered the dispute her brother had had with the girls, and she should have known Aurelia would use it to her advantage. Just as Valora had used the information she'd gathered about Mona and Myrcella to make her job easier the night before, Aurelia and Juno would no doubt do the same. It was how they'd managed to get her to go into the forest in the first place. They'd manipulated her weaknesses—Valora's desire to please her friends.

They were doing the same to Bo, using his defensive outburst as the grounds.

Who else would have a motive to go against the girls? As far as the people of Norlyn knew, Valora had died months ago, and for whatever reason, not many others disliked her old group of friends. Valora had always found that hard to believe—even *she'd* thought Aurelia had her moments. Others probably kept their opinions more guarded, though. For all Valora knew, the whole village hated her old friends. Why would they have told *her* their negative stances? She had been one of them.

Bo, however, had expressed his opinions. He'd called them out in front of a group. He'd posed a threat to Mona and

Myrcella and *still* posed a threat to Aurelia and Juno's secret. And Valora had provided them with the perfect excuse to rid themselves of that threat by killing Mona and Myrcella.

Her little brother—accused of murder. Because of her….

"He was there," Ryker continued. Valora looked up. "He was there and defended himself. His parents and friends were there as well. The dad…he was really upset. Looked ready to jump on the brunette girl, yelling about stuff I didn't know. Called her a few names before the wife took over and kept—are you crying?"

Silent tears ran down Valora's cheeks. She sniffled as Ryker watched and waited for her to compose herself, his face relaxed and patient.

Ryker sat still, though—not reaching for her, not saying anything. Just waiting until Valora wanted to talk again. She wiped her nose with the back of her hand, not caring how disgusting it was.

"Bo is my little brother," Valora finally choked out. Something like relief flashed in Ryker's eyes before they filled with sympathy once more. "They fought a few days ago—Aurelia and Bo—and she threatened him. He's so kind…he never would have stood a chance against them. But I just…I put him in more danger by acting out."

She sniffled again and inhaled a shaky breath. It caught when Ryker placed his hand on her knee. Valora stared at it, trying to remember the last time anyone had done anything to comfort her. Console her. No matter how simple.

"They know, Valora," Ryker whispered. "Your brother… the man and his wife were your parents?" Valora nodded. She didn't need names or descriptions. She knew her parents' steadfast defense of their children anywhere. "They all know the girls did something to you. That much is obvious, even from the little I saw."

Valora gazed up at his sympathetic amber eyes. She watched him as he struggled to keep eye contact with her. She knew he hated her actions—apparently could hardly stand to look at her knowing about the blood now on her hands. He'd been kind enough to help her clean up her injuries the night before, and all the other times before that. And his claim that he didn't think she'd use the training for her mission—Valora knew not even Ryker could admit that was the full truth. Somewhere, deep down, he'd had to have known what she wanted to do, even if he didn't want to believe it.

When Valora reached out and placed her hand atop his, Ryker let out a shuddered breath.

More silent tears trailed down Valora's cheeks as she said, "I need your help training. After what happened today…I can't risk anymore mistakes. I can't have them finding any reason to blame Bo. I want to use this time to become stronger and learn more about my abilities."

A tear dropped onto Ryker's thumb, but he didn't move it. He didn't pull away from Valora's touch, as if knowing she needed him at that moment. She needed something to ground her, to make her feel as though she weren't asking the impossible or, worse, something completely embarrassing.

She knew, based off his reaction the day before and given his aversion to her mission, the likelihood of him declining her request was high. Valora might have thought it higher had he removed himself from the space again, though. That Ryker remained in his seat, staring at the teardrop on his hand gave Valora a little glimmer of hope.

She would never admit it to him—for fear of inflating his already gigantic ego—but Valora needed Ryker if she wanted to succeed.

Ryker nodded slowly. "I can help." He placed his other hand atop hers. "I *will* help," he assured her.

The glow in his eyes made Valora believe he was holding back from telling her something more, and for once, Valora didn't care. She would get it from him eventually. From that moment forward, Valora had a feeling a lot of things would change between the two of them. For the first time since he had rescued her, she and Ryker were on the same team.

## CHAPTER 13

"**P**UT YOUR BACK into it! C'mon! Okay, okay, maybe not your back *literally*, but show me what you got, shadow bender!"

Valora glared at Ryker as he pushed his fire against her shadows. They broke the moment the light hit them, as expected. She grew more frustrated with each failed attempt to the point where her head had started to hurt. If she kept up much longer, Valora thought her skull might actually burst. But as with all new skills, Valora needed to hone in on learning how to manipulate the darkness in ways she never tried before. Ways that would work against the light of Ryker's abilities.

She cast up another shield as Ryker's flames came at her once more—but in a form different than what he'd used before.

"What was that?" she asked.

"What was what?" Ryker replied, his flames still formed into the same shape he'd struck with.

Valora weakened the shadows swirling around her hands until they disappeared entirely, blending back into the near darkness around them. Some of the sun's rays managed to leak through the canopy, providing their training session some light, the rest provided by Ryker.

She pointed to the fire coming from his hands, shaped into thin strands of flame that had lashed out at her the same way a whip would.

"What are those?" she asked.

Ryker's attention tilted down to the fire. He shrugged, then returned his focus to his training partner. "I don't know if they have an official name. I just figured out how to do it one day when I was bored."

Valora eyed the dancing flames. "How do you concentrate the fire like that? So it's solid."

The corner of Ryker's lip twitched upwards. "Like weapons?"

Valora cocked her head, unamused. "If that's what you want to call them."

"That's what they are." Ryker grinned, flicking his wrists so the whips reacted, waves of orange and yellow light. "Weapons. Except instead of being man-made, I've learned how to create them from my abilities." His eyes narrowed speculatively at Valora. "I bet you could do this too."

She huffed a laugh, letting the shadows appear once more around her hands. "I don't know if you've noticed, but my shadows don't exactly have much substance to them."

Ryker chuckled as he extinguished his whips. Valora loosened her control of her abilities as well as he approached her.

"No, no—bring them back," Ryker instructed.

Valora narrowed her eyes at him, unsure which direction his training was going to go, but did as instructed.

A fresh ball of fire appeared in Ryker's palm. The heat of it radiated onto Valora, its glow cast over both of their faces.

"Hold up a shield against this," Ryker instructed.

Slowly, Ryker eased his palm forward, not by way of striking, but as if trying to test something. Valora followed his orders, though she wasn't sure why. He'd seen her throw up a shield before, her shadows just barely strong enough to hold against the light of his fire.

The same result came about when Ryker tossed a small ball of flame into the shield. It dissolved with a sizzle, lost in the darkness.

He nodded slowly. "Okay, now do that thing where you trap me inside the shadows." When she neglected to fulfill that request as well, Ryker added, "Humor me, Valora."

She sighed but did as he wanted, holding out her hands to let the shadows find their place around Ryker, trapping him in a sphere of darkness.

"Hold tight," Ryker commanded. "Bring as many shadows around me as you can. I'm going to try to break free."

Valora nodded pointlessly. With as many shadows as he wanted her to trap him in, there was no chance he could see her. But Valora could see Ryker, the glow of his hands giving away his position within the translucent mass surrounding him.

The shadows swirled as Valora brought forth more of them, conjured both from her natural abilities and drawn in from the darkness of the forest. Even so, Ryker's fire continued to glow within them as he attempted to break free.

Then Valora felt it—the push of his abilities against hers.

She'd never felt that before, not even the day he'd initiated their sudden sparring session. What normally appeared as flimsy tendrils suddenly held enough strength to withhold the light that Ryker tried to push through in his attempt to free himself.

Something told Valora he very easily could have if he ignited his abilities just a bit more, but that wasn't Ryker's intention. No, Valora knew he was holding back so that she could feel the push of his fire against the shadows. To prove their solidity.

The light dimmed before Ryker called out, "Okay, you can take the shadows away."

Soon, Ryker's grinning figure emerged from the dwindling tendrils Valora set free from her control.

"Did you feel that?" he asked.

"It was…it was like I was pressing against the flames," Valora replied.

"Exactly." Ryker took two steps towards Valora. "I remembered the shield you put up a few days ago and wanted to test it. The exercise we just performed was for extra confirmation that your shadows can act the same way my fire does."

"And what way is that?"

"They solidify into a weapon you can control and utilize unlike any man-made weapon you might own," Ryker explained. "It requires a different kind of concentration, but based off what you just demonstrated, I have a feeling you can pick up the skill quickly."

One of Valora's brows quirked in curiosity as she asked, "What can I do with solid shadows?"

Ryker shrugged. "As someone with different abilities, I suppose that's up to you to decide. I, personally, don't use the whips outside of training, but your abilities…." He regarded her for a moment before finishing, "I imagine there's a lot you can do if you master the shadow whip technique."

Valora's brow furrowed. "Shadow whips?"

"You have a better name for them?"

She didn't answer because she did not.

Ryker grinned at the silence, then took up a defensive stance.

"C'mon," he encouraged. "Let's see if you can do it. Channel your focus into the whips—as though they are an extension of you rather than just your given ability. Hone them like a weapon instead of a shield."

Fresh flames lit Ryker's palms as he waited for Valora to go back on the defensive. Her shadows curled around her, coiling around her legs and forming around her palms in the likeness of Ryker's fire. She allowed the purple-black tendrils to grow, extending beyond her normal confines, until they stretched as long as the whips Ryker utilized before.

Ryker eyed the whips and smirked.

"Show me what you've got, sunshine."

Then he sent a ball of fire Valora's way.

She dodged out of the way at the same time she flicked her wrist, the shadow whip growing even longer as it reached for Ryker. It fell just short of what she'd hoped would be a successful latch around his ankle, and he knew it.

"Close," he said. "Again."

He launched another two fireballs in succession, each one missing Valora with enough breadth that she knew he'd never intended to hit a target. His mercy, however, didn't prevent Valora from lashing out stronger than before, more determined.

Valora struck with whips of darkness each time Ryker acted. They danced around the clearing—her darkness against his light—in attempts to win the battle of opposing abilities.

Ryker laughed at her and threw more of his fire around. Valora suspected that after so many years of having only the forest predators and a slab of iron to fight against, having a decent opponent was nice. She had to admit she'd missed squaring off against someone with decent talent. Even facing off against the other talented warriors in Norlyn had grown tiresome once Valora mastered the techniques to beat the select abilities.

Ryker proved to be a much-needed challenge.

His taunts and confidence bothered her. Much like Aurelia, Valora hated being second best. She would never murder someone for it—Valora knew when to pick her battles and admit she might actually be weaker than her opponent—but she would also never let Ryker get away with it.

She scanned the surrounding forest. Luckily for her, the dense canopy created plentiful shadows even in the middle of the day. Valora grinned, and Ryker stopped smiling. He knew well enough to fear her when she felt confident, even with an ailing back.

Valora watched the shadows creep up behind Ryker and wrap silently and successfully around his ankles. They may not have been aimed at him in the form of a whip, but they did the job easily enough.

She jerked her chin up, and Ryker's feet shot out from under him. He crashed onto the ground with a gasp and a grunt, the fire in his palms fading to nothing but embers. Valora watched with pride as he moved up onto his elbows, grinning with his white teeth.

"You proud of yourself?" he asked.

Valora shrugged and turned on her heels, taking a few steps

away, an extra swing added to her hips. "Not yet."

When she heard Ryker try to stand, she jerked her chin up again and aimed her palm down at the ground. He grunted again, and when Valora turned back over her shoulder, she found the shadows pressing him down in place. Ryker's body shook with silent laughter.

"Now I'm content." She smiled. "This training session has given me wonderful ideas of how to keep you quiet."

Ryker's hands ignited. He ran them over the shadows, making them fade in the light. Valora did nothing further to stop him as he sat up and leaned back onto his doused palms.

"And I thought you were beginning to warm up to me." She raised a brow at him. "No pun intended."

Valora rolled her eyes and shook her head. "Guess again."

She turned away and swirled a small cloud of darkness with her fingers like a cyclone. With a flick of her wrist, she sent it spinning toward where Ryker sat, making sure it disappeared just before it would have hit him. A reciprocating burst of flames shot past her shoulder and Valora jumped. She turned to glare at him and found Ryker wearing a shit-eating grin.

"I definitely don't like you," Valora concluded.

Ryker got to his feet, and she turned away again, hoping to actually make it back to the house on her third attempt. It seemed like her companion planned to allow as much as he fell into step beside her.

"Not even a little bit?"

"Nope, not even a little."

"You sure about that?"

"Positive."

Ryker shrugged. "You'll like me eventually. And besides," he said, nudging her with his shoulder, "I got you to smile, and that's all I've been going for."

Valora peered up at him. He stood at least five inches taller than her. She didn't say anything, though—just stared—and it took Ryker a moment to realize he'd earned her attention. But after a double take, he grinned and nudged her again.

"You *do* realize you're a somewhat…moody person, don't you? I mean, it's taken me months just to get you to crack a smile. I'm just glad to be the one to prove you could."

Valora kept her head down, guilty for bringing such negativity into his house. Ryker—who never seemed to be without a smile—had invited a girl who neglected to do so for *months* to stay with him. Valora didn't feel guilty for not being happy. She had the right to be sad, what with everything that had happened. But Valora couldn't help feeling some guilt for acting sorrowful enough that Ryker had made a personal goal of making her smile.

"Hey," Ryker whispered and grabbed her shoulders. When he refused to let go, Valora finally looked up at him again. "You did great today. I've never known a shadow bender that could do what you did."

"I was unaware you knew any other shadow benders."

"I don't. But I suspect that if I did, you'd still outshine them."

Valora couldn't handle the way he stared at her with his amber eyes. They were like liquid fire—while they could be comforting at times, now they only burned her. Valora looked down, shielding her emotions in the only way she knew how without pulling shadows around her. Ryker was kind, but she didn't need empty compliments to make her feel better.

"Same time tomorrow?" Valora asked, using her own attempt at changing the subject.

Ryker released her shoulders and started to undo the wrappings from his wrists. Heat radiated from his body, covered with nothing but his typical rolled up, ratty trousers. He needed a new pair soon. Given the state of the stitching, Valora suspected one stray ember would have them falling apart.

"I look forward to besting you." He grinned, then breakfast became his priority.

"Like today, right?"

Ryker turned over his shoulder while he reached for some plates.

"Moody but spirited." He smirked. "We'll see how long it lasts after tomorrow."

# CHAPTER 14

**R**YKER KEPT HIS word.

Valora found herself on her rear more than she found herself victorious. The fire never touched her, but Ryker knew enough about his abilities to figure out what scared people.

And Valora assumed rapid fireballs scared just about anyone.

The onslaught continued day after day after day until Valora got so upset with her inability to fight off the fire that she neglected to leave her bed. Being a warrior had always come so easily for her, but it seemed lately she could get nothing right when training with her housemate. Then again, it wasn't only Ryker who gave her a difficult time. Valora had also been careless when dealing with the twins.

She needed to develop her skills again if she wanted to continue on with the mission, and that meant getting to a point where she could go hand-in-hand in combat with Ryker. Valora refused to let him keep beating her—she just didn't know how to make it stop at her current caliber.

Ryker, having gotten up far before Valora and the sun that morning, marched right into the shared room and pulled her from the comfort of her blankets, not caring how upset she was. Valora fought in her pajamas that day.

His power and what he'd learned to do with it amazed her. Valora knew the warriors of Norlyn acted as nothing more than a precautionary security system. If trouble came to the village, the warriors would fend it off.

Knowing Ryker had once acted as a part of that system made Valora fear for anyone who might have thought of attacking. The standing peace treaty meant that neighboring villages rarely caused any ruckus—Valora only remembered one instance years before, where a visiting man had drunk a little too much and killed someone in a fight at the tavern. The man had received no greater punishment than jail time, but Valora wondered what would have happened had the Master decided to utilize Ryker's ability as punishment.

As powerful as he was, Valora couldn't imagine her housemate as a killer.

They only stopped their training when Ryker decided to. After that, they'd return to the house, make breakfast, and prepare for the day. Valora went back to bed for the first few days of practice, if only to keep herself from running after Ryker to accompany him on his watch over Norlyn. With her back still not quite strong enough to climb trees—but apparently plenty strong enough to train for three or four hours every morning—Ryker volunteered for the task. He kept an eye on Juno and

Aurelia and kept an ear out for any word on the accusations against Bo.

On the third day of his spying, Ryker returned with both good and bad news.

"You left some evidence behind in the bedroom," he informed her.

As terrifying as her encounter with Ash had been, it had ended up working in Valora's favor. In her haste, she'd stepped directly in Myrcella's blood, and the retreating footprints provided enough proof to clear the accusations against Bo.

"They measured Bo's footprint against the ones left behind," Ryker continued. "Thankfully, the villagers are smart enough to tell a male footprint from a female footprint."

"It's a good thing they think I'm dead then," Valora said, taking in the new information before she went to the bedroom to sharpen her weapons.

When she was not waiting for Ryker to return, Valora used her time to train. The morning sessions helped enough with strengthening her abilities, but Valora needed to make sure she could also use her weapons. Valora knew Ryker preferred his natural abilities to man-made tools, but she didn't believe anything would be as satisfying as successfully sticking a knife in the intended target.

The targets initially consisted of the sides of the meat shed. Then Valora moved onto a harder target: the trunks of oak trees. Finally, she moved onto the thin, white trunks of the birch trees randomly dispersed around the clearing.

When she felt particularly confident, Valora would sit and wait for a rabbit or a squirrel to enter the confines of the clearing. As soon as the poor creature came just a little too close, Valora would throw her knife or shoot an arrow, not wanting to repeat what had happened the last time she tried to capture prey with her shadows. Most days, she succeeded in her hunt. Others, she moved too slowly and needed to wait for the next round of prey to unwittingly stroll to its potential doom.

"And all this time I thought you were getting sick of the rodents."

She and Ryker sat outside at the end of the thirteenth day. His cupped palms contained a small blaze. Valora turned a stick with two skinned squirrels she killed earlier that day above the flames.

"I *am* sick of them, but I'm also bored during the day."

"Do you mean to tell me you miss me?" Ryker grinned. The fire in his palms made his eyes glow.

"Not even a little bit," Valora assured him. "But I do appreciate you doing all the dirty work."

"You're getting soft on me, Valora. Could our morning training and more frequent conversations be melting the icing on your cold, dark heart?"

She peered up at him from under her lashes. When she returned her attention to the cooking squirrels, her lips curled slightly at the corners. If Ryker didn't pay such close attention to her, Valora suspected he never would have noticed the moment of weakness.

"Maybe a little bit."

"And here I was thinking you despised talking to me."

Valora shrugged. "Not all the time."

They ate the squirrels in near silence. Every so often, Ryker would attempt a joke. It took him almost his whole squirrel to finally say something that broke Valora's straight face again.

Then, satisfied with his success, he stayed quiet.

That was how the routine worked. Train. Taunt. Eat. Go about their separate daily activities. Eat. Heal. Sleep. Repeat. Valora and Ryker moved in that rhythm, going about their days the same way with only the meals and reports from the village changing. But more often than not, Ryker came home with no new information. And Valora didn't venture further than the clearing to hunt. The last thing she wanted was another run-in with the wolves while Ryker remained indisposed at the other side of the forest.

The solitary lifestyle started to grow on her. She understood Ryker's fondness of it, enjoying the peace it gave her so much so that she often found herself partaking in activities she otherwise wouldn't have. In the village and as a member of her old group of friends, she had often felt forced to go along with whatever they planned. Every so often, Valora didn't mind a night out, a bit of shameless flirting with one of the boys she met there, and the chance to dress in something nicer than her usual black leggings and cotton tunic, but not all the time.

In the forest, though, no one forced Valora to do anything other than Ryker's morning training. She filled her time how she wanted to, not with what others expected of her. It helped that she lived with Ryker. They expected nothing of each other because they knew nothing about each other.

But the seclusion—especially when Ryker left to play lookout, as Valora wasn't yet desperate enough to speak to the squirrels before she killed them—also left her with plenty of time to think. Time and again, she found herself recalling happy memories about her family or training or old friends. But generally, they revolved around darker thoughts: loneliness, abandonment, pain, loss.

No matter how much time passed, Valora couldn't help but dwell. Memories of her old life, spurred by Ryker's reports, always arose.

That afternoon, while waiting for Ryker to return, Valora found her thoughts wandering back to a memory of her friends. Only Juno and Aurelia had accompanied her at the time. They'd been fighting about something so pointless Valora couldn't remember the exact reason, but it had resulted in a rift between the girls. Always the faithful sidekick, Juno had taken Aurelia's side, leaving Valora on her own. She remembered feeling as alone that day as she had on the first days after the attack.

She should have realized it then—that day when she'd admitted how the darkness went beyond her abilities. The inky, swirling heaviness that often found its way into her head, entrapping her thoughts the same way she entrapped her enemies within her shadows, and made her overthink miniscule events and details. Valora had seen their faces. Her honesty had scared them, and she knew in that moment they would never understand her, no matter how adamantly they claimed they did.

Their *advice*—though Valora could hardly call it such in recollection—had held as many cryptic messages as their attempt to lure her into the forest. They had planned the attack, lying to her all the while, making her believe they were still her friends.

*Stop doing this, Valora.*
*Start doing that, Valora.*
*You're so depressing, Valora.*
*You're so different, Valora.*
*You don't fit in with us, Valora.*
*Valora, Valora, Valora—*

"Valora!"

She woke with a start, her skin slick with sweat and her chest rising and falling heavily. She looked around the room, the vivid nightmare making her forget her location. Only when her eyes found Ryker's did Valora realize she was not in Norlyn but sleeping inside a cabin in the forest.

Ryker continued to watch her with concern-filled eyes. His hands felt oddly cold where he'd placed them on her shoulders, or maybe that was just her skin refusing to accept the warmth.

"Valora...." he breathed.

Her lip trembled, and Valora let out a desperate whimper, like an animal in pain. Ryker moved quickly, going to his bed to remove his only wolf-pelt blanket to wrap around her. Despite being covered in sweat, Valora's body shook with violent shivers. Or did she shake in fear?

The sobs escaped beyond her control, and Ryker collected her in his arms. Under any other circumstances, Valora would have immediately pushed him away. But at that moment she didn't think she held enough strength to give him even a little shove.

"Shhhh," Ryker comforted. "It's alright. It was just a nightmare. It's all right. You're safe."

But she wasn't safe. Not until she killed the last two girls would Valora feel safe anywhere but in the depths of the forest. Until then, the memories and threat of being found would constantly haunt her.

"You need to stop, Valora," Ryker whispered. "You need to let this go. It's just going to keep getting to you."

Valora shuddered a breath, her whole body shaking within Ryker's hold. "They left me in the forest to *die*, Ryker. You *saw* what they did to me." Her lip quivered again. Her voice lowered, weakened. "I should have seen it coming."

It didn't matter how many times Ryker tried to guilt-trip her out of her mission. Valora needed to complete her task and return home. He had made his choice to stay, and likewise, Valora wanted to make her choice too.

"What they did to you was horrific. I will never argue that." He sounded so stern in comparison to mere moments before. "But getting back at them by doing the same...." He paused, deciding what to say. "You'll go the rest of your life knowing you killed them. It will consume you. It already is."

"What do you know about what I'm going through?" Valora challenged. "You keep acting like you know what it's like, but how could you? You live alone in a forest that only murderers and thieves and the banished retreat to."

"I come from somewhere, too, you know." He stuck his neck forward, trying to see around the side of Valora's face. "I have parents and friends that I left behind."

Valora leaned back into his shoulder so she could look up at him. Her lips pursed, and her brow furrowed in confusion. Ryker wiped sweat from her forehead, prolonging the silence.

"I lived in Norlyn too. I remember you—just beginning your training with the Master before I left. When I first rescued you, I didn't know. But then you used your shadows...." He grinned. "The only shadow bender I've ever met."

Valora had always wondered if he knew her the same way she'd known him—vaguely, but enough to leave an impression. Instead of dwelling on that remark, though, she didn't do anything. She stayed still, facing forward, her head resting against the front of his shoulder, his arms wrapped around her, holding the blanket in place. Ryker was finally opening up, and as much as she hated how intimate their positioning felt, Valora knew if she pushed him away, she might not receive another chance to get answers.

Even though she faced away from him, Valora could sense Ryker's nerves by the change in his breathing. His arms tightened around her, and she tensed but did nothing to stop him.

"I was involved with someone romantically at the time. We had been together since we were thirteen. I loved her—so much so that, after five years, I asked her to marry me."

Valora fought the urge to turn to him. She hated how she couldn't remember the girl he spoke of. It could all be a lie, but something deep inside her told Valora she wanted to keep listening.

"We were only eighteen, and I know that's young by typical standards, but I figured after so many years, what was there to lose? We had talked about our plans for the future before, and I was certain she felt the same way. How could she not? After all we had shared...." Ryker shifted. His hold tightened.

"She said yes. I proposed to her right in the middle of our house one evening, and we celebrated the rest of the night. Drinking, dancing...*other* activities. We were both so elated and distracted by our joy that neither one of us remembered to douse our fireplace before we went to bed."

Pain laced every word he spoke. Ryker hung his head so that his forehead rested on the back of Valora's skull. "Do you remember during the wolf attack a few weeks ago? When you looked at me like I was a monster? That was exactly how I felt the next morning, when I woke up and realized I was all that remained of the house. I'm so used to the heat—the fire—that I hadn't even noticed what happened. And she always slept much deeper after drinking, so she didn't wake either.

"I was too stunned to talk about anything, and no one pushed me to. Her parents, my parents—they knew our history. They kept telling me I did everything I could, and if I could have saved her, I would have. It wasn't *my* fault I can withstand fire.

"She was an empath—someone who could feel others' emotions," Ryker continued. "I think that's what drew me to her. Even from a young age, she was capable of calming me. She knew when I was angry or upset. I believed from the day we met that we were meant for one another, since I'm sure you know the rumors surrounding fire benders. Our tempers. She kept me in line—taught me how to handle the anger that sometimes flared in me. That's why I have such a strong control on it. I'd always considered my abilities a curse until I met her, and in the end…in the end they still ended up being just that. A curse.

"I left not long after the house burnt down. I couldn't stomach looking at the pile of ashes that used to be the house, thinking somewhere hers were mixed within them. I couldn't handle seeing her parents crying or deal with the coddling from mine. So, I packed up what I thought I would need and went into the forest.

"I knew the tales as well as anyone else—the death, the creatures, the darkness that waited in the trees. But I didn't believe anything could be worse than what I felt at that moment. If I met my death in the forest…maybe it would be better that way. I wouldn't be around to cause anyone harm.

"But death never came. It took my first encounter with a hungry wolf to realize I did not, in fact, want to die. When I was about to be torn apart, I thought *not yet*. So, I killed the wolf instead. Thus was the beginning of my life in solitude.

"I created this clearing by slicing down the trees with fire whips. I built the house and shed from the trunks. I began collecting berries and shrubs that I thought might be useful, based on what the Master had taught in training. Eventually it all came together—this life alone—and I kept telling myself this was how it had to be. I couldn't return in fear of hurting someone else I loved.

"It wasn't an easy transition, by any means. I went from having a family—having friends—to having no one. I hated it. Every minute of it. But I'd made my decision and needed to live with it. Anything, no matter how lonely I felt at some points, was better than knowing someone else could fall victim to my abilities.

"That's when I started learning how to heal. My ma—she has the ability to revive plants. Isn't that funny? A woman who was literally born to save living things, no matter how small, gave birth to someone so destructive. But I figured that meant there had to be some part of her in me, so I gave it a try. I started with small creatures first, then started trying to heal some of my own wounds. It worked out well enough that I figured…well, I decided I would use that aspect of the fire more than the destructive part, if possible.

"Then, three years later, I was training and heard a scream." Valora's breath caught. "The tales of this forest are not false, but I'd never heard anything like that scream before. There'd been plenty before it but this one…it sounded so…heartbroken. Like nothing had hurt the person it belonged to more than the present danger.

"So, like any sensible person, I ran towards it. I followed the sounds of the voices until I nearly broke through the brush. I stopped myself and watched, the worst of the damage already done, and I couldn't understand for the life of me how the girls could do that to someone.

"I waited until they left, then emerged from where I hid. The girl had lost a lot of blood, but she was still breathing. So, I…well, I suppose the rest is history, right? Here you are, alive and…*well* wouldn't be an appropriate adjective at the moment, I don't think. But you're alive, just like I knew you would be. I could tell you were a fighter, Valora."

For a fighter, she felt very weak. Ryker couldn't have made up that story. He'd finally told her how he'd come to live in the forest—the reasons behind his strange way of life and the guilt that followed him all these years later.

Valora had suffered from nightmares, or at least ones bad enough to have Ryker wake her. She couldn't tell where the thoughts from her day ended and the ones from the night began, if any separation existed at all. And maybe it made her a terrible person, but the thoughts did not revolve around guilt. They revolved around the parts of her life that had so clearly warned of the betrayal she would face. They constantly reminded her how blind she had been to something unfolding right in front of her.

"If you say I'm a fighter," Valora whispered, "then you must know why I have to continue. No matter what it does to me."

"Valora, I—"

"No. I don't care what you have to say." She twisted in his arms, freeing herself, and kneeled in front of him, holding the blanket around her shoulders on her own. "You held feelings for…" Valora realized she didn't know his partner's name and didn't have the heart to ask, in fear of bringing about lingering pain. "My situation is different. And I know you think it's hurting me, but I promise you it's not. The darkness goes beyond my abilities. It always has. They could never understand that, but I'm no longer going to use it as the weakness they think it is. I intend to come out stronger."

Ryker stared at her—her mussed hair, her sweat-slick skin, her desperate eyes. His eyes left her face to examine the space around them. Shadows moved like mist around her, tendrils spreading out into the room and reaching for Ryker. She'd summoned them in her anger just as Ryker summoned fire when he lost control of his emotions. Given what he'd said, though, Ryker seemed oddly calm in that moment, even after relaying his tale.

Valora watched him swipe his hand through the dark clouds. They did nothing, but when she performed the same action, they followed her hand like smoke, allowing her to bend them every way she wanted.

She twirled the shadows through her fingers as she asked, "How do you keep it at bay? The anger. The power."

Ryker shrugged. "Training helps, but I've found having company has also been beneficial. It keeps me from my thoughts."

Valora peered up at him from under her lashes. She would never admit she held the same opinion, but maybe he could figure it out himself.

"Before you so kindly interrupted to defend yourself," Ryker said, "I was going to tell you I would keep helping you. I think it's brave to face your problems rather than run from them like I did."

Suddenly, she understood his reaction when she'd called him

a coward prior to the wolf attack.

"Ryker, I didn't mean—"

He held up his hand. "I will help," he repeated. "We'll train. I will spy until your back is healed. Then you'll continue on. I can't say I would necessarily face the problems the same way, though."

Valora leaned forward and shoved his shoulder lightly. Ryker chuckled and got off the bed.

"Do you think you'll be able to stay quiet the rest of the night? I need my beauty rest."

She shook her head at him, making sure to lift her shadows to make sure he could see. "Asshole."

Ryker chuckled again as he crawled into bed. "Goodnight, Valora."

He slept through the rest of the night.

So did Valora.

# CHAPTER 15

**THE NEXT MORNING**, Valora woke on her own feeling surprisingly well-rested. She smiled to herself, wondering if she'd only dreamed Ryker's confession, but the extra blanket on her bed proved he really had come to comfort her after her nightmare.

She turned her head to the side, expecting to find Ryker still asleep. Valora wanted to take the opportunity to wake him before he dragged her out of bed for training.

Ryker's bed sat empty, and sunlight replaced the darkness Valora usually saw when she first looked out the window in the morning.

Valora threw off her blanket and scrambled to pull on her chest wrappings and sweater. If Ryker surprised her with a sneak attack, she wanted to have at least a little support for her breasts. If she needed to dodge fire whips in her pajama pants, so be it.

Prepared for her housemate's antics, Valora crept through the kitchen. The room was empty, even of Ryker's usual breakfast of forest vermin.

Valora straightened her posture, her brow furrowed and her curiosity piqued as she surveyed the room. She turned back towards the bedroom to double-check that she hadn't missed Ryker standing out in the open.

Nothing.

Growing frustrated—though whether from her confusion or Ryker's antics, she wasn't sure—Valora ventured out of the house. She stopped just beyond the doorway and gave the clearing the same inspection she'd given the kitchen.

Valora took another cautious step out of the safety of the house. "Ryker?" she called.

She heard nothing. Her housemate had probably gone to hunt or spy—it was far too late in the day for training according to the usual schedule—without waking her first. Ryker probably saw it as a strange way of showing sympathy for the night before. Or to avoid talking about it altogether. As much as she remembered his confessions, Valora also remembered the way Ryker had held her while he told the tale of his ex-partner. How she'd let herself be held within his strong embrace, in fear of scaring away the rare openness he'd shown her.

She concentrated so hard on the forest before her that Valora didn't hear the soft thud behind her, even with her expert hearing.

The new shadow that appeared alerted her, and Valora spun around just seconds before a whip of fire would have knocked her in the head. She fell on her back—and regretted it immediately.

Valora cringed as her back arched, and she twisted in discomfort to try to dull the pain that arose from her wounds. Ryker, who had busied himself with laughing at his sneak-attack, stopped instantly and rushed to her side. He sank to one knee and tried to place a helpful hand on her back. Valora swatted it away.

"Why did you think that would be a good idea?" she asked through gritted teeth. Just like that, all positive memories from the night before vanished, replaced by the fluctuating disdain Valora held for her housemate.

"I said I would help you, didn't I?" he countered, trying again to help Valora up. Again, she hit his hand away. "You have to be ready for anything when dealing with people with abilities."

"Clearly," Valora ground out. She sat up and rested her weight on her palms, staring Ryker down with cold eyes, her jaw tight. "Did you ever think that I maybe *wouldn't* be facing someone with abilities?"

"Huh?"

"Aurelia and Juno don't have any powers."

Ryker stared at her in silence. "Oh," he said after a beat.

"Oh," Valora mocked before she pushed herself to her feet. She let Ryker help her that time, the movement making her wounds sting almost unbearably. "If anything reopened, I swear, Ryker…."

"Sounds like I've made the kill list. I'm honored—truly. I hear it's a wonderful place to be." The sarcastic bastard placed his hands over his heart and smiled as though he were genuinely pleased. "But I'm afraid I'll have to ask you to move out if that's the case. Can't have you in the next bed over, you see. Makes your job far too easy."

Valora dusted herself off while she said, "You won't even need to ask me to go. I'll be out the moment I run my knife through Aurelia."

"So, she'll be the last?"

"Apparently, you're now the last." Ryker grinned. Valora returned her attention to her dusty pajama pants. "But yes. She is the last of my assassins to go."

"And how will you do it? Kill the ringleader." Ryker waggled his brows. "I imagine you've thought about it."

Valora stopped cleaning off her pants and looked up at him. "No, I haven't actually," she admitted. "You might think I'm insane, but I don't dream about killing people. It's just…I have to do it."

"You don't *have* to do anything—except die at some point," Ryker teased. "And you've done a pretty good job of not doing that so far."

Valora growled as she brushed past her companion. Just to spite him, she pulled the shadows from the ground and wrapped them around his ankles. She thought after using the maneuver so many times during their training sessions, she should have grown tired of it. But Valora still smiled when she heard Ryker land with a satisfying *thud* and groan on the ground.

"Too bad you're mad at me," Ryker called to her as she made her way back to the house. "I was going to ask you to join me on my little fieldtrip to the forest edge."

Valora stopped in her tracks. She didn't need to turn around to know Ryker was grinning.

**He continued grinning** as they both sat on Valora's favorite tree branch to watch over Norlyn. At first, the combined weight frightened Valora, but the branch seemed to hold up without trouble. Ryker was fit but heavy with muscles. Once it was determined they wouldn't crash to their doom, they sat side by side, hidden beneath the unnecessary shadows—or so Ryker claimed.

Valora vowed that should anyone find them in the tree, Ryker would play the role of the sacrifice while she made her escape.

While she straddled the branch, Ryker elected to sit back. He leaned against the trunk, one leg dangling casually over the side of the branch, the other pulled up with his arm resting over his knee. Small marble-sized balls of fire shot up out of his fingertips as he moved them in a waving motion. Then he moved onto twirling fire through his fingers. Then around his arms. Then suddenly a fire snake slithered up in front of Valora.

"You do realize we're in a tree, right?" she asked as she batted the snake away. It stuck its tongue out at her before Ryker made it disappear. "Trees burn. Very easily."

Ryker chuckled, a low rumbling sound from behind her. "I wanted to see how we'd escape that particular knock on death's door."

"Well, I don't, so cut it out."

He chuckled again but stopped. When Valora glanced quickly back at him in her peripheral vision, she found her companion lounging casually against the tree trunk, his hands behind his head, elbows out. He let out a contented sigh and closed his eyes.

Valora enjoyed the silence at first, using it to her advantage. Her focus narrowed in on the village where she worked to find

Juno and Aurelia's figures in the vast space.

Norlyn was one of the larger, more affluent villages on the continent, though it hadn't always been so populous. Valora remembered her childhood when houses had slowly but surely popped up around her family's property. She'd loved watching the village grow into the near five-hundred-person settlement it stood at presently and meeting all the new families. Especially when the families included children with abilities.

Her parents had decided to live in Norlyn before it became so successful. They had set up their candle shop soon after they married and kept it going over the years, while also deciding to have two kids somewhere in the mix. Valora and Bo had always gotten to voice their opinions on what scents should be created. Valora favored lavender. The store never ran out of that scent. Bo's varying taste in scents gave the shop most of its options. If it had been up to Valora and her parents alone, the shop would never sell anything but lavender and pine.

Valora set her eyes on the little store in the shopping hub of Norlyn, trying her best to sneak a peek inside one of the windows. Patron after patron entered the shop and exited with product in hand, making Valora smile. She loved witnessing her parents' success.

It was around the time of the year where her aunt and uncle up in Wolfden would ask for a shipment via the Bo express. Normally, Valora would attend as well, but seeing as the world believed her dead....

She'd never considered her extended family's reactions or learned if they'd even received the news. Valora couldn't imagine her mother *not* writing to inform the others, but it had been four months, and no one had visited. Her family was close. If they knew, Valora thought at least a few of her relatives would make the trek to Norlyn.

Given her parents' suspicions, though, maybe they wanted to wait until they received a clear confirmation. Based on what she and Ryker gathered, she knew her immediate family thought she'd died, but they also suspected foul play. Ryker said he'd heard gossip about the conspiracy theories flying around after Mona and Myrcella's death. At first, they'd mostly blamed Bo. Once he got cleared, though, rumors of the walking dead arose.

Valora snorted at the thought. Even those with powers that allowed them to heal or regenerate couldn't raise people from the dead.

As much as she wanted to catch a glimpse of her family, Valora couldn't help but let her attention stray. Young warriors and those training for other occupations often frequented the tavern on days off, meaning Juno and Aurelia would be busy at least until supper time.

She glanced over her shoulder to make sure Ryker paid no attention before Valora found the spot in the village that belonged to the largest catastrophe within recent years.

The house hadn't been rebuilt after it burned down, but volunteers had cleared the remains away. Talk of using the property for more shops and new houses for the expanding village had occurred, but the family of the girl refused any new building on the plot.

Valora remembered hearing about the girl who died in the house fire. Enough random tragedies happened in the village that it had earned little attention—much less than a double murder, anyhow. But word still traveled, especially in a village of Norlyn's size.

If the girl had been an empath as Ryker said, she could have become a warrior. Rarely did those without any abilities make it into the ranks. Juno possessed superior athletic ability, so the Master giving her a chance didn't surprise Valora. But Aurelia…that decision had always shocked Valora. She'd accepted it without question, though, especially since Aurelia joining the warriors meant all her friends could train together.

The girl, though, had likely trained to be a doctor or counselor. Most empaths took that path—not that Valora knew many of them. She based her assumptions on what the Master and her parents had told her about those with abilities. Having been the only one in her immediate family gifted with them, she'd gotten information from anyone and anything that offered it.

She couldn't imagine it—the always-careful Ryker acting carelessly enough that someone had died as a result. The more she stared at the empty plot, the more her mind drifted back to the wolf attack. It had brought out a side of Ryker that Valora didn't normally see, but she accredited it to adrenaline. She remembered the fire in his amber eyes, consuming his hands and arms, burning the life out of the wolf in his grasp—

"What are you staring at?"

Valora jumped so dramatically that she would have fallen off the branch had Ryker not grabbed her. His hands stayed on her waist until she stopped wobbling on their perch one hundred feet above the ground.

"I just—I—my parents' shop." Valora fought the urge to hit her palm to her forehead.

Ryker's head tilted to the side. If he found her suspicious at all, he didn't let it show as he said, "I didn't know your parents owned a shop. Which one?"

"They sell candles." Saying it out loud made it sound so uninteresting.

Ryker's lips turned up in a small smile. "I think I've bought from them before. Are they the shop on the corner near the bakery?" Valora nodded her confirmation. "Then I have. My mom loved the lavender candle I got her for her birthday."

Valora let out a small, embarrassed laugh and turned back to the village. She wrapped her shadows tighter around them both and let herself focus on the shop again, her eyes darting between it and the tavern. She didn't want to miss her old friends' exit.

"Looks like they're doing well," Ryker commented.

Valora didn't reply as she watched patrons move in and out of the shop. Her breath caught when, finally, Bo and his friends walked out the door, roughhousing as teenage boys did. Weeks had passed since she'd last seen him, and Valora felt relief at seeing him happy and unharmed.

Then her mother exited the shop.

Her mom rarely left the shop during Valora's spying sessions. She had little reason to do so, but Bo apparently created some inspiration.

Her brother and his friends ran away from her, most of them towering over the small woman with her brown bob. Valora's mother stood at the same height as Juno, if not shorter. Valora and Bo often teased her about it.

Valora almost felt like crying when she saw her dad appear in the doorway behind her mother. He put his hand on her shoulder, towering over her by at least a foot. The raven-haired man yelled something to the boys as they ran away, trying to assist his wife.

It did no good. The boys would have continued on no matter

if one parent, two, or every parent in the village had yelled at them to stop.

She watched until Bo disappeared with his friends, and her parents retreated back within the shop to help their customers. She watched after them, unable to look away.

When she did finally manage, Valora found Ryker's gaze intently focused on something in the village as well. She thought it might be Juno and Aurelia, finally emerged from their afternoon of drinking—he was staring off in that same direction—but when she followed his stare, she found it focused elsewhere.

A man and woman spoke with another couple—laughing, smiling, and relaxing as they should be on their days off. Valora couldn't place the one pair, but she could pick out Ryker's parents easily, especially given the resemblance between him and his mother.

As if he knew she'd found the people he watched over, Ryker said, "I would be lying if I said I spent all my time up here watching your targets."

"I'm sure they miss you," Valora replied.

Ryker shrugged. "They probably think I'm dead."

After so many years, Valora didn't doubt that. It had only been months for her family, and already it seemed they'd adjusted their lives to fit her absence.

"Would you ever go back?" Valora asked. "If given the chance, would you return to Norlyn?"

Ryker let out a soft huff. "After so long, I would need a pretty damn good reason to return."

He did not grin. He did not smirk. He certainly did not smile. Just like the night before, Ryker appeared haunted by his past, confessing more than he'd probably ever admitted to anyone else before. Valora watched the pain flicker in his eyes as he continued to stare at his parents and the other couple. How many days had he voluntarily gone to the hiding spot in the tree to watch the village, knowing full well what he would see? Valora had her reasons, but why would Ryker put himself through that kind of pain?

"I'm getting bored," Valora said. Ryker slowly turned to her, one brow raised. "I found a clearing not too long ago when I was trying to train—found some does in it. Care to go hunting? Might do us well to eat something other than rabbit or squirrel."

Ryker's eyes lightened. Valora felt comforted by it, and even more so by the small smile that spread on his lips.

"Let's go, shadow bender. Show me you can hunt something other than rodents for a change."

**T**HEY RETURNED HOME with two does and spent the remainder of the day in the meat shed with Ryker teaching Valora how to properly prepare an animal so that they might get the best use of everything it offered.

While preparing the meat, Ryker thought it would be a grand idea to throw a small, bloody piece of deer at Valora. She screeched and ran off her stool to avoid it, only to later find out it was part of the animal's intestines. The following hissy fit consisted of wiping all light from the room and refusing to replace it until Ryker apologized.

He did no such thing, but he did remind her that if he

couldn't prepare the meat, she couldn't eat.

"So," said Ryker as he chewed a bite of previously dried venison used for dinner that evening. He'd explained that the deer meat needed to sit at least a week before it would taste its best. "It was warmer today."

Valora put her hand under her chin—the signal she gave her housemate when he chewed with his mouth open. Ryker blushed, having worked very hard in recent weeks to break the habit, and Valora smiled a little.

"Have our conversations grown so boring that you're resorting to talking about the weather?"

"What conversations?" Ryker retorted once he swallowed. Valora gave him a look, but failed to make it as cold as she would have liked, given his success in not showing her bits of chewed doe meat. "What I mean to say is spring is around the corner."

"That *does* happen after winter."

Ryker took his turn to give her a look. He set his fork down on his plate while Valora continued to pick off small bites of her dinner, eyeing him every now and again from under her lashes. His stare was so unrelenting that Valora had no choice but to challenge it.

"Calm." Ryker smiled when her eyes found his. Then he went back to his meal. "The mountains are nice this time of year. And there are some berries and things that I've discovered up there. Maybe—if you're up for it—we could go collect some in the near future."

He didn't meet her eyes once while he asked. Valora mimicked his actions from before, setting her fork down and staring at him. Unlike her, he didn't give in; Ryker continued to make little cuts of his meat and take dramatic bites.

Too much time passed before he finally broke the silence. Only when Ryker finished eating did he finally peer up at Valora. She sat back in her chair, her arms crossed over her chest, irritated from having to wait so long for some kind of follow-up on his end.

"It's secluded, if that's what you're worried about." It was not. "But your shadows can help us out to an extent."

Valora's mouth twitched in the desire to answer, but she didn't know how. She wanted to say she would go—she needed some kind of distraction from her thoughts and the fresh, light air of the mountains would do her good. She wanted to say that going into the mountains excited her; she had never been before.

More than anything, Valora felt inclined to thank Ryker for inviting her rather than simply going on his own. But doing that would ruin the wall she had so successfully created, and after the minor intimacy the night before, Valora could absolutely, under no circumstance, break that wall.

That intimacy was likely the reason why the invitation felt as though it carried an odd sort of tension.

"Yes…?" Ryker prompted. "You can say no, if you'd like. I won't be *too* offended."

His accompanying grin and eventual pout when Valora neglected to respond made it near impossible to keep a straight face. She rolled her eyes, tilted her head to the side, and smiled softly.

"I guess if you insist…." Ryker's smile spread from ear to ear. "Didn't you mention mountain lions at some point or another?"

"I did." Ryker nodded. He sounded excited almost.

"And have you ever had the pleasure of running into one?"

"Unfortunately not."

"Do you think they'll be as fun to face as the wolves?"

"I think they'll be *more* fun to face."

Valora let out a small laugh and shook her head at him. As the laughter faded, she let out a prolonged, "Ah." Ryker watched her in amusement, joy lighting his eyes.

"And you say *I'm* the crazy one," Valora chuckled.

Ryker shrugged. "We're both crazy. Just in different ways."

He took a sip of his water. Valora noticed the way his eyes became saddened, and his smile fell behind the rim of the cup. But the moment his eyes found her again, Ryker's lips curled back up, clearly forced, and clearly trying to mask whatever he was thinking. His still-empty eyes gave him away.

Valora, not wanting to fall victim to another emotional night, cleared her throat and turned her attention to her dinner. She picked up her plate, still halfway filled with the food that would surely satisfy her grumbling stomach.

"So, when would you like to go?" Valora asked, starting to clear up the table.

She heard Ryker shift in his seat. He too cleared his throat before speaking. "What would be the best time for you?"

"Oh, you know me and my tight schedule," she tried joking. When Valora glanced back at her companion, she found him fidgeting nervously. He had no idea she saw him. "Should we see what the weather looks like in a couple of days then head out? Warm weather means rain is upon us."

"A couple of days? Does that mean—?"

"I wanted to get one more out of the way—yes." Valora sighed and stood up. "It's been long enough since Mona and Myrcella. Bo has been cleared. My back is healed…enough. I see no point in waiting."

She leaned back against the counter, crossing her arms over her chest. Ryker didn't look at her. Instead, he watched his hands as he continued to fidget.

"You're still planning on leaving as soon as they're all dead?"

"That's always been the plan, so yes. I am."

Knowing that only Aurelia would remain when she returned from the trip to the mountains would hopefully make going on the excursion easier. Her job would almost be done, then only one person would stand in the way of Valora returning home to her family.

And she *would* return—no matter how many ideas Ryker thought of to prolong her stay within the forest. She was finding she no longer loathed his company and sometimes looked forward to the training sessions in the mornings, even if he did wake her up before the sun sometimes. That still didn't mean she was going to give up on her original plan.

At the very least, Valora owed him for those training sessions and for allowing her to stay with him while she healed. If going to the mountains to pick berries accomplished that, then so be it.

Ryker glanced up quickly then back down at his hands. His veins began to glow orange-red beneath his skin, traveling from his fingertips to his elbows. Valora watched his illuminated blood, the shades of orange changing depending on the flow, becoming darker where the blood ran thicker in his veins. It resembled lava running in the cracks and crevices down a volcanic mountain.

Valora had never seen anything like it before.

It was beautiful.

Small flames no bigger than those belonging on the wick of a candle appeared on each of his fingertips. Valora inhaled deeply, audibly, and turned away.

"That's going to be soon," Ryker whispered. "They'll all be dead soon."

"Soon enough," Valora agreed. She paused. "But not before our trip to the mountains."

Her and Ryker's eyes met at precisely the same time. The shadows began to swirl around her, just like his fire began to consume him.

"You promise?"

Valora nodded slowly. Then quicker. Then stopped. Ryker stared at her, assessing if she had told the truth. He sighed after a moment, turning away to stare longingly at the kitchen counter.

"I wish I had flour. And sugar."

"*What?*"

Ryker's mind never ceased to amaze Valora. She had never met someone whose brain went so many different directions so quickly.

"We are going to collect berries," he said as though that would help clarify. "I wish I had flour and sugar so I could have my mom's pie. I haven't had it in years."

"Are you suggesting now that you have a woman in the house, you can have it again?" Valora felt the shadows pulling towards her. If that were the case, she would have no issue showing her housemate that she was the kind of woman who would kick his ass before she baked him a pie.

"I'm suggesting," Ryker started, "that I miss it and would like it again." He looked at the counter again. "There are a lot of things I miss that you being here reminds me of."

Valora raised a brow. "I remind you of pie?"

Ryker chuckled and shook his head. Valora watched his lips spread in a smile. It shrank when he turned to her again.

"You remind me of home."

Valora relaxed after his response set in. She blinked at him, trying to read the emotions etched in his face, shining in his eyes, but Ryker appeared sincere. Maybe she had misjudged the meaning behind his rain comment from the night before. Valora had faced so much rejection in the recent past that maybe her subconscious craving of acceptance made her believe Ryker wanted *her* to stay. She hadn't thought that he wanted her around because she connected him to the home he felt he could never return to. He wanted the memory, not the person.

The realization hurt Valora more than she'd thought it would. She had thought that, maybe—just maybe—she could find a place she belonged once more, even if only temporarily. Finding friends had never been her strong suit. Valora got along with nearly everyone she met, but finding people that wanted to stay....

Just when she'd thought she found those people, they'd left her in the most brutal way possible. Valora had dealt with friendships that ended naturally over time. She had dealt with heartbreak. She had even dealt with people who told her she didn't belong in their group. But having Ryker become one of those people so soon after those she trusted the most stabbed her in the back....

She didn't know she was crying until Ryker came around the table and grabbed her shoulders. Valora peered at him through tear-blurred vision—at the concern controlling every inch of his face.

He took her into his arms then, holding her tight against his chest, his hand cupping the back of her head to keep her cradled there. Valora wrapped her arms around his torso in return, not able to find the strength to tell him her thoughts. In that moment, she didn't want to let go of the one human she believed accepted her immediately. The one human she would leave in a matter of weeks.

Valora inhaled a shuddered breath. Ryker continued to soothe her without any explanation as to why but simply because he was kind—because he had lost so much already and gave up so much. Valora didn't know why she continued to let him do so.

She pushed back. Again. It took three tries to get Ryker to finally let go, and when he did, Valora took a step back and wiped at her eyes. Her breathing continued to come in and out in ragged gasps.

"I have to go sharpen my weapons," she whispered after a few moments of silence, aside from her sniffling and obnoxiously loud breathing.

"Would you like me to—?"

"No," Valora said before he could finish the sentence. "No, I just—I...."

She glanced up at him. His features shared his every emotion, and she couldn't bear to look at them for too long.

Valora rushed away and went to shut the bedroom door quickly behind her.

"Just so you know, I hate the rain," Ryker said abruptly before the door closed. Valora caught the door, brow furrowed, confused at the sudden change of topic. Ryker shrugged at her. "I hate the rain," he said again. "You know—fire, water—not a good mix. But if it starts soon like you believe—if our trip gets pushed out days, weeks, months—I think I wouldn't mind."

Valora stared at him a moment more through the cracked opening before she closed the door the rest of the way.

# CHAPTER 16

**SILENCE CONSUMED THE** village, but Valora didn't take that or the time that had passed between attacks for granted. She made sure she stayed wrapped in her darkness, moving quickly in spots of moonlight where it would be easier to pick her out. The pitch of the night and the dense clouds covering the moon that evening created plenty of natural shadows, but Valora still found herself sprinting through the village square and gathering spots.

She had heard no news of a curfew—Ryker had reported the same—but Norlyn seemed oddly quiet for a village of its size. Valora remembered the stragglers returning home from the tavern the night she'd killed Mona and Myrcella. Now, as she continued almost unnecessarily sneaking from shadow to shadow, Valora felt as though she had entered a deserted village by mistake.

Something crashed behind her and Valora covered her mouth with her palms to suppress her shriek. When she turned, she found a stray cat perched on the window ledge behind her. It sat unconcerned beside a broken flowerpot and unaware its actions had caused any sort of fright.

Valora scowled at the animal. Between her encounter with the cat on the current trip and Ash on the previous, she didn't think she could consider herself a cat *or* a dog person any longer. They seemed to cause more trouble than good as of late, even if in miniscule ways.

Juno's family lived the furthest from the rest of the group. For the most part, her friends lived within a few streets of each other. Not Juno. Her family had gotten to Norlyn only when it had already begun to bloom, meaning they'd gotten stuck on the near outskirts of the village, at least a ten-minute walk from Valora's family home.

It was clear precautions had been put in place—by the village, by Juno's family, or by Juno and Aurelia after suspicions had arisen—when Valora made it to the house and saw no easy way to enter.

She rattled the front door lightly, not expecting it open but wanting to try, just in case her luck turned. Valora crept around the perimeter, checking for any open window or loose board in the siding that might provide her entry but found nothing. Mona and Myrcella had made her task easy, so Valora hadn't anticipated the challenge of actually breaking into the home.

She swore under her breath and tilted her head back, defeated for the moment—just enough to see the stone chimney peeking over the roof. She smiled to herself at the wonderful sight.

The newer-model house provided fewer window ledges and footholds in the siding for Valora to utilize on her climb up to the roof. But Valora also spent most days scaling a hundred-foot tree to spy on her victims—she didn't believe anything could prove more difficult than that.

Valora regretted her confidence when she slipped and fell backwards, shoving a knife into the roof at the last minute to secure her hold.

She bit down on her bottom lip and fought against the pain-induced groan that wanted to escape as the wounds on her back pulled. Wolves were dogs—big vicious dogs that liked to try to eat her face and claw her back. Maybe Valora *could* consider herself more of a cat person.

She checked her shadows, making sure with all her distractions they remained strong. The fall had made enough noise to wake the household, and she needed to guarantee no one could see her if they decided to come outside. But no one stirred inside the house. Valora waited five minutes—holding onto the hilt of her knife, dangling from the side of the house, the wounds on her back on fire—to be sure of it.

After adjusting her grip on the knife, she removed another from her belt and swung up to stick it higher in the roof. Valora had heard stories of people using similar tactics to scale the mountains, and as she didn't know where Ryker planned to take her, she figured the practice might help.

Moments later, Valora found herself standing on the roof. The moon emerged from behind a thin cloud, casting her in a blue glow. She watched it while she pulled the darkness around her, hiding in a shadow it couldn't wipe out. It was a beautiful, powerful feeling to be able to best nature.

The chimney appeared large enough to fit a moderately sized human being, much like the one on Valora's childhood home. She remembered figuring out she could fit when she and Bo played hide and seek. If she stuck out her hands and legs like a star, the applied pressure kept her in place. The addition of her shadows had made it nearly impossible for her little brother to ever find her. Bo had gotten so upset by it that Valora had eventually stopped using the chimney as her go-to hiding spot.

Sneaking down the chimney at Juno's house would be the ultimate game of hide and seek, except if someone found her, she would face greater consequences than forfeiting her pride.

Valora hoisted herself up and over the edge of the chimney so her legs dangled within it. She'd traveled up the length of the house without considering having to go right back down in a much more challenging way.

However, she saw no other quiet way in—no matter how much the present idea made Valora's nerves swirl. Breaking a window, though much easier, would draw too much attention, and Norlyn made all families double-bolt their doors. Not to mention whatever extra precautions the family took.

Valora took a deep breath and replaced her knives before she spread her legs out, pressing her feet securely against either side of the chimney. Her knees bent much more than when she was younger, but she could still slide down easily enough.

Valora inched her way down, careful to keep the rhythm of her movements consistent. Right foot. Left foot. Right hand. Left hand. Each limb hardly seemed to move, but she would rather take all night, get down safely, and make a swift kill than fall down however many feet into the fireplace and get caught.

Only when she saw the faint, blue glow coming from the

windowed room where the chimney let out into the fireplace did Valora dare release her hold. She fell a few feet before landing in ashes, a cloud of them rising around her.

Valora crept through the house, careful to avoid faulty floorboards or anything else that might give her away. Even concealed in her shadows, Valora took extra precautions. In a house where the occupants knew her abilities, she needed to do all she could to ensure they didn't catch her. She refused to make the same mistake as before, almost revealing herself due to carelessness. If it happened again, Juno would know. She'd figure out that Valora had survived the attack.

Her shadows had never felt so heavy as when Valora found herself standing outside Juno's bedroom door. She silently twisted the doorknob and slowly pushed the door open. She slithered through the small crack she'd created for herself and closed herself in.

Juno slept peacefully in her bed. As Valora moved closer, she could see the distinct rise and fall of the bed covers with each of the small, blonde girl's breaths. Each tiptoed step made Valora's blood boil, and when she finally saw Juno's sleeping face, her fists balled at her sides.

Valora ground her teeth together, fighting the anger bubbling inside her at the sight of the girl she had once considered a friend. She had not thought much about Juno in the days since the attack—only that she still needed to meet justice, even if she had been the most reluctant to act.

Valora released the shadows that covered her, letting them instead swirl around her legs like a dark cloud. With all the anger she felt for the sleeping girl, she wondered if her insides looked a similar way.

Juno may not have been the first to stab Valora's back, but she had been the first to do so metaphorically. Juno could have told Valora to run when they'd been stopped outside the forest edge together. She could have warned Valora what would come should she decide to enter into the darkness with them. In that brief moment, Juno could have put an end to it all, but she had not. Instead, she'd made Valora believe everything would be okay.

Valora remembered sensing Juno's fear—the desire to warn her—but nothing had come of it. For all the time Valora had spent helping Juno when she struggled to keep up with the powerful warriors, when she drank too much at the tavern, when she needed general life advice, warning Valora would have been the least Juno could do to repay her.

But as Aurelia's ever-loyal pet, she hadn't. No matter how close they were, Valora would always come second. The Master may have seen her as his first choice, but everyone else considered her as secondary, unimportant, worthless where Aurelia was involved.

Juno stirred and Valora inched even closer to the foot of the bed, shadows spreading. As they slithered up over Juno, the girl began to thrash and shiver, feeling the chill the darkness brought with it—the same chill that haunted Valora day in and day out.

Eventually, the cold became too much, and Juno opened her eyes. Valora stood there, watching, waiting until Juno shot up in bed. The surprising sight of her guest spooked her.

Valora tilted her head to the side slowly. Her mouth remained a straight line. Her tight-fisted hands made her fingernails dig into her palms.

Mona and Myrcella's deaths had come so swiftly that Valora

hadn't seen their faces, only heard the small gasps that came with slitting their throats. But there Juno was, the same as she'd always been, except for the fear that now controlled her face, brought on by her unexpected visitor.

"Valora?" Juno breathed. She squinted into the darkness. "Val?"

The shadow bender said nothing as she tilted her head further to the side.

"Is it really you?" Juno asked. "We thought you were dead. We thought you—"

Valora cut her off by sticking an arm out towards the defenseless girl. The shadows crawling over the bedding instantly turned into the whips Ryker had taught her to make. They wrapped around Juno's neck, squeezing the air from her throat a little more each time Valora turned her hand.

Juno clawed at the shadows but could not grasp them. No one could hold onto the darkness like Valora could.

She kept her arm extended as she moved around the side of the bed. While doing so, Valora lifted her hand, making the shadows pull Juno out from under her covers. She hovered above the mattress, still fruitlessly trying to free herself, while, for once in her life, Valora stared up at tiny Juno.

Tears fell down the choking girl's cheeks. Her eyes moved to her captor, silently pleading for release, but Valora did not succumb.

"You thought wrong, Juno," Valora taunted. She used her other hand to bring more shadows around her one-time friend. Juno let out a choked whimper.

"Why didn't you stop them?" Valora asked. "Why didn't you tell me to turn around when you had the chance? Aurelia wasn't there. We could have blamed it on my fear, and this wouldn't have needed to happen."

Valora twisted her hand and the shadows around Juno's throat tightened. The girl kicked and attempted whatever kind of scream her half-closed throat would allow. Realizing the risk of allowing as much to happen, Valora sent her darkness to wrap around Juno's mouth like a gag. More tied themselves around the girl's ankles.

"After all I did for you, Juno, you repaid me by *killing me*," Valora spat. She followed it with a huffed, humorless laugh. "Well, *almost* killing me. Looks like second best is still the best you all can do."

She twisted her hand more and watched as Juno's face turned from red to purple. Valora lowered Juno to eye level.

"Because unlike all of you, I will not fail in my task." She put her face directly next to Juno's ear. "Killing each of you, one by one."

Juno's eyes widened, either because of the sudden awareness of what had happened to Mona and Myrcella—what was about to happen to her as well—or because her body was receiving no air.

Valora took a step back. "Goodbye, Juno."

Juno's skin purpled as Valora twisted her hand just a little more, but not quite enough to cut off her victim's airways completely. She stared into the eyes of the girl she'd once considered a friend, watching and waiting for the life to leave them. Valora could imagine what Juno was seeing—the slowly blurring form of her killer in front of her. She'd seen the same thing when she'd been left on the forest ground, thinking she'd bleed out.

Except, unlike the girls who had left her there to die, Valora didn't move. She didn't walk away. She watched and waited for life to leave Juno, for the confirmation she'd succeeded, just as she'd promised she would.

Valora could end it so fast. The shadows could choke Juno enough that no more air could get in or out of her lungs.

All Valora needed to do was give her wrist one more tiny twist.

As she stared up at the girl, desperately clinging to the last bit of life she might be allowed, Valora found herself unable to follow through.

"No."

Juno fell onto her bed with a desperate gasp as Valora's shadows recoiled, pulled back by their master. Valora stared at her hands as the darkness she'd just controlled blended in with the rest that occupied the room.

She couldn't bring herself to look at Juno just yet—at the eyes that had just been flooded with desperation, a silent plea for mercy. They'd not thought twice when Valora had directed the same eyes at them, but something about knowing what it felt like…the betrayal….

"Why?" Juno panted. "You…you killed Mona and Myrcella. Why not…why not me?"

Valora lifted her gaze from her hands, left that evening with less blood on them than she'd anticipated. She…she *had* failed in her mission.

Valora rushed to the window, taking advantage of Juno's shock to make her escape. The thud when Juno had landed back on her bed could have been heard by any number of the others living inside the house, and Valora had taken enough risks that night.

One of them stared at her from her bed, alive and wide-eyed, while she continued to regain the breath that had nearly been stolen from her.

Valora unlocked the window and shoved it open. Climbing back up the chimney sounded much worse than going down.

She hopped out, using her shadows to conceal her from anyone who might possibly be awake at such an hour, and closed the window behind her.

Each of Valora's steps felt much heavier that evening. Perhaps she might have felt worse after she'd killed Mona and Myrcella if she hadn't needed to worry about escaping their crazy dog. Or, perhaps, she only felt worse having spared Juno because she knew what that meant.

She'd left a witness.

Valora used the familiarity of being home again, even if it only lasted for a short time, to distract her from those worries. Instead of focusing on what might come of her choice, she passed the shops she used to visit, the taverns she used to eat at, the school she used to attend, the bakery she used to—

Valora doubled back to the bakery and pulled a knife from the belt at her hip, using the tip to pick the old lock on the shop's door.

It clicked open in the most satisfying way.

**W**HEN VALORA PUSHED through the brush surrounding the clearing, she found Ryker training against his iron slab. He paused the moment he heard her arrive, and looked more than ready to scold her for returning home in the light of dawn. But he stopped upon seeing the burlap sack slung over Valora's shoulder.

She said nothing to him as she walked through the clearing and into the house. Ryker followed behind, and paused in the doorway while she continued on her way to the opposite end of the table.

Careful to protect her cargo, Valora removed the covered basket of eggs that sat atop the rest of her goodies and set it on the table. Ryker's brow rose and the other followed shortly after when Valora continued to dump out the contents of the sack. Flour, sugar, salt, baking powder, butter—she'd grabbed everything she could find.

Ryker stared at everything on the table in silence before looking up at Valora.

"We'd better collect enough berries to make a decent pie or else I will be thoroughly pissed off that I carried all this home," she said flatly.

Ryker only stared at her in return, until finally, he tried, "Valora—"

"I should get to bed," she deflected. "There's a long day ahead of us."

He didn't try again, and she didn't feel like talking. Without another word, Valora retreated to the bedroom, leaving Ryker alone with the supplies and his thoughts.

## CHAPTER 17

**UNFORTUNATELY, THEY** couldn't treat themselves to a well-deserved meal until they made their trip to the mountains. As it turned out, Ryker was incapable of improvising with his cooking. She watched him contemplate what to do with the ingredients she'd brought home when she woke, but for all the talk, he stood there doing nothing.

Valora guessed that meant he had no inkling of how to cook beyond using his abilities to roast meat.

So instead of wasting both of their time, Valora sent him on his way to the tree perch while she began to pack for their trip. Dismissing him served the dual purpose of also stopping her from blowing up at him for casually dropping that the mountain trip would last almost a week.

"Think of it like a vacation," Ryker had said.

Valora huffed. Yes—a vacation indeed. A vacation where the two of them—*only* the two of them—would be stuck in the mountains together under the one tent she found stored with some other camping supplies.

She'd only made it through half the packing when Ryker returned.

"She's not dead," he announced.

Valora didn't respond right away, finishing folding a wolf-pelt blanket and stuffing it into a bag before saying, "I know."

"Why didn't you say something?"

Valora shrugged. "I didn't feel the need to."

Ryker was silent for a moment, then said, "You think you failed, don't you?" Valora's answering silence gave him enough reason to continue. "Valora…I don't believe you failed. You *refuse* to fail."

Valora peered up from where she was reaching for the next blanket in the pile when Ryker's hand landed atop hers, pushing it back down.

"You chose to spare her," he whispered. "Why?"

"I don't know."

And it was the truth. Valora had spent the better part of the morning trying to figure out why she'd made the decision to let Juno live, and come up with nothing substantial.

Valora brushed Ryker's hand away and reached for the blanket.

"I think I've decided I'm excited for our trip," she said, her sad expression completely contradicting her claim.

One of Ryker's brows rose. "You don't want to hear any more of what I learned?"

"I…I didn't think there would be more." How could there

have been when the target had been left alive?

"Oh, there's more," Ryker assured with a grin. "No marks were left on the girl, so her claims of attack were very hard to believe. I also enjoyed watching her squirm while she tried to explain the situation without revealing that you survived the assassination attempt she took part in."

Valora hadn't thought of that part. Juno could only give so many details of her attack without incriminating herself in the process. Not many killers could say their weapon of choice was shadow whips, which would mean revealing Valora still lived. She couldn't imagine Aurelia would be okay with Juno doing that, so the most Juno could say was that her room had been broken into.

Valora had never been so relieved in all her life, knowing her abilities had potentially bought her a little more time.

"You'll have to tell me how you managed to leave no physical evidence behind on our way up the mountain," Ryker continued as he brought a few shirts over to the bed to fold and pack. "It'll be a good way to kill time."

"Ryker...." Valora pressed, more interested in the repercussions of her visit to Norlyn than his interest in her violent tendencies.

"Right. Sorry. Anyhow, they've imposed a curfew, which I think is absurd. Clearly, the girl was targeted while already in bed for the night. But it's there, along with increased warrior patrols. Oh, and they found a cloud of ashes in the family sitting room." Ryker peered up at Valora under his eyelashes, smirking. "Down the chimney, huh?" Valora nodded. "Impressive, sunshine."

"You can kiss the ground I walk on later, fire boy," she retorted. "Please do continue with the story."

Ryker chuckled and stuffed a shirt into a bag. "All families are advised to have fires going at night from now on."

"Isn't that dangerous?"

"Depends on who lives in the house, I suppose." Ryker shrugged. He hid the pain that Valora saw flash in his eyes by dropping his next shirt and producing a ball of fire in his palm. "I would have no issues. But yes, most others might find it a dangerous solution."

"Are you trying to impress me with your abilities?"

"Is it working?"

A grin slowly spread across Valora's lips. She shook her head and went back to her tasks. "Is that all that happened?"

"It seems so." Ryker moved to stand next to her. She refused to look up. "I'd say if you hadn't been so messy with the fireplace, nothing would have happened. The girl didn't have enough proof without naming you outright to help her case." He nudged her with his shoulder. Valora glanced up then moved her eyes back down to her clothing and blankets, not wanting Ryker to notice her blush. "You're becoming quite the expert murderess."

"Ah, yes—just what every young woman loves to hear. I'd also like to remind you that my victim from last night is still alive."

Ryker said nothing more, but she felt his eyes on her. The discomfort of being watched became so strong that Valora felt the need to finally look up at him.

"Stop that," she said, hitting him with the blanket she'd worked on folding.

"Stop what?"

"Stop staring at me like that."

"Like what?"

She turned to face him and placed her hands on her hips, not amused in the slightest. Ryker grinned down at her. She could tell he fought against a desire to reach out based off the way his arms kept twitching at his sides.

"I'm not looking for praise," Valora said.

"I'm not giving it to you."

"Ryker, honestly—"

He held up his hand to silence her—a gesture Valora certainly did not appreciate, but allowed nonetheless. She remained silent while she waited for whatever smart response he'd thought up. He was at a particular disadvantage, having been secluded from women for so many years.

"I think what you're doing is courageous," he admitted. "I think facing your fears and those who wronged you is very brave. I think it's even braver what you did last night."

"Not very long ago you were telling me what a terrible human being I was for wanting to do all this."

"I said no such thing," Ryker defended himself, wagging his index finger at her. "I would never tell you you're a terrible human being because I'm the *last* person with the right to do so." Valora's expression softened at that. Ryker noticed and grinned. "If I worried about sleeping in the bed next to you before, imagine how I feel now, knowing you can kill without leaving evidence." He punched her shoulder lightly. "Murderess."

Valora punched him right back. Harder. Then she shoved the few articles of clothing she possessed into a knapsack.

"Hurry up," she said while she slung one of the straps over her shoulder. "If this journey is as terrible as you're making it sound, we should get going while there's still enough daylight."

**R**YKER HAD NOT been lying. Valora didn't know if she could have made the trek up the mountains had it not been for her companion. She couldn't imagine making the journey alone, but then again, Ryker probably hadn't travelled with still-healing gashes on his back. Paths worn into the mountainside by past travelers luckily kept the scaling to a minimum. Still, Valora asked for a healing session when they arrived at a decent campsite.

They finally settled on a plateau Ryker recommended from trips past, making quick work of setting up the tent and collecting enough wood for a fire.

Valora sat on a rock while Ryker prepared the disinfecting poultice with the ingredients she had packed earlier in the day. She watched him crush them together in the mortar. When that bored her, Valora watched the dancing flames of the fire Ryker had started. Her shadows kept them hidden from any watching eyes down below.

It was unnerving, living in the middle of nowhere. Ironic, really, considering she lived in the middle of a supposedly haunted forest. But in her time at Ryker's hidden home, Valora had become used to the forest. The mountains were unexplored terrain, and Valora couldn't shake the irrational fear of the mountain lions Ryker had once mentioned.

She knew his fire could scare any predator away, yet Valora strengthened the shield of darkness around them—just to make sure no predator found them to begin with.

Ryker finished the poultice and made his way over to her. Distracted by providing the shield, she didn't notice him. He cleared his throat, and when Valora looked up at him, he motioned with his index finger for her to turn around.

Valora did as instructed and only when her back faced him did she remove her shirt. The action had become so customary after the incident with the wolves that it no longer bothered her.

She shuddered when the cold poultice touched her skin, then relaxed when she felt Ryker's warm palm. He must have noticed her aversion to the temperature, as he adjusted the heat in his fingertips. A tingle of warmth accompanied the ointment in the spots he applied it.

Ryker went about his routine as usual, touching her back gently, moving his hands over each of the wounds in his methodical way. But something had changed from the way he first treated her wounds. Ryker used to talk endlessly to her during the sessions—badgered Valora about this and that. Ever since the attack with the wolves, he'd worked in near silence, his hands moving over the ridges that had formed where some of her wounds had closed. That seemed to be the case for most of the gashes, both from the wolves and the girls.

The excuses to stay away from Norlyn were running out. With the wounds healed and her old friends almost all dead, she could return as soon as their excursion in the mountains ended. She could finish her mission that same night—hopefully with more success than the night prior—and move back home in the morning.

Ryker's hands continued roaming, grazing, warming. Valora leaned back into it, and he paused just long enough for her to realize what she had done. Quickly, she made her back rod-straight and cleared her throat.

"A copper for your thoughts?" Valora said, trying to distract from her moment of unsound judgment.

"What?"

"It's...." Valora sighed. "When I would catch Bo while he was upset, I would ask him what was wrong. At first, he never gave anything up. He's not a very emotional person. Then I offered to give him something in return. A copper for a thought. He has nearly a whole jar full of coins in his bedroom now."

Ryker remained silent. Valora did as well, not wanting to give up any more information without prompting.

"You and your brother...it seems like you were very close. *Are* very close, I suppose."

"Yes," Valora whispered. "We fight sometimes. Obviously—all siblings do. But we need to get along. It's only the two of us. If we didn't, we would have no one else to turn to."

"What of your parents? Were you close with them?" His hands continued to wander across her back, warm and inviting.

Valora let out a deep breath. "Yes. Mom and I have always been close. Dad and I became close when I got older. I think he was happy I decided to use my abilities to become a warrior, but I've always helped them run the shop."

"What scents were your favorites?" Valora heard the smile in his voice.

"Lavender." She paused, letting him connect the dots. "I always liked pine as well. I blame that on my fascination with the legends of the forest. Though I can't say I ever thought I would be living in it."

Ryker chuckled. His palms flattened on her back. He moved them up and down along her skin. Valora's jaw tightened, and she clenched her teeth together.

"What about you?" she asked, fighting against the taut muscles in her face. "I've given you more than a couple of thoughts. It's your turn now."

"I never agreed to your game, you know."

Valora scowled and reached blindly back to try to hit him. It took her three tries to finally connect her palm with his leg. Ryker chuckled again, then sighed while he ran his hands up her bare back to her shoulders. He massaged them, and Valora couldn't help but enjoy it. Carrying a bag full of heavy baking items and climbing a mountain in one day had taken its toll on her muscles.

"Let's see…" Ryker began. "Well, I sadly don't have any siblings to tell stories about, but I do have Ma and Pa. They're a couple of young souls trapped in aging bodies. Always managed to keep things interesting enough, I suppose. Pa used to play the fiddle after supper sometimes. Ma would dance. When I was little, I would too, but then I started to grow and got clumsier and I decided it'd be safer for everyone if I stayed in my chair."

Valora laughed softly, desperately wanting the chance to see Ryker stumble over his own two feet while dancing with the woman who could have been his twin, the golden-haired man they'd seen in the village playing his fiddle by the fire, the family laughing and clapping….

"I've never known two people more in love," Ryker continued. "They married young—knew right from the beginning they were the ones for each other. I guess that's why I hoped my first love would be the same."

He paused for a moment, and Valora waited for his follow-up question. Instead, she got, "I walked in on them once."

Valora beamed from ear to ear. The image of Ryker walking in on his parents was far more entertaining than that of him trying to dance. "No way."

"I couldn't have been more than ten," Ryker laughed.

"Scarred for life from that moment forward. Though the talk Pa had with me the next day gave me a leg up on my friends. And with the ladies."

"Oh, I'm sure of it, you scoundrel." Valora rolled her eyes and laughed with him.

When the laughter faded, Ryker, sounding embarrassed, asked, "Have you…have you ever been in love?"

Valora stayed quiet for a moment before she admitted, "Once." Ryker's hands tensed. "It was a long time ago. A few years now, I think. We were together for a couple of years—romantically…physically." She didn't know why she felt the need to admit that part of her private life, but it slipped out anyway. "Then his family moved to Doonatel. We tried to keep it going, but the distance… he claimed it wouldn't work for him. I cried for days."

"I'm sorry," Ryker whispered.

Valora shrugged. "Looking back on it, I think it's stupid. We would have never worked out. Him moving away was a blessing in disguise, really. I think I would have married him simply because it was comfortable." *Because he was one of the few people that initially didn't push me away.*

They were both silent, lost in the memories of their pasts. Only the crackling of the fire and the sound of nighttime insects surrounded them. The sun finally sank below the horizon and darkness took over the wilderness. Without Valora's shield, the orange blaze behind them would have given away their position immediately.

Ryker's hands stopped their focus on her shoulders and roamed around the bare skin of her back again. Valora stared out blankly into the darkness while she leaned back into the touch once more. The second time, she didn't stop when Ryker temporarily paused.

The warmth of his hands—his touch—felt incredible in the chill of the night. The fire helped, but Ryker helped more. And with her shirt gone—her entire upper half exposed to the elements—Valora wanted all the warmth she could get. As his hands continued exploring her scars, she imagined just how warm she would be pulled back against his chest, his heated arms holding her, warm breath on her neck, his hands moving to trace patterns on her stomach rather than her back until they eventually moved up to her—

Valora gasped in a sharp breath and stood quickly. Ryker stayed on the ground while she tossed her shirt over her head and pulled it down firmly. When she turned back to him, her arms crossed over her chest, he watched her with concerned eyes, his arms still slightly outstretched as they had been while he touched her.

"I'm sorry, I'm just—it's just that I'm getting tired. It's been a long few days for me."

"Of course," Ryker said. "Yeah, of course," he repeated, shaking his head to clear away whatever daze her sudden movements had left him in. He rubbed the back of his neck while he continued, "The tent should be good to go. Pallets are out. And all the blankets are in there as well."

Valora nodded slowly. "Perfect. Well—um…." She shifted her eyes off to the side, wanting some kind of distraction but found nothing in the pitch black of the night. "Well, goodnight."

"Goodnight, Valora."

They stared at each other in tense silence before Valora strode past him to the tent. It could easily fit the two of them, with room to spare, but still, she preferred having more space.

With one of the tent flaps pulled back, Valora hesitated and turned back over her shoulder. She found Ryker still sitting by the fire.

"Ryker?" she called to him. He turned slowly to her. "Call me Val."

She didn't know what made her give him that kind of permission. Only those closest to her called her Val, and, well…she supposed Ryker had become one of those people. Or he was becoming one—slowly but surely. And allowing him to call her by a nickname would be the easiest way to repay him for all his healing, she supposed.

Before Valora could see how he would react to her request, she ducked into their tent.

## CHAPTER 18

**VALORA STRETCHED THE** sleep from her limbs, a soft, contented groan escaping from the back of her throat as she did. She hadn't slept so well in what felt like a very long time—or at least she had once Ryker had started heating the tent. Her sweater and pants did well enough at the house, but in the elevated, colder wilderness of the mountains, Valora had found herself using all the available blankets. Her companion must have noticed her shivering at some point during the night and removed the one blanket he used to cover himself and turned up his natural heat. It radiated off his body, making Valora feel like she slept beside a roaring fire.

Using the blanket to shield against the chilly morning air, Valora stepped outside the tent. Ryker was still asleep, which Valora attributed to his staying out hours after she'd called it a night.

The sun rose over the forest, giving the sky a beautiful blue-purple-pink tint. Low-floating clouds hovered over the tops of the mix of pines and spruces and birches. Every so often a wolf's howl found Valora's ears, and a flock of birds took flight, soaring amongst and above the clouds, little black dots against the vastness of the scenery.

Only the smoke from chimneys alerted Valora to Norlyn's location in perspective to her current position. She'd never thought her home village small until she witnessed it from such heights.

It was strange, feeling so at peace, even though she knew her life was anything but. In that moment, while watching the world wake, Valora could have forgotten everything that had happened in the past months. It amazed her how everything that seemed so significant to her was utterly insignificant in the grand scheme of things.

She stared down at Norlyn. Watching as though she resided in her tree perch, Valora waited for her eyes to find her targets as they always seemed to. She and the girls were connected, more so than through the friendship they once possessed. They'd started something more—something that would not break until a clear winner remained. That winner could have been so much more evident had Valora succeeded the night before, a one-on-one battle between her and Aurelia all that stood between her and her chance to return to the village.

Instead, the odds continued to sway out of Valora's favor.

"I make this trip once a year, and the view never gets old."

Valora jumped when she heard Ryker. He grinned down at her and apologized while she adjusted the hold on her blanket, pulling it tighter around her shoulders. She looked away from him after a moment, unable to shake the thoughts of the previous night from her head.

"Are you still alright to go berry-picking today?" he asked. Valora turned back to him, waiting for his explanation as to why she would *not* be fine to partake in such a simple task. "I was just wondering since your back was bothering you yesterday. We need to do a bit more climbing—"

"I'll manage," Valora assured him.

Ryker nodded once and stuffed his hands in the pockets of his cotton pants. He rocked back and forth from the balls of his feet to his heels, staring out over the expanse in front of them. His eyes didn't find Norlyn nearly as frequently as Valora's.

He subtly sidestepped towards her, acting as though his rocking made him stumble. Valora casually sidestepped away. She pulled the blanket further around her like a cocoon.

"Are you cold?" Ryker asked, innocently. "I sometimes forget how bad it is up here at this height. I can get you another blanket if you'd—"

"I'm fine, Ryker. Don't worry."

She meant it. The blanket provided her plenty of warmth—along with her growing embarrassment. She felt like her every move gave away her thoughts from the previous night—the real reason she'd retired to the tent so early.

But if Ryker figured anything out, he didn't show it. His standing so close to her was nothing out of the ordinary. He tended to forget that Valora didn't always want affection, no matter how many times she told him. No—he ignored that request as always and continued to stand on the edge of the mountainside, fidgeting on his feet.

Valora dared a glance down and regretted it immediately. Her legs turned to instant pudding, and she took a cautious step back from the ledge of the mountain. Heights didn't bother her. The idea of falling victim to the massive boulders and jagged edges that covered the mountainside did.

Of course, Ryker noticed.

"Afraid of heights, sunshine?" He smirked.

"I climb hundred-foot trees," Valora retorted. "What do you think, fire boy?"

Ryker's smirk grew, and Valora's brow furrowed. Immediately, he turned away, moving his eyes up to the sky and pursing his lips. Valora tilted her head, not amused, and waited to see the result of whatever plan Ryker was no doubt formulating.

"So if I were to—let's just say—do this…."

Ryker knocked the side of his body into hers, making Valora stumble towards the edge of the cliff, a bit too close for comfort. She quickly shuffled back, her eyes wide and her heart racing.

"Ryker, I swear—"

"But you're not afraid of heights!" He smiled. "So it wouldn't be an issue if I did something like this…."

Before Valora could argue that any further action would be subject to her wrath, she found herself picked up off the ground and dangling over the edge of the cliff. She yelled Ryker's name while she thrashed in his hold, wanting to do anything in her power to get him to put her down. Valora dared another glance down at the rocks, imagining what would happen should her captor's hold slip—on accident or on purpose. How the rocks would feel as she crashed among them, all the blood, all the new wounds….

The reopening of wounds freshly healed.

Valora's heart pounded against her chest as Ryker finally set her back on the ground, laughing at her tantrum.

"That wasn't funny!" Valora yelled as she gifted him with a series of punches to the arms and chest.

He held his hands up defensively—or maybe in surrender—and Valora used them as new targets. The blanket fell from around her shoulders while her actions pushed them back away from the edge. Unless Ryker wanted the pummeling to continue, he needed to keep moving.

"Calm down, tiger," he laughed. "You're going to give us away."

"Don't *ever* do that again, understood?" Valora reprimanded him. He finally got ahold of her wrists, but she continued to fight, kicking one of her legs forward with the intention of hitting him where it would hurt most. Ryker curved his body to avoid the blow. "You scared me half to death!"

"Death is probably getting very tired of you toying with him all the time. How many times have you evaded his clutches now?" He laughed as she tried to kick him again and missed. "My count is at least three."

"He'll forgive me when I give you up as a sacrifice instead!"

Valora thrashed violently in his grasp, but to no avail. Ryker held strong—so strong that Valora felt like she provided little to no challenge.

Soon, she yelped and pulled away on her own. Her wrists glowed faint red and stung where Ryker had burned her. He *burned* her—not in healing but in harm. In self-defense.

Valora stared at him in awe. Ryker, having realized what he'd done, slowly released his hold on her, his eyes first set on the burned wrists, then moving to the hands that had caused the damage.

"You burned me," Valora whispered.

"Valora, I—I didn't mean—"

"You *burned me*," she repeated, her jaw tense with an emotion stuck somewhere between shock and hurt.

Ryker looked up from his hands, his shining amber eyes meeting Valora's. They didn't shine with the joy that usually radiated from Ryker. Instead, she caught a rare sight of the pain that haunted him.

"I didn't mean to harm you," whispered Ryker. "It…it was a natural reaction—a defense. I'm not your enemy."

"When you feel the need to defend yourself from me, you become my enemy," Valora spat right back. "So, if it hurts you to see me as such, I'd suggest refraining from dangling me over the edge of a cliff to avoid any future issues."

"It was a *joke*, Valora."

"I was *scared*, Ryker."

His brow rose. Valora never admitted her weaknesses. Ryker could have figured it out on his own, surely, based off her reaction, but to have Valora say outright that the cliff frightened her….

She looked down, ashamed of herself for saying as much, and rubbed her wrists. Amidst the newfound silence, Valora could hear each of Ryker's heavy breaths. She moved her eyes to watch his chest rise and fall but refused to go any higher.

A foot came towards her and Valora took a step back. Ryker paused and held up his hands again in truce.

"Let me take a look at them," he offered.

"You've done enough."

Valora turned and walked back to the tent. Ryker wisely

remained at the cliff edge and stayed there until he came to find her an hour later to ask if she still wanted to pick berries. Valora noted the hurt in his eyes as he stared at the damp wrappings around her wrists. The temperature of the elevated mountain air kept the wrappings cool enough that Valora hoped no blistering would occur.

Saying nothing, she grabbed an empty sack from the corner of the tent and exited past Ryker. Originally, Valora had planned to go all the way to the berry patch, until she stopped, realizing Ryker never told her where it was.

Ryker must have known that too because he took far longer than normal to emerge from the tent. When he did, he was grinning from ear to ear, his own sack slung back over his shoulder.

Valora waited with her arms crossed over her chest and her foot tapping impatiently. Her lips, in pure opposition to Ryker's, were pursed angrily. It got worse when she saw the swagger he chose to add to his step that morning.

"Ready, Val?" he asked as he passed, clapping his hand on her shoulder.

Ryker continued on his way towards the berry patch, whistling while he went. The cheery melody matched the sickening little bounce in his step.

Valora scowled at his back. She didn't believe she would ever stop hating herself for allowing him, in her moment of sympathetic weakness, to use her nickname.

"Val?" he called back in a sing-song voice.

Valora rolled her eyes, tossed her sack back over her shoulder, and followed after her companion.

Ryker's warning about the additional climbing had been

warranted, Valora realized. How he'd managed to find the berry patch in the first place baffled her, as she couldn't imagine reaching it without anyone's help. By the end of the trek, her back hurt and her muscles ached more so than after their journey the day before.

Ryker, on the other hand, acted as if he'd just woken from the world's most contented night of sleep. He stretched his arms above his head and sighed, his lips curled in a great smile.

"Did it get warmer out, or is it just me?" he asked when Valora finally made her aching way to his side. She glared at him sidelong, and he winked. "First one to fill their sack wins."

Ryker must have known the challenge would entice Valora because she got straight to work after that. She would never back down from a competition—especially when it included the chance to best her housemate.

Considering the time of season, Valora hadn't expected to find so many blueberries, strawberries, and raspberries. The longer she worked at plucking the small fruits, the more aware she became that perhaps Ryker's comment about the weather hadn't been intended as a joke.

The particular part of the mountain where the patch resided was a diamond in the rough. From the ground, Valora saw some of the greener areas, but the berry clearing hid among mountainside brushes and trees stubborn enough to grow among the rocks. Most of them grew sideways before they decided it best to shoot up towards the sun, thus creating a natural wall around the clearing.

She imagined if any of the cooks in the village knew of the clearing's existence, she and Ryker wouldn't have been so lucky with their harvesting. Ryker had found his own little secret oasis full of mouth-watering treats. Just from the vibrancy of the berries Valora tossed into her bag, she could tell each one would explode in her mouth with sweet flavor.

Valora busied herself with examining a handful of blueberries when another, larger hand filled with strawberries appeared in front of her. She nudged it to the side without looking up at its owner, but the hand refused to give up so easily.

When she glanced up, she found Ryker standing there, another one of his stupid grins on his face, trying to persuade her to take the berries. Valora, ever stubborn, turned away slightly and went back to picking her blueberries. She flicked her long, black hair back over her shoulder as a further show of her solidarity of ignorance. The stinging pain in her wrist caused by the action only further reminded her why she should be mad.

Her one ally had harmed her, and a couple of stupid berries would do little to make her forget that.

"Oh, c'mon, Valora." Ryker crouched down beside her. "This is my peace offering. My apology, more than anything."

The berries appeared under her nose again. Valora turned her head away from them, fighting the urge to grab every single succulent strawberry and devour them instantly. Their sweet aroma wafted up to her nose.

In a show of defiance, Valora tossed a couple of blueberries into her mouth. Though delicious, their slight bitterness didn't live up to her expectations, making Ryker's offering even more enticing.

"I really am sorry," he tried again.

Valora turned almost entirely away from him and his berries. She heard him sigh. Any normal person would know to give up, but Ryker was no normal person. Not even close. So when she felt little, soft balls hitting her head, shoulders, and back, Valora used every ounce of willpower not to turn around. They were locked in a battle of stubborn against stubborn.

Eventually it became too much, and Valora whirled around. "Would you stop tha—"

With her mouth wide open, in the middle of reprimanding him, Ryker took the chance to plop a strawberry in. Shocked by his audacity, Valora sat there, staring at him with wide eyes, the strawberry sitting in her mouth unchewed.

"Eat it." Her companion smiled. He tossed a strawberry into his mouth. "They're delicious."

He chomped at his berry and continued to pile them into his mouth without swallowing the previous ones. Valora scowled at the half-chewed food he put on display for her then placed her hand under her chin. She couldn't recall the last time she'd needed to use the silent cue.

Ryker paused and swallowed whatever food he held in his mouth. His cheeks filled with a blush and Valora couldn't stop herself from smiling—just a little. The same man that had burned her wrists only hours before always managed to react to the most innocent things.

"There we go." Ryker wiped his mouth with the back of his hand. "Some progress has been made."

It got better. In his attempt to wipe away excess berry, Ryker only made it worse. His hands were covered in the red and purple juices from hours of picking, and they'd made his face look like a painting.

"What?" Ryker asked when Valora covered her mouth with her palm to hide her growing smile. "Is there something on my face?"

His worry only made him smear more juices on his skin. The worse it got, the more Valora fought against her laughter until finally she couldn't help throwing her head back. Despite his desperation to clean his face, Ryker stopped. His smile grew as he watched her. She tried to make it stop—tried to conceal it with her hands—but failed. His colorful face was so ridiculous that Valora couldn't help but laugh.

Ryker did nothing to stop her—for a while. When he saw no end to her fit, he picked a handful of blueberries from her sack and threw them at her. Valora gasped at him through her smile.

"That's what you get," he said firmly, wearing his own grin.

Valora shook her head at him and reached for her bag of berries, taking out a handful to return fire. Ryker turned away to dodge the ammunition. When he spun around again, he held a new handful and launched a mixture of berries, one at a time, at her.

She laughed at him to stop, but her companion showed no signs of giving in. Desperate to get away from the berry attack, Valora stood, grabbing her bag, and jogged away through the bushes and vines. Ryker followed after retrieving his collection, and the two continued their assaults.

Laughter filled the clearing in the mountains. Valora didn't have her shields up, and for one of the first times since Ryker had found her in the forest, she didn't care about being unprotected. No one would find them in the mountains. Norlyn busied itself with other tasks, too far away to hear any antics taking place in a hidden berry patch.

She and Ryker stood alone amongst the berries that they continued to throw at each other until their entire day's work lay scattered and squished on the ground.

**On their way** back to the camp, bags empty of berries after the small bout of warfare, Ryker managed to kill an opossum. The delicious scent of cooking meat made Valora realize how little they had eaten that day. Aside from berries, she couldn't remember eating anything at all.

When she gazed across the flames of their campfire, she caught Ryker's hungry eyes focused on the creature rotating on a stick. She watched him for a while, the orange glow of the fire dancing on his skin and making his fiery amber eyes burn even brighter.

Having noticed her staring, Ryker looked up at her across the flames. The ravenous glaze that his eyes had possessed while he stared at his dinner faded, and he met Valora with nothing but kindness. He smiled softly, and she turned away, tucking some obsidian hair behind her ear.

They ate in silence, enjoying meat that didn't belong to their usual forest findings. As soon as they had returned to the familiar territory of the camp, silence reigned. Whatever carefree parts of themselves they'd allowed to break free in the berry patch went dormant once more.

And still, neither one of them left the other's side. Valora could have gone to the tent. Ryker could have gone on a walk. Instead, they sat there on rocks on opposite sides of the fire.

Valora pulled her knees up to her chest and rested her chin on them as she stared blankly into the dancing flames. Her whole body ached from the activity of the day, but she refused to say anything about it. She didn't want to complain anymore. She'd done enough to last a lifetime since that morning.

Ryker was right. Valora should feel lucky that she had evaded death so many times in recent months, but instead, she took her luck for granted. If she'd met death when the girls intended it, she would have missed out on opportunities like watching the forest at sunrise or strawberry wars. Everyone had the right to complain, but she took advantage of it—and of Ryker's ability to listen.

Valora didn't know many others that would be given so many chances to keep living. Multiple stab wounds, an attack by a wolf pack…no wonder so many feared the forest. The darkness within it expanded beyond the physical sense.

And somehow, she had managed to find the one source of light within it.

"Do they hurt?"

Valora, drawn from her distraction, peered up, confused by Ryker's sudden question until she noticed her subconscious action. Her hand was running over her wounds, likely as the result of her thoughts. They felt like nothing more than ridges of raised skin. They didn't hurt any more than usual, but she nodded anyway.

Ryker removed the opossum from the heat and moved towards her. Valora removed her shirt and positioned herself kneeling with her back to him by the time he sat down behind her. When his fingertips grazed over the same wounds she had just touched, Valora bit her lower lip.

"They look good," Ryker pointed out. "As good as they can, anyway. Even the ones from the wolf."

"That's good," Valora whispered.

Ryker continued to run his fingers over them, the temperature of his fingertips rising as he did. Fresh calluses and cuts covered his hands. He must have gotten in trouble with the berry bushes. The thought made her smile a little. Big, bad, fire-bending Ryker—bested by a plant.

"How do your muscles not ache?" Valora asked.

Valora didn't need to turn around to know her companion was grinning. "Is that what's wrong? You're sore?"

Valora nodded, and she felt Ryker's palms flatten on her back. They remained there as he decided what to do. She wouldn't have known how to remedy the problem either if she was dealing with a back as mutilated as hers. No matter how well her injuries had healed, she wouldn't want to take unnecessary risks. Apparently, neither did Ryker.

Soon enough, his hands ran up her skin to her shoulders. He kneaded her muscles like dough, working out each of the kinks created over the past few days. The massage the night before had been nice, but now that Ryker knew the issue, Valora felt the difference in the way he worked. She shut her eyes, narrowing her attention to the brilliant pain he caused.

"Feel that?" Ryker asked, referring to the growing heat in his palms. "That's how I don't get muscle aches. I heat them. Constant muscle relaxant...."

His voice was nothing more than a breath in her ear. Valora's body rose and fell drastically under his hands.

"Does this feel alright?" he whispered.

"Yes," Valora replied breathlessly. She wondered if he could feel her heartbeat through her back. It picked up as her thoughts from the night before returned, except this time they didn't scare her away.

Ryker's hands ran back down her skin, over her wounds, to rest on her hips. The same lips that whispered in her ear placed a gentle kiss just below her jaw. Valora's breath shuddered out from her lungs.

"Still alright?"

Valora nodded, and Ryker's hands tightened on her hips. His head nudged hers to the side so he could continue to kiss her jaw and neck. She slowly lowered the shirt she held against her bare chest, exposing herself to the darkness.

She knew he noticed by the way his hands wrapped around the front of her hips, hooked down between her thighs, and pulled her back towards him. Valora wobbled a bit and reached back to hold onto him, only as a way to steady herself. Her arm somehow found its way around his neck, her fingers in the hair at the back of his head.

"Where did you say the aches were?" Ryker rasped in a newly husky voice.

"Everywhere," Valora sighed. She leaned her head back on his shoulder.

Aches. Burning. Want. They coursed through her veins the same way Ryker's fire coursed through his.

His hand made its way up and down her thigh, a different heat than the one Ryker produced remaining behind. The other hand made its way up her stomach, making a chill run down Valora's spine. His gentle touch tickled her.

"We're going to have to fix that, aren't we?"

"Mhm." Her agreement turned into a prolonged hum when he bit her neck.

Ryker moaned against her skin. Valora let her mouth hang open, the tease of her own moan lingering in the back of her throat. One more move from Ryker and it would escape.

His tongue ran over her neck as he kissed it, and she could

take no more. The only sensations she felt were those of his mouth and hands, one still caressing the curve in her side, the other curving in and out between her thighs.

When he bit her neck again, Valora lost control.

"Dammit, Ryker," she whispered before she tugged on his hair and brought his head up.

Their lips met in a hungry crash. Valora turned around, both of them still kneeling on the large rock she'd used as a seat. His hands continued to roam over her exposed skin while her fingers tangled in his shaggy brown hair.

Valora cared about nothing except the two of them—where they touched—in that moment.

They broke away only long enough for Valora to tug Ryker's shirt off. The muscled arms she watched during training everyday pulled her closer until their chests pressed up against each other. They were so close that Valora had no choice but to straddle his lap if she wanted them to keep going.

And she did.

Ryker's hand moved to her lower back. The other tangled in her hair. Then his lips once again found her neck and Valora tilted her head back to moan.

"Come here," Ryker hissed as he brought his lips back to hers.

Valora had never been a particularly sexual person. She wasn't completely inexperienced, but the idea of letting someone get close to her that way—see her vulnerable in that way—made her uneasy. She'd never understood Aurelia's ability to bring home men that she'd just met that night. Meaningless affairs, while fun, were too much of a risk.

But in that moment, feeling the heat of Ryker's hands and his breath and his tongue, Valora was convinced that the risk was far outweighed by the reward. She knew Ryker. She trusted Ryker. He'd seen her at her most vulnerable time and time again and had never violated that trust.

She wanted this. She wanted him.

Valora slid her hands down Ryker's chiseled chest to the band of his pants. He didn't stop her. That was how they worked. Without the other's permission, nothing would happen. That was how they had operated together—managed to live together—since the day Valora had grown strong enough to leave her bed. Even before, when Ryker first began his heat therapy on her fresh wounds.

She stopped, pulling away with a gasp when she heard the bushes rustle. Her eyes, the widest they had been since Ryker started his massaging, darted around the camp, searching for the source of the sound. It had been too loud for the soft breeze to cause.

"Ryker." Valora hit his shoulder softly, repeatedly, trying to capture his attention as he went back to kissing her neck. It would have made sense for him to mistake the cause of the gasp. "Ryker. Stop. I think I heard something."

His head popped up again, but Valora didn't meet his eyes. She continued to scan the area. Whatever tension the bout of pleasure had released returned in full force.

When she felt Ryker's hand cup the side of her face, she finally looked at him. Concern filled his eyes.

"No one can find us, Val," he whispered. "Not with your shield up."

Valora's tension grew. She knew he felt it—saw it in her eyes.

His other hand joined the first, forcing her to face him.

"Your shield *is* up, isn't it?" The tenderness in his voice was gone, replaced entirely with worry.

It very obviously grew worse when Valora didn't respond. She couldn't bring herself to. The shield had originally been up—she knew it had been in order to hide the fire dancing behind them. But then she'd lost her focus, concentrating on only Ryker, and….

"Shit," Ryker hissed. He practically pushed her off him. "Shit."

Ryker grabbed his shirt in his fist and stood. Valora scooted back on the rock, feeling for her own shirt and quickly bringing it back over her exposed chest. She watched Ryker run through the camp, collecting their things, knocking the tent down and shoving it haphazardly into a sack.

With a swipe of his hand, he doused the fire. Valora temporarily lost sight of him until his skin began to glow, his veins filled with the orange embers of his abilities.

He stalked towards her and tossed a sack her way. "Well, don't just sit there. Get dressed. We have to go."

Valora snapped out of her daze and pulled her shirt back over her head. She got up and brought the sack with her. She and Ryker packed up the few belongings of the camp in a rush, tossing anything into any of the bags they'd brought. When nicely folded, everything had fit. In their hurry, nothing did.

Ryker continued to curse under his breath, the glow in his veins creating the only light source to work off. It was hardly anything at all, which forced Valora to work directly beside him. Wherever Ryker went, she went.

They both jumped and froze when the bushes rustled again. Ryker dimmed his skin just enough for Valora to see the approaching glow of what appeared to be a torch or a lantern.

"Run," Ryker breathed. He rushed to grab one of the mostly packed bags and shoved it against her chest. "Run!"

## CHAPTER 19

**VALORA TRIED TO** grab ahold of the darkness around them to use it as a disguise while they ran hopelessly up the mountain path, anywhere out of the open camp.

She ran as fast as she could, knowing she wasn't moving as quickly as Ryker probably wanted. Still, he always remained at her back, keeping himself between her and the male voice that chased after them.

Someone had found them. Because of her carelessness, the fire had given away their position, acting as a beacon for any traveler or villager to track them down.

How could she have been so stupid? One careless moment—one moment of weakness—and she and Ryker found themselves running for their lives.

The mountainside suddenly loomed in front of her, its

shadows having blended into the surrounding darkness until they were right upon it. Valora skidded to a halt just in time, but didn't have a chance to warn Ryker before he crashed into her back. She jolted forward at the impact, nearly hitting the wall before he caught her and wrapped her in his arms.

"What do we do?" she asked frantically when he released her. "Where do we go?"

They found themselves in an alcove made entirely of mountain. No matter which way they turned, they met another obstacle. The only way out was the path from which they'd just come—which led straight to their pursuer's arms.

Ryker's mouth hung open. Valora heard a sound coming from it while he decided what to say. For once, after all the trouble they'd gotten into, it seemed Ryker didn't know what to do.

He glanced at the bag Valora carried on her back, then met her eyes. The bag was filled with their weapons, and she realized what he was thinking.

It was all wrong. Valora knew Ryker wouldn't kill anyone—he hid himself away in the forest in order to avoid it. And Valora refused to murder beyond what was necessary for her return home. She'd already made that harder for herself as it was.

Valora heard the cracking twigs and rustling of bushes and knew their pursuer grew closer. Her eyes darted to where she knew he would appear in the alcove. Ryker's head peered over his shoulder to follow her gaze. When he turned back to her, he placed a hand on her shoulder.

"Follow my lead," he instructed and then removed a knife from her bag. "No shadows. Nothing that can give us away."

Ryker stepped in front of Valora defensively, one hand

reaching back to hold onto hers. The other held the knife up, ready to strike.

The light from the lantern grew brighter. Valora sidled closer to Ryker, increasing their contact by grabbing onto his wrist with her free hand. She saw him glance back at her for a second before the light appeared in front of them.

Valora scrutinized its owner. He appeared to be in his forties with a full, dark beard and shaggy hair to match. The fine quality and tailoring of his clothing indicated he had likely traveled from Norlyn.

On his back, he carried a large knapsack, the lantern in his hand the only source of light to guide him through the night. It cast a circular glow of orange around the three of them.

Ryker let out a relieved sigh and began to chuckle. He lowered his knife and the man looked at him like he was insane. Valora wondered the same.

"Oh my." Ryker smiled. He let out another sigh and turned halfway to Valora. "Darling—I told you we shouldn't worry."

Valora said nothing, trying not to let her confusion show for the stranger. He raised his lantern higher to better see her and Ryker.

"Hello to you too," the man said. He sounded unsure of what to do. "Might I ask who exactly I've stumbled upon?"

Ryker exuded confidence, his smile still spread across his face as he took a daring step towards the man. Valora made sure to keep the hold on his hand, not wanting to be without a shield and definitely not wanting him to get too close.

"My name is Wesley." Ryker introduced himself, placing a hand on his chest. "This is my wife, Harmony."

He pulled the cautious Valora forwards to stand at his side

and snaked the arm previously holding her hand around her waist. Valora continued to stare at the man, unable to think of anything to say, her face blank. When Ryker pinched her side, she managed to crack a small smile and play along. Why did he have to say she was his wife?

The man didn't seem to buy it. His eyes darted between them, most noticeably focusing on their hands. Valora realized they wore no rings to corroborate their story, and she tried to put on a more convincing act. She leaned her head on Ryker's shoulder.

"Kind of young to be married, aren't you?" the man asked.

"You sound like our parents," Ryker chuckled. "Love knows no age, my friend. Isn't that right, darling?"

Valora giggled like a dumb, lovestruck teenager and gazed adoringly at Ryker. At least she hoped that was how it appeared. "How could I resist him?" she asked, turning to the stranger.

His stare unnerved her, as though he could see right through her, down to every little fiber of her being. Valora's smile almost faltered, but Ryker pulled her closer before that could happen. He smiled and dared to kiss her before sighing contentedly again.

Valora felt the eyes of the stranger still on her, unrelenting. If Ryker noticed, he didn't let it break his character.

"Harms and I are on the run," Ryker continued, "hopping from village to village, trying to find a home that accepts us and our decision."

"You've missed Norlyn by a few miles, then," the stranger pointed out, nodding in the direction of the village. "What made you think it was a good idea to camp out in the mountains?"

"If we're being honest, it was the privacy." Valora giggled and turned into Ryker's shoulder, trying to feign embarrassment. "We planned on arriving in the village tomorrow."

"And where are you two originally from?"

"Up north in Wolfden. We're working our way down to Black Hallows. But enough about us!" Ryker extended an inviting hand towards the stranger. "What about you? What brings you to the mountains at this time of night?"

The stranger lowered his lantern. The angle of the light cast eerie shadows over his face and reminded Valora of when she and Bo would tell ghost stories to their parents as children.

"My name is Kent," the stranger said. "I live in Norlyn." He grinned. "That's all you need to know about me."

Valora clutched Ryker's shirt in her fist, her smile wiped from her face and any chance of trusting the stranger gone. Ryker squeezed her hip, and she felt his tension all the way in his fingertips.

"Pleasure to meet you, Kent," Ryker said in a tone that didn't match his rigidity. "Hey—do you think there's any chance for us in Norlyn, or should we pack up and be on our way?"

Valora knew Ryker well enough to pick up on his attempt at a joke. Kent didn't react accordingly. He didn't so much as crack a smile as his eyes continued to dart between the couple in front of him. Valora wanted to shrink away from his stare. There was something about this man… it was as though he knew every detail of her life from one look.

"You appeared to be in quite the hurry to leave your camp." Kent raised a suspicious brow.

Valora's breath caught, but Ryker, ever quick on his feet, seemed prepared for even that remark.

"I told you you were being ridiculous." Ryker smiled down at her. He flicked Valora's nose with the pad of his index finger then turned back to Kent. "My wife thought you were a mountain lion," he added with a chuckle.

The pinch on her hip cued Valora in that Ryker wanted her to join. They stood there, wrapped in each other's arms, laughing at her false stupidity, while Kent continued to stare at them, completely untrusting. Valora's smile faltered as she laughed, albeit very weakly. She felt closer to the verge of tears than anything else.

The man came from Norlyn, and despite the growing population, there were ways for him to determine her and Ryker's identities. She hadn't been gone long enough to be forgotten entirely. Citizens born with abilities were often well-known, and being the daughter of popular shop owners gave Valora an additional disadvantage.

Then there was the dilemma of the both of them being involved with the deaths of multiple young women. Though hers were unattached to her name, Valora remembered the scandal surrounding the girl who had burned with her house. Ryker's name had never reached her ears when she'd heard of the tragic story, but that same might not be true for Kent. Something told Valora the man knew much more than he let on.

She felt Ryker's knife pressed against her back. She wished he would use it to end Kent immediately rather than keep them trapped in such an elaborate lie. With the weapons and both of their powers combined, they could make quick work of the stranger. Though Valora didn't know what such thoughts said about her increasingly convoluted morals….

As if he were aware of her inner monologue, Kent smiled mischievously. Valora tucked herself closer to Ryker, her hand reaching for the knife. He pulled it away from her and took a step forward.

"Have you been traveling for long? Harmony and I have some food left over at our camp. Now that we know there isn't a man-eater stalking us, we really should be getting back there."

"Yes, you two certainly wouldn't want anyone to find you up here," Kent agreed. He glanced sidelong at Valora before finally smiling at Ryker. "I would love to eat something decent. Thank you for the invitation."

"Of course, my friend! Of course!" Ryker took another few steps towards Kent, away from Valora. She was glad her companion blocked the light from Kent's lantern, or he might have seen her nerves written all over her face. "Why don't you lead the way back, seeing as you have that handy light source there?"

Valora watched from a few steps behind, almost entirely out of the light as Ryker ushered Kent back towards the camp and away from her. He clapped his hand on the man's shoulder like an old friend then stopped short.

"Come on, darling. No, no—you can go ahead, Kent. We'll be there in a moment."

Valora didn't move. She kept her eyes trained on the retreating light of the stranger as Ryker made his way back to her. He grabbed her wrist rather than her hand like before. She moved her eyes to his, barely able to make out any of his features in the new darkness.

"Do you trust him?" Valora asked.

"Not even a little," Ryker confirmed. "But if we want to escape this alive and with our secrets intact, we need to act as though we do. He'll leave. We'll finish collecting berries, maybe some more meat, then head back into the forest where no one will dare to come search for us."

"And when the two nomadic newly-weds refuse to join him in Norlyn in the morning?"

Ryker paused. During the silence, he tried to grab hold of Valora's hand, but she pulled back. Even in the darkness she could see the flash of hurt caused by the rejection. Their moment had passed. It had been a quick release of building desire that would not—could not—escalate to anything more. Valora knew that, and she needed Ryker to understand as well.

He took a step back. "We'll figure that out when the time comes. Now, c'mon. He thinks we're following after him. And as much as you dislike it, he also thinks we're in love."

Ryker extended his hand to her. Valora stared at it, remembering all-too-vividly how that same hand had felt against her skin not too long ago. With a sigh, she hesitantly accepted the offer a moment later.

"Next time your brilliant mind thinks up some kind of plan," Valora began as they followed after Kent, "try using something more casual like *brother and sister* or *mortal enemies*. Not spouses."

"Mortal enemies it is."

Silence fell for a heartbeat before Valora asked, "Where did you get the names from?"

Whatever amusement her previous comment had caused vanished. The small curl of his lips fell and Ryker stared straight ahead into the darkness before them as he replied, "They're my parents' names."

They said nothing more the rest of the way to their campsite.

**Considering their** activities not long before, Valora felt quite uneasy in her seat cuddled up next to Ryker. She watched Kent eat the leftover opossum, reheated after using his lantern flame to get the fire going again. She knew Ryker used restraint in taking charge of lighting the fire as always, and she cast him warning glances every so often to make sure he held strong.

She understood, though. It felt strange not having her shield up. With the fire ablaze once more, she knew that the encampment was in full view of anyone who might be on the mountain or watching from down below—a bright beacon of orange in the otherwise dark wilderness beyond Norlyn.

Ryker shifted and pulled Valora closer to him. Reluctantly, she snuggled into his side. With his arm wrapped around her shoulders the way it was, she found she didn't have many options when it came to sitting comfortably.

Kent devoured his food. He acted as though he had not eaten in days, but if Valora knew the Norlynian lifestyle—and she did—Kent had probably eaten enough in the past day alone to last a person in a poorer village a week.

His presence made her grow more and more wary of his intentions. She knew Ryker watched the guest as well, scrutinizing his every detail, every action. Valora always thought her companion trusted easily, unlike herself. He had accepted her into his home without much second thought, after all. But she supposed the circumstances had been different. If Valora had posed a threat, he could have defended himself without any problems, with her being unable to stand on her own for some time and all. On the other hand, Kent was a grown, able-bodied man that they knew relatively nothing about.

Her warrior senses kicked in, trying to determine if Kent had been born with an ability. Nothing about him indicated as much—he didn't have the physique of an average warrior, and no other physical signs pointed that direction. Sometimes, those with abilities possessed traits that indicated their powers, like Ryker's fiery amber eyes. Kent looked like any normal person Valora would pass on the street.

Perhaps he could disguise his power, like she and Ryker were. Valora wondered just how hard Ryker fought to keep his elemental power hidden, though, as she felt his hand on her arm heat. His whole body began to heat.

Valora tilted her head up to her companion. He watched Kent too diligently to notice he earned her attention and continued to chew on his lower lip. She inhaled sharply at the sight of it, remembering instantly where those same lips had been earlier in the night.

Her mouth hung open ever-so-slightly when Ryker finally looked down at her. Valora blushed, and he smiled before giving her forehead a chaste kiss. Before she could object, Ryker rested his forehead on hers and shut his eyes.

"We'll get him to leave soon," Ryker whispered so softly that Valora almost couldn't hear him over the crackling flames, "since it seems that being next to me is becoming too much for you."

"Don't flatter yourself, fire boy," Valora replied in an equally quiet tone.

Ryker shushed her before he kissed her forehead again. She wanted to argue it but then saw the benefit of the show of affection. Kent had finally finished his opossum and watched them just as intently as they had surveyed him.

"Now I understand why you two were looking for privacy,"

Kent commented monotonously.

"Young love," Ryker replied with a shrug. "What can we say?"

Kent grunted his response and picked scraps of meat off the opossum bone.

"Tell me," Kent continued. "How did you two meet? I'm a sucker for a good love story."

Valora tensed under Ryker's hold. He gave her shoulder a reassuring squeeze and said, "Oh, we're nothing special. Just your classic love at first sight story. Isn't that right, darling?"

Valora nodded slowly. "He had me at hello," she added, her voice sounding weak even to her own ears.

Kent eyed her, and Valora stared back until Ryker pulled her tighter against his side. She looked up at him briefly, feeling the heat rising again, before resting her forehead on his shoulder, turned almost completely away from Kent.

"I'd appreciate it if you didn't stare at my wife like that, sir."

"I meant no harm," Kent assured him. "Simply trying to figure out where I know her from, is all."

Valora's tension grew, and she buried her face further against Ryker. He pulled her closer, knowing full well that her worst fear was coming true. She had been recognized. Somehow the man knew her identity, even without the revelation of her abilities.

"If you've lived in Norlyn your whole life, I highly doubt you've ever seen my Harms. We were in Black Hallows up until our parents rejected our decision to wed."

Kent smirked and raised a brow. "I thought, Wesley, that you said you and your young bride hailed from Wolfden?"

Valora wrapped her arms tightly around Ryker's torso. She needed to get away. Nothing in her body would allow her to remain calm—not with Kent's questioning. So, Valora looked up, resting her chin on Ryker's shoulder to get his attention. She tried to disguise the emotion in her eyes, but knew Ryker saw it for what it was: fear.

"Sweetheart," she fought out, "I'm cold. Don't you think we could go into our tent?"

"But we have this nice, warm fire before us." Kent tossed his cleaned bone into the flames then narrowed his eyes at them. "And how can you be cold sitting next to a fire bender?"

Both Valora and Ryker slowly turned to Kent. So, he recognized them both—and apparently their abilities as well—but how, Valora did not know. The silence that fell over the trio said enough. Not even Ryker could think up a convincing enough lie to steer clear of Kent's claim. His smirk widened.

"Hello, Valora Bellemore," he said. "For such a talented shadow bender—or so some say—you clearly need practice. Finding your camp was far too easy once that fire suddenly appeared. You also have quite the piercing scream."

Ryker tensed. So that was how Kent had found them in the mountains—not because of the fire, but because he'd heard Valora scream when Ryker threatened to push her off the edge of the cliff. It made sense. If Norlyn was the two-mile journey Kent claimed it to be, he couldn't have made the trek in the night. It would have taken him all day when combined with his trek up the mountain.

The guest turned his attention on Ryker. "And hello, Ryker Falkov. Wesley and Harmony have missed you in your time away. They've never seemed to come to terms with the fact that their son left them. Even after all these years." The man shrugged. "Such is the case with fire benders. Even if I didn't already know what you were, I could have guessed it. Your kind tends to show very little remorse for your actions...."

It took Valora a moment to process what was happening. This man knew everything about them. She wouldn't have been shocked if he had told her what she'd received as a gift for her fourth birthday after having revealed such details.

Ryker uncurled from Valora, all pretenses dropped. Kent had known their identities the entire time, and had probably only gone along with their act to receive an invitation back to their camp so he could....

Valora didn't want to think about what the man planned to do.

"Okay, so you know who we are," Ryker said. "What do you want from us?"

Kent smirked. "It's very interesting how you two, of all those who flee—though I suppose you did not necessarily choose to initially leave Norlyn, Miss Bellemore—ended up finding each other." The man narrowed his attention in on Valora. "Did Mr. Falkov's story inspire you to go on your own murderous rampage? That's one thing of which I am unclear and have been aching to know."

Ryker stood quickly, pulling Valora with him. With the truth out in the open, he didn't refrain from igniting his arms. But even though Ryker showed the first signs of aggression, Valora spoke first.

"You know nothing about his story," she hissed. "You know nothing about either of us."

Kent chuckled again and slowly stood from his seat. "On the contrary, child. I know *everything*."

Suddenly, all Kent said up until that point made sense. Her

shock had blinded her to his absolute knowledge of what happened to her. He knew she hadn't chosen to leave Norlyn, and that she had taken matters into her own hands to return. And the words he used when talking of Ryker's abilities….

*If I did not already know….*

"You're omniscient," Valora breathed. "You have the ability of infinite knowledge."

"Smart girl," Kent complimented. "And this whole time I thought you would never figure out an ability practically waved in front of your face."

"What do you want from us?" Ryker repeated. Valora could tell he wanted to push her behind him but refused to douse his flames. She wouldn't have allowed it anyways. She wanted to fight beside him, should the confrontation lead to violence.

"The same thing your friend wants," Kent said with a nod in Valora's direction. "Revenge."

He stalked around the fire, closer to where Valora and Ryker stood. She pulled the shadows around the scene, disguising the encampment from the rest of the world, as it should have been all night.

More shadows collected around her, in her palms, summoned from the night. She and Ryker stood strong—light and dark—ready to defend themselves against the man that knew all.

## CHAPTER 20

KENT CIRCLED THEM like a lion, ready to attack at any unforeseen moment. Ryker, never touching her, guided Valora around the fire between them and the enemy. She knew so long as the fire remained in the middle, Kent couldn't get to her. Ryker wouldn't allow it. He would use his power to make absolutely sure of it.

"You can't keep this up forever, shadow bender," Kent called from across the flames. "You and the fire bender will have to stop eventually."

"If you lay one finger on her, you die," Ryker threatened. "One. Finger."

Kent chuckled manically. "Do you miss the thrill, Ryker? Jealous that your little girlfriend gets to have all the fun? Or will it be easier to watch this one die?" Kent grinned. It disappeared seconds later. "Give her up, Ryker! She's not worth saving."

"If you knew half as much as you say you do, you'd know I would fight to the last breath to protect her."

Valora stumbled over her ankle and quickly regained her balance. Ryker stopped short of helping her steady herself when he remembered his flames.

The momentary lapse in concentration allowed Kent to gain some ground in Valora's direction. Ryker quickly pushed her to the side with his shoulder, extremely careful of avoiding any other contact. Her memory cut to that morning, when she'd seen the flash of pain in his eyes at the sight of the burns—her bandaged wrists. He would never harm her again if he could help it.

"She killed them!" Kent yelled, his pent-up anger finally filling his every feature. "Justice needs to be met! For my nieces!"

*Them. Nieces.* Mona and Myrcella. Kent was their uncle. It explained the cognitive ability similarity. But how he'd figured out Valora's connection to the deaths....

Ryker eyed his companion, clearly wondering the same. The both of them had seen the repercussions from Mona and Myrcella's murders. A bloody mess—yes. But nothing had come of it other than Bo's brief moment of blame and—well, and two deaths.

When she began her mission, Valora had never thought of anyone else but her family. Valora wanted to return home to her mom and dad and brother so terribly that she'd forgotten the girls had families as well. Somewhere, people mourned Mona and Myrcella. They should have been mourning Juno as well. Little did they know, though, their precious deceased were nearly as guilty as their killer.

"I knew the minute I saw the footprint in the blood," Kent grit out. "My ability—it lets me figure out such details. Connect the dots where others may struggle. I know each moment, each following decision. I can *see* them. And from there...well, the events wove their path straight to you, little shadow bender." He made to jump, but Ryker stuck out his flaming arm. Kent slowed and continued to glare at Valora.

"I would have told everyone immediately," he continued, "but everyone believed you dead. *I* believed you dead. And I knew what Mona and Myrcella did—I knew the minute that group of girls came back to the village crying over your demise. Lost to the creatures of the forest, they said. Everyone believed it, because who would think those little girls killed their friend?" Kent paused and straightened his posture. "But I knew. I swear this ability is a curse. I knew, and I could tell no one because those were my sister's girls—what would she think of me turning her twins in for murder?

"Then *they* were murdered, and I knew it could not be a coincidence. I went to the house, consoled my sister, and took a look at the room. When I saw the footprints of blood...." He shook his head and scowled at Valora. "You couldn't have picked a messier way to kill those girls."

Valora fought to keep moving. Her legs wanted nothing more than to collapse from beneath her as Kent relayed the aftermath of the Mona and Myrcella's deaths. From what Ryker had told her—what she had witnessed with him from the tree—nothing had gone catastrophically wrong. Yet here was a man completely shattered and willing to seek revenge for his deceased family. He wanted to kill.

The girls had done more than create a new kind of bond with Valora when they tried to kill her, she realized. They had started a chain of death, spurred by the desire for revenge. One that stretched further than they might have ever imagined.

"I tried to find more clues that would lead me to you. The only information I got from my brother-in-law was that the dog ran right up to the forest. Even an animal should know not to go in there. Little did *I* know you were actually camping out in the mountains." Kent grinned. "How did you manage to trick me, shadow bender? Hiding in the darkness?"

Valora couldn't provide a response because if she did, she would willingly admit to everything Kent guessed. And whatever information she gave him would only give him more knowledge—knowledge of her plans, her strategy, her eventual desire to return home. If he learned that, he would never allow it to happen. Between the word of an omniscient and that of Juno and Aurelia, Valora might not stand the slim chance she believed she possessed.

The thought of Kent, Juno, and Aurelia exposing her—even if they incriminated themselves in the process—made Valora sick to her stomach. The whole village would come after her, because while Aurelia and Juno had attempted to kill her in the forest, that was all it had ended up being. An attempt. They'd failed. Their failure, though, would not haunt them in the way Valora's would. No—she'd only failed in killing Juno. Mona and Myrcella were dead, and Kent's ability would be all they needed to prove for certain Valora had done it.

Kent took daring steps towards her, and Ryker reacted immediately. With a sweep of his arms, he brought the fire from the camp swooping between them and the other man. Valora took a step back from the roaring heat, as did Kent.

"One finger," Ryker repeated through gritted teeth.

Valora strengthened her reformed shield. With his new

display of power, Ryker put them at greater risk of visibility. Kent must have been thinking the same thing. He looked around the camp, at the flames swirling between him and Valora, at Ryker partially ablaze and growing worse. The flames spread all the way up his arms to the point where even his neck gave off a faint orange glow.

Kent chuckled and withdrew his only mean of defense—a knife that resembled one from a butcher's shop. Valora eyed the shining, sharpened edge as the orange glow of the flames danced in the reflection.

"I have to admit, I'm impressed, Mr. Falkov." Valora watched Kent move closer, but the flames partially obstructed her view. Still, the knife seemed to glow beyond the wall of heat, never entirely leaving Valora's sight. "You have been practicing over the years. Much more control than before. But just *how* much more?"

It all happened so quickly. One moment, Ryker stood in front of her; the next, he'd fallen to the ground, and Valora felt Kent's arms wrapping around her. He pressed a knife to her neck and pulled her away from the groaning Ryker, whose fire had vanished the moment he collapsed. Valora strained her neck, trying to keep the blade away from her throat, but that only made Kent press it harder against her skin.

Focusing her attention on Ryker, Valora noticed the rock on the ground beside him and the reddening wound on his forehead.

Kent kept Valora's arms pinned to her sides, obviously aware of her preferred method of shadow bending. She still retained some level of mental control over them, but he must have realized from her earlier lapse that her mental abilities were lacking in comparison.

Ryker slowly sat up, dazed and confused from the blow. His hands reignited up to his wrists when he saw Valora in Kent's hold, and Valora was relieved to see that he was well enough to react instinctually.

He rose unsteadily to his feet, trying to keep focus on Kent while Valora struggled to free herself. Movement was near impossible with the knife so close to her throat. It pressed in harder each time she shifted, making her breath come out in fear-filled shudders.

"How about I save you the trouble with this one, fire bender?" Kent taunted. "You keep your conscience clear and I get revenge for the death of my nieces. We both win."

Despite his unsteady focus, Valora saw Ryker's threat shining in his amber eyes. *One finger.* Kent had her entirely within his grasp.

"Valora, stop moving, alright?" Ryker commanded. "Stop trying to free yourself."

Valora locked eyes with him, frantic that he'd decided to take the deal and side with Kent. When she saw the concern on his face, she let out as much of a relieved sigh as the blade would allow. Ryker needed time to think of one of his wonderful plans—time that he would not receive if the knife cut across Valora's flesh too soon.

It needed to be well thought out but secretive. Kent, as an omniscient, would see anything coming. He knew everything that might happen—he could watch one move and predict the next strike. That was probably how he'd managed to knock Ryker out long enough to grab Valora—he saw the chronology of events beforehand and knew which path of action to take.

"Ryker," Valora breathed, not bothering to hide her fear.

Tears brimmed in her eyes.

How would they beat a man who knew everything? Who saw everything? Kent would always be one step ahead, no matter what brilliant idea Ryker thought of.

Ryker's hands remained ablaze, two small beacons in the dark. Valora watched them while he paced back and forth. She knew she had time until Ryker took some course of action. Kent wanted to see how everything played out. Valora could tell from his over-confident smirk.

Ryker knew it too. He knew he couldn't use a tactic as obvious as his fire, which seemed to trouble him. Valora saw it shift in his palms from orbs to coils to the flaming ropes he used against her in training.

Valora's eyes widened but she willed her thoughts elsewhere—anywhere other than the plan she had just formulated, just as she had the night of Mona and Myrcella's murders. She wondered if Ryker had used those shapes on purpose, trying to appear unsure to throw Kent off his trail.

"Ryker, do something!" Valora called out.

Ryker continued to pace, then suddenly threw his fiery fists down to his sides. "Let her go, you bastard! Your nieces are better off dead for what they did to her!"

Kent chuckled. "If you want me, you have to go through Valora. And I would very much like to see that happen."

"Ryker!"

"Shut up, girl!" Kent hissed. "C'mon, fire bender. Burn her like you did the last girl. Watch her murderous flesh char and crumble. Watch her heart stop beating. Do your duty to your home and kill her. Avenge your reputation."

The knife pressed harder against Valora's throat, and she

tilted her head back, trying to get away from it. Ryker's hands began to glow brighter, the flames creeping back up his arms. Kent chuckled in Valora's ear.

"Ryker, just do it! Don't worry about me! Kill him!"

"*Would* you kill me, Ryker? Would you be able to live with yourself if you killed another innocent soul?"

"Valora is innocent!"

"She's a murderer! She's—"

Valora fell back with Kent, careful to prevent the knife from going into her throat when they hit the ground. She shoved her elbow back into his face after she pushed the weapon away.

They needed something he couldn't see coming. They needed darkness.

Valora released the shadows from around Kent's ankles and stood, running over to Ryker. He pushed past her to the man on the ground. Kent's face bled from an unknown source. Most likely a broken nose, though Valora believed it could have also been a knocked-out tooth.

Ryker kicked the weapon from the man's weak grip and summoned more flames. He towered over Kent like a fiery predator, ready to kill his prey. Valora watched him from a safe distance.

"Go ahead," Kent prompted. "Kill me."

Ryker stood there, unmoving aside from the heavy rising and falling of his shoulders as he breathed.

Valora waited for something—anything—to happen. She wouldn't have blamed Ryker if he chose to kill Kent. The man held an endless supply of knowledge against them. He would return to Norlyn and reveal that they were both alive and hiding. The Norlynians would organize a search party. Ryker would be forced to return home. Valora would be captured, charged for murder, and—

"Go home," Ryker said, extinguishing his hands. The camp went dark aside from the embers still burning in the preexisting fire. "Go live your miserable life. You said it before, Kent. If you expose Valora, you expose what the girls tried to do to her. Your precious nieces will be remembered as nothing more than killers."

"And you?" Kent pressed. "What if I go back—say nothing about the girl, but tell your parents that you are alive? Tell the parents of the girl you loved that you were responsible for her death?"

"Then I will be met with a just punishment," Ryker replied flatly. "And you can continue believing you saved the day when really all you did was condemn a young man to an untimely death."

"Isn't that why we are all here? Because of the untimely deaths of the young?"

"Not me," Ryker said. "Not Valora. *We* are trying to start our lives anew."

Kent stayed silent. Ryker stared at him a moment longer before he turned his back and made his way toward Valora. When they locked eyes, she hoped he could see the relief in hers.

Valora was ready to reach for her companion's hand when something behind him startled her.

"Ryker, watch out!"

Without a second thought, Ryker spun around, flames shooting out of his palms in streams towards Kent's body, the man's arm raised and ready to strike with the retrieved knife. It only took seconds for his body to burn enough to kill him.

Kent fell to the ground, hardly recognizable beyond the burns and blackened flesh.

The flames died down and darkness fell over the camp once more. Valora stared at Ryker as he examined the corpse. When he turned around to finally face her, he let out a shuddering breath. Silent tears fell down Valora's cheeks in response.

She reached him just after he fell to his knees and took him in her arms. Ryker embraced her firmly, tucking his head into the crook of her neck and tangling his fingers in her hair. Valora ran her hand down the back of his head, a poor attempt at soothing him.

"It's okay," she whispered. "It's all okay. Ryker, you are so brave. You are so good."

She continued to reassure him as he cried into her shoulder, promising him that he'd done the right thing—that attacking Kent after he'd tried to kill them didn't make him a monster.

She wondered if the same could be said about her.

*You are not a monster.*

*You are not a monster....*

# CHAPTER 21

AFTER EXTENSIVE ARGUING, Ryker decided it was best he slept outside that night. Valora opened her mouth, ready to continue the argument and tell him he needed to stop acting so crazy—it was too cold for him to sleep outside the tent. But Ryker silenced her with a raised brow and a blow of smoke out of his mouth.

She argued no further, tossed him a blanket, and retreated into the tent, dreaming of fire-breathing dragons—and fire-breathing men.

When Valora woke the next morning, she found herself covered in sweat. She turned, convinced Ryker had snuck into the tent at some point, but she was alone. Completely alone.

Valora sat up and ran her fingers back through her hair. The mountains sounded as peaceful as they had the day before, but she knew things were different. Instead of finding a beautiful sunrise when she walked outside the flaps of the tent, Valora would find Ryker sleeping on a pile of rocks. Nearby, she would find the half-charred body of a man who had tried to kill her—the uncle of her now-dead friends.

She buried her face in her palms and groaned before throwing off her blankets. Valora slipped into her shoes and ventured outside the comfort of her tent.

The crisp morning air hit her sweat-slick skin with a vengeance, making a shiver run down her spine. She hugged herself tight and rubbed her arms, trying to use the friction to create some warmth.

Her eyes instantly found the discarded blanket and balled-up shirt Ryker had used in lieu of a pillow. Valora retrieved both, wrapping the blanket around her shoulders and keeping the shirt in her grasp so she could bring it to Ryker. He was sitting on the edge of the cliff with his legs dangling off.

Valora tried to ignore the presence of the charred body on the campsite as she made her way over and took a seat beside her companion.

"Not going to push me over the edge?" he asked.

"No," Valora replied. She grinned as she placed his shirt on his lap. "Unlike you, I try to avoid acting like an asshole when I can."

Ryker chuckled and took his shirt. He put it on a few seconds later, making Valora feel much more comfortable about sitting next to him, despite being fully covered herself. Out of everything that happened the night before, her time with Ryker still haunted her the most. Valora couldn't quite shake the feel of his hands on her skin, his lips on hers and on her neck....

She wondered if she haunted him as well.

They sat there in silence, staring out into the expanse before them.

"What are we going to do?" she asked. When Ryker raised a brow at her, Valora quickly added, "About the body."

Ryker nodded slowly, clearly disappointed. Valora folded her hands in her lap and twiddled her thumbs nervously.

"We can leave it here for now," he said, and Valora tensed. "Or I can move it somewhere more…hidden. So we don't have to see it all the time."

Valora nodded her agreement. Ryker said nothing more and peered down at his lap as well. He remained silent for all of two minutes—*a new personal record,* Valora thought.

"Thank you," he said softly. "For what you said last night. I…I needed it."

Valora continued to stare at her hands as she said, "You've saved my life on more than one account. And after what Kent kept saying to you…" She finally looked up. "You've never been a monster to me, Ryker. Not even after you told me your story. Sometimes you're a pain in my ass"—Ryker chuckled and shook his head—"but never a monster."

Much to her surprise, Valora didn't flinch when he reached out and placed his hand on hers. Instead, she undid her hands and turned one over so her palm connected with Ryker's. They held onto each other, both of them staring at the place they touched. Valora felt each of his calluses, developed over the years of taking care of himself in the forest, especially when he brushed his thumb along the back of her hand.

"We make quite the team," he commented.

"Yes, if someone considers two people who are utter opposites a good team."

Ryker smiled. "Well, you know what they say. Opposites attract...."

He leaned in, his lips coming far too close to Valora's for her liking. Seconds before they made contact, Valora cleared her throat and pulled her hand away from his. Ryker sat back. The same pain her rejection had caused the night before in the alcove flashed in his eyes once more.

If he asked, Valora would never deny she'd enjoyed their brief time together. Even with the boy she had once loved, she'd never once experienced such strong desire before. But until the time came to admit that maybe—just maybe—some part of her was not opposed to spending more romantic time with her housemate....

"Maybe today we can pick berries without showering each other with them?" she asked as she stood.

Valora extended her hand to him to help him to his feet. Ryker took it—Valora believed he would take anything she offered him—and followed her lead, careful not to slip on the edge of the cliff. She watched his eyes flit to Kent's body.

"We're going to have to try if we want a pie when we get home."

Valora smiled softly, trying to receive a similar reaction from Ryker. Since he was unable to remain serious or upset for more than a few minutes, she eventually got it. Reluctant. But it was there. And that was all Valora could hope for.

THEY RETURNED TO the camp a few hours later with two

knapsacks filled with berries. Valora had worried they'd wasted all the good ones on their small berry war but found herself very satisfied with their success.

Ryker held back a low-hanging branch that stood as their final obstacle before the campsite. Valora passed through the cleared space and gasped as soon as she walked onto the plateaued cliff. Her bag of berries dropped to the ground and spilled out the top.

Ryker moved beside the frozen Valora, worry etched all over his face, but the same fear that flooded her soon replaced it.

Kent's body remained in the open space on the side of the camp furthest from their tent, covered with a few blankets. They'd talked about moving it but ultimately decided not to. Neither one of them had wanted to touch it and relive the memories of the previous night.

The wisest option might have been simply tossing the body over the edge of the cliff, Valora thought. Even if someone found it, the burns put Kent well past the point of recognition. Even if they hadn't, Valora believed Ryker could have performed further damage to guarantee that. She would never ask him to burn the body completely, afraid of what dark memories doing so would bring back, though the thought had come to mind.

But because they had taken no precautions—because they'd left fresh meat out in the open wilderness—Valora and Ryker had unwittingly attracted the attention of a mountain lion.

Ryker placed his hands on Valora's shoulders, guiding her back into the brush. The big cat was too preoccupied with devouring Kent's remains to notice them. It snarled as it continued to rip flesh from bone. Valora felt sick when she caught sight of the bloody remains—ribs protruding, muscles torn, bloodied footprints on the ground around the corpse where the cat had walked.

"Stay calm," Ryker breathed. "We'll leave—give it time to finish eating. It should be gone when we return in an hour." The mountain lion took a particularly vicious bite of Kent's remaining flesh. "On second thought, maybe we should return tomorrow," he corrected.

Valora nodded once and backed up faster. Ryker, not as affected by the carnage as Valora, struggled to keep up with her pace. He stumbled, muttering her name in an attempt to get her to stop but failed. It only made Valora move quicker, causing him to back into the bushes and branches.

A stick snapped under his weight.

The lion paused. It whipped its head around to them.

Valora gasped at the sight of the bloody maw of the animal. Suddenly, everything that Ryker had once warned her about became very, very real. And even more real was Valora's chance of becoming lion food if she didn't get away right that moment.

She turned on her heels but walked into Ryker's chest. Valora tried her best to shove past him, but Ryker did the job for her. He pushed her to the side and strode out into the campsite on the cliff, his hands and arms igniting more with each step. The wild cat snarled and advanced on its approaching target, not seeing a fiery threat so much as it saw its next meal.

"Ryker!" Valora called. He didn't acknowledge her. "Ryker, stop!"

The fire bender continued to ignore her. She saw his determination in each of his strides. Her stupid companion just *had* to be the savior all the time. But this time, his opponent was not a wolf or a vengeful man from Norlyn. He faced a large cat with teeth that could and *would* tear him limb from limb, even if he were still alive. Food was food, after all.

While Ryker continued to advance on the mountain lion, Valora scurried across the ground. If she could retrieve her bow and arrows from the tent while Ryker distracted the cat, she could bring down the beast with one well-aimed—

The lion snarled again and charged towards her. It brought Valora back to her early days in the forest, when the mere presence of wolves had terrified her, only because she'd never faced them before. Knowing she had defeated a whole pack of wolves didn't calm her nerves about doing the same with the approaching mountain lion.

Valora fell back off her knees and screamed, only for the cat to be knocked away by a blast of fire. The beast shook it off and glared at Valora in the dim light of the dusk, its green eyes glowing like emerald lanterns. It bared its bloodied teeth to her, a growl rumbling in its throat.

Another ball of fire hit the cat's back and it spun away from Valora towards Ryker. He launched two more rounds, making the cat lose its interest in his previous target. Before it could go for the easy meal, the beast needed to defeat the only thing keeping it from food.

Valora watched in dread as the cat picked up speed and launched itself at Ryker, knocking them both to the ground. She covered her gasp with her hands as the mountain lion lunged towards Ryker's face. He placed both his fiery hands on the side of its face, trying to push it back.

Ryker kicked his legs out, sending the lion flying until it landed a few feet away. Unlike the wolves, the cat found its way back onto its feet almost instantly, not afraid to take another go against the fire. Valora saw the burnt fur on its face and back where Ryker had already managed to harm the predator.

Coming to her senses, Valora crawled towards the tent and disappeared. With the cat completely preoccupied fighting Ryker, it didn't try to come for her again. Even so, thinking about Ryker facing off against the cat made Valora's hands shake as she tried to nock her first arrow.

She heard his scream before she exited the tent. Valora's head whipped around to the flaps where, somewhere beyond them, the lion had bested Ryker in one way or another. She held her breath, wondering if her companion had finally met his match, then exhaled when she heard the oddly comforting sound of his struggles.

Ryker would not go down so easily.

Valora finally managed to set her arrow and exited the tent, a fresh wave of adrenaline coursing through her veins. She steadied herself in a defensive stance, the sharpened arrowhead aimed at the snarling mountain lion. Blood oozed from one of Ryker's new wounds as he continued to wrestle with the cat. The rapid movements made it difficult to get a good aim at the beast without fear of accidentally hitting Ryker instead.

The arrow moved in tandem with the lion—left, right, up, down—always pointed at the cat's head. If she only got one chance, Valora wanted to make sure she got the kill. She knew a blow to the head would guarantee that. The way Ryker wrestled the cat made a shot at the heart too risky, even with her practiced precision.

But one move from Ryker had her gasping. Valora finally saw where the blood came from—a long series of gashes across his chest. By some miracle, he continued to fend the mountain lion off from his back, continually chancing another scrape of its claws against his flesh.

She threw the bow down and extended her palms towards the animal. Shadows crawled towards it, forming themselves into the whips she had used during training with Ryker and to take down Kent. Valora knew she could handle bringing down a human, but she had yet to try out her abilities on a mountain cat, let alone a very angry, very hungry mountain cat.

The darkness snaked around the oblivious animal, wrapping itself around its limbs and neck until Valora locked them in place by clenching her fists. The cat threw its head back and snarled again, teeth bared and claws scraping at itself in a desperate attempt to be free of whatever force harmed it.

Valora's fist loosened when, for a moment, she found herself back in Norlyn, her shadows wrapped around Juno's neck, squeezing, tightening, while the girl clawed for her freedom. For the last chance of a breath.

A breath—and then some—that Valora had allowed her.

From the brief moment she dared to look away from the cat to Ryker, Valora knew he realized how her most recent target had escaped without visible harm—and how easily Juno's life could have ended.

The mountain lion threw itself off Ryker and thrashed on the ground while it continued its futile attempt at escape. Letting her determination to survive outweigh her emotions, Valora clutched her fists tighter, causing the shadow whips to act in accord with her command. The hold on the animal became so strong that the flailing calmed as the cat tired out. Soon, it did not move at all.

Valora held on for a reassuring moment longer, making sure the beast wasn't playing dead. She knew mountain lions were smart creatures, but this one had met its end at her hands and, once Valora pulled back her shadows, remained motionless beside Kent's ripped-open corpse.

Ryker's groan brought Valora back to reality.

She rushed to his side to find his injury was worse than she'd thought. The gashes left behind by the lion's claws ran diagonally across his chest, from the top of his left pectoral down to the right side of his ribcage. Luckily, they didn't look too deep, but they still bled enough to make Valora queasy.

Standing in a pool of her former friends' blood—fine. Placing a bare hand directly on Ryker's bloodied chest—never.

Valora rushed over to the tent and grabbed whatever she could find—her sweater, her blanket, his shirt—and hurried back to Ryker's side. She kneeled down and pressed her sweater over the parts of the wounds that were releasing the most blood. The wool instantly shifted from off-white to bright crimson.

Ryker's body twitched in pain. His neck stretched back, and his teeth gritted in an attempt to keep from crying out. With his adrenaline wearing off, Valora assumed the pain had finally caught up to him.

"Hold still," Valora soothed. "Please, try to hold still, Ryker."

"Yarrow," he ground out. Ryker lifted his head ever-so-slightly, got sight of his wound, and lay back down. "There's yarrow in the tent. In my bag."

It took Valora a moment to realize what he wanted her to do. Yarrow—a plant used to clot blood and prevent infection in open wounds. She remembered learning about it in one of her survival lessons during warrior training. Ryker must have packed some.

Valora moved Ryker's hand atop the sweater to keep pressure

on the wound before she took off towards the tent again. She returned with a whole bag of various plants Ryker had packed, his mortar, and a deerskin canteen. She might have remembered their capabilities during her warrior training, but that didn't mean Valora could recognize each plant. She'd taken greater interest in strengthening her abilities than in botany.

Trying her best to recall *some* of her lessons, Valora sifted through the bag, desperately hoping for Ryker's sake that the sight of one plant or another would jog her memory. Ryker continued to groan all the while.

"That one," Valora heard him say. "That one."

With shaking hands, Valora pulled the yarrow from the bunch and put some of the flowers in the mortar. There were hundreds of them. How many did she use? She had never made a poultice before. Judging by the length of the gashes, though, she figured generosity wouldn't hurt.

Ryker guided her through the process when he found enough strength to sit up, though it never lasted long. Valora removed her sweater from the gashes and replaced it with his shirt. It too soaked up the blood, which thankfully was exiting the wound slower than before.

She worked on the poultice, taking Ryker's instructions while he held the shirt to his wounds. When she'd finished mixing everything together in the mortar, Valora removed the bloodied shirt from the gashes. Ryker's skin felt warm to the touch; he must have been using the same heat treatment he used on Valora's wounds to heal his own.

Not wanting to risk infection, Valora poured some of the water from the canteen over her hands to clean them. She poured more on the extra shirt she'd brought from the tent and began to clean the blood that remained on Ryker's wounds.

He winced when the water touched his open skin, but Valora didn't bother apologizing. She needed to keep moving—keep working without the distractions of conversation. In his weakened state, Valora doubted Ryker could provide her any light and the darkness only continued to grow as night fell. She needed to work under the little sunlight that remained—and work fast.

Ryker's blood mixed with the poultice as Valora applied it. Ryker winced again. Again, Valora didn't apologize for any pain. He had never apologized during their many sessions for *her* wounds. But soon, Valora realized it didn't matter. Ryker stayed quiet, laying on his back and staring up at the sky. Until—

"Does it make me look tough?"

Valora almost hit him. She almost hit him right on his fresh wound for making such an idiotic comment. Almost. But she most definitely did not shy away from giving Ryker one of her infamous glares. It wasn't the time for jokes.

"Lighten up, sunshine." Somehow, Ryker managed one of his grins. He even had the audacity to place his arms under his head, looking perfectly relaxed. "Your life can't be *all* blood and darkness. Sometimes there needs to be a little fun."

"Can the fun wait until after you're healed?"

His grin widened and slowly shifted into a smirk. "What kind of fun do you have in mind?"

Valora shook her head and continued her work. "Jokes. The knock-knock kind. Lots of them. Now, shush. I need to concentrate."

The quiet and surprising stillness lasted all of five minutes before Ryker began to look around for something, tilting his head from side to side. Valora tried to ignore it, but sometimes she found her eyes straying from where she continued to lightly apply the poultice to her companion's wounds.

Ryker moved one arm out from behind his head and pointed. He tried to sit up, but Valora didn't allow it. She put one finger on his chest and pushed him back down. The fire bender grinned at her then returned his attention to whatever he had found. Valora refused to give him her full attention.

"Kent's bag," Ryker said. "It's over there."

"How observant," she deadpanned.

Ryker sat up again. He only winced once while he situated his weight onto his elbows. Valora did nothing to stop him that time and continued her work. She felt his eyes on her hands while they applied the poultice to his bare chest.

"Didn't you smell his breath last night?" Valora raised her brow but didn't look up. "He reeked of alcohol. He was drinking before he found us."

A relative of Mona and Myrcella that clung to the drink? Not surprising.

Valora glanced at where Ryker had pointed and saw the bag. In the midst of having her life threatened she must not have cared to pay attention to the scent of Kent's breath. But sure enough, she made out the shape of a bottle underneath the flimsy fabric of the knapsack.

"Wanna go get his drink of choice for me?" Ryker continued.

Valora finally looked at him, and an attempt at an innocent smile spread across his face.

"I might be helping you with your injury, but I'm not your servant."

Ryker chuckled. "I was going to share with you. I'm not the selfish bastard you want to believe I am."

Valora rolled her eyes and pushed him down again. Ryker popped right back up onto his elbows, the same shit-eating grin gracing his lips. Valora's lips quirked up ever so slightly in return.

"I'm in pain, Val," he continued with a pout.

"You're healing the wound with your heat."

The warmth cut off. Valora shivered, not realizing how dependent she'd been on his body heat to stay warm until it disappeared. When she glanced down at the wound, she couldn't deny the yarrow and his heat-healing had already made a significant impact. What had been a bloodied mess not long ago already looked like it'd had days to heal. It wasn't perfect, by any means, but enough to calm Valora's worries a bit.

Ryker moved his weight to one elbow and took the mortar from Valora's grasp. He set it on the ground behind his head, out of her reach. She stared at it, then at his wound. It did look substantially better.

"We can share," Ryker repeated. "C'mon. I bet you're fun when you're drunk." Valora raised a brow. "Not that you aren't an absolute pleasure to be around when sober."

Valora lowered her eyes and shook her head, a full smile appearing. She sighed when Ryker nudged her arm with the back of his hand then stood. He smiled triumphantly and watched her as she went to retrieve the bottle.

It felt wrong—stealing from a dead man. Valora refused to let her eyes settle on Kent's torn body as she removed the half-empty bottle of amber liquid from his bag. She swirled it around, examining it, remembering the once-familiar drink. Just seeing the liquid made her throat burn in memory of the many nights spent at the village tavern with her old friends.

Valora plastered a fake smile on her face and spun around on her heels. She shook the bottle, sloshing the liquid around in the glass. Ryker eyed it, the contents of the bottle glowing in the increasing moonlight.

"Get ready—Falkov, was it?" Ryker grinned and nodded. Valora tilted her head to the side and popped the cork stopper from the top of the bottle. "You're in for a show."

Valora brought the lip of the bottle to her mouth and took a large swig. It had been months since she'd tasted a drink so strong—even before her friends had attacked—and the sensation burned her throat. Rum, she guessed. Perhaps whiskey. Either way, Kent's drink of choice left her throat on fire and her head already feeling light.

She passed the bottle to Ryker who knocked it back like a champion. If he had been alone in the forest for years, his last experience with alcohol must have been *way* before Valora's. That proved true when he lowered the bottle after the second swig and shook his head, his face twisted in disgust.

Valora placed a hand over her mouth to muffle her laughter.

"It definitely distracts from any other pain, that's for sure," Ryker said. "*Gah*—that's rough."

"Man up, fire bender," Valora teased. She snatched the bottle from his grasp. "Let a professional show you how it's done."

Valora hated the feeling of the next drink as much as the first. The third as much as its predecessor. And so on and so forth, until she and Ryker had exchanged possession of the bottle so many times that she no longer felt anything at all aside from the spinning in her head.

They poked fun at each other while they tried to outdrink one another. Death had not yet learned to take Valora out through her competitive nature. Stabbings, mountain lions, and wolves—

those were no problem.

Valora would find her downfall at the hands of the self-induced challenge to finish off a bottle of liquor.

She handed the nearly empty bottle to Ryker while giggling like a schoolgirl and fell back onto the ground. She heard him laugh along with her, the contents of the bottle taking a similar effect on his senses, then groan. Valora didn't need to look at him to know he'd finished the drink.

"It's gone," he slurred. "I'm sorry."

"You're such a selfish bastard." Valora laughed. She sat up for a moment to hit Ryker's leg.

Ryker laughed with her and leaned back. Valora couldn't imagine the pain he was in from sitting up for so long, advanced healing or not. His warmth had disappeared when he convinced her to grab the bottle from Kent's bag, so Valora assumed he'd paused his heat-healing.

They lay there on their backs, staring up at the sky, laughing at nothing. Valora shut her eyes and when she opened them, she found the stars spinning above her. They looked like they belonged in a painting—blurring together and creating an abstract semi-circular pattern of blue and white light.

Her grandmother had owned a painting like that—one of a red barn in winter with the night sky behind it, the stars little dots and dashes against the black and navy. She would stare at it for hours when they visited, just as she did all her grandmother's artwork. But while the ones of wildflowers and prairies were nice, Valora always felt more drawn to the darker images. She imagined it had something to do with her abilities. Her mother had always told her she was a bright light, yet Valora couldn't help but feel like darkness always shrouded her.

"A copper for your thoughts."

Valora sat up only to find Ryker staring at her. Her eyes could not focus, and thankfully neither could his.

Not only her eyes had difficulty concentrating on any one thing, though. Her mind also struggled to comprehend Ryker's comment and create a coherent response.

Ryker must have taken the silence as ignorance and spoke in her place. "There are few times I've felt more ashamed of myself than when I burned you yesterday morning," he said with his head down.

When his eyes settled on her again, Valora saw the sincerity in them. She subconsciously grabbed for the bandages at her wrists, trying to twist them like a bracelet. Her palms ran over them, igniting the pain of the blisters beneath. In the midst of everything else, she'd forgotten all about Ryker burning her.

Finally, his eyes remembered how to focus—right on the bandages. Valora sat up—not without a great deal of dizziness—and put her hands between her legs to hide them from him. When he looked up, he met her already waiting eyes.

"I feel bad that I'm leaving," she admitted softly. "At first, I wanted nothing more than to go back home…but now I feel guilty that I'm taking away your one connection to Norlyn."

Ryker's brows furrowed. Valora watched his face twist in pain, then moved her attention to the long gashes that ran from his pectoral across to his ribcage. They both certainly had their fair share of injuries.

"Is that what you think you are to me? My connection to Norlyn?" he asked, sounding incredulous. "Is that why you think I saved you—let you live with me?"

Valora shrugged and pulled her knees up to her chest. She

rested her chin on them and refused to meet Ryker's stare—partially out of shame and partially because she felt that if she did, she would lose the little food in her stomach.

Ryker inched forward, little by little, probably trying to avoid the same fate. When he came close enough, he placed his hand on her boot-clad foot. Valora stared at it for a moment, then at her companion's injury, then finally at his amber eyes. They were nearly the exact color of the alcohol they had successfully finished.

"I saved you out of guilt for my past," Ryker admitted. "But I let you stay because..." He faded off. "No one knows where I live—where I went all those years ago—and I never wanted anyone to. The minute I found you breathing, I knew I couldn't leave you there, dying alone. No one deserves that...that kind of betrayal." Valora swallowed, fighting back her tears, as Ryker's eyes glowed with guilt. "Even if that meant exposing where I'd been hiding, I planned to save you. And, now, I'm glad I did."

He took Valora's hand from its hiding place, running his thumb over the underside of her wrist before lacing their fingers together. She did nothing to stop it, not because she didn't want to, but because she couldn't move without feeling sick.

"Valora," he whispered. During the pause, Valora managed to move her eyes back to his. "I think I—"

"Don't," she commanded, instantly turning away. She shut her eyes tight. "Don't say anything to me now that you wouldn't say sober."

She pulled her hand away and stood, fighting to quell the nausea that came with the sudden movement. Ryker hardly looked as though he cared. The alcohol held enough power over him that anything she did would seem inconsequential in the moment. That, or he was simply so used to her rejection that it didn't bother him anymore. Valora hoped it was the former.

"I'm going to bed," she announced, stumbling slightly to the side with her first step. Ryker tried to get up to help her but winced when his injury prevented such quick movement. "Do you need any more help tonight?"

Ryker shook his head, his expression utterly dejected, then lay back down on his back. He moved an arm behind his head, using it as a pillow. That was when Valora realized he had no intention of sleeping in the tent.

If he hadn't just tried to confess his feelings, Valora imagined she might have told him he could. Instead, she watched him for a few seconds more, then stumbled off to her shelter.

# CHAPTER 22

VALORA SLEPT FITFULLY that night and woke with a headache and a churning stomach. She left the tent to find that Ryker had vomited at some point during the night, and the smell on top of the sight of the corpses that still rested outside their camp nearly made her sick.

Feeling that neither of their attackers deserved much respect in their disposal, Valora summoned shadow ropes that wrapped themselves around the bodies. With a flick of her wrist, she sent the corpses over the edge of the cliff and listened as they tumbled down the side of the mountain over boulders and through the random greenery that had decided to sprout up through the rocks. Anyone who found them would believe Kent had been attacked, with the cat having ripped off most of his charred flesh. The lion could have met one of many ends as a wild predator.

The shadows disappeared into thin air, and Valora clapped her hands together, clearing them of nonexistent dirt. Only when she lifted one of her arms did she realize maybe the corpses hadn't been the main cause of the stench.

She smelled absolutely horrible.

Valora expected nothing less after cleaning herself with only a wet cloth for the past few days. Her hair had long since gotten used to not being washed frequently and rarely caused her any issues. The rest of Valora's body, on the other hand….

She remembered seeing a stream on one of the journeys to the berry patch. If she snuck away while Ryker slept, she could maybe manage to get some laundry done while properly washing herself. She'd discovered plenty of flowers after her adventures in Ryker's medicine bag that she could use to get herself—and her clothes—smelling pleasant again. She would need to move quickly if she intended to get Ryker's blood out of her sweater.

Valora quickly and quietly gathered her things from around Ryker and in the tent. Much to her great surprise, Ryker had some lavender stored away in his bag, which Valora took a generous helping of.

With a change of clothes, dirty laundry, some stray rope to use as a clothesline, and an extra oversized sweater in hand, Valora took off into the brushes that surrounded the cliff-top encampment. She thought she heard Ryker stir but didn't look back. Valora had dealt with her mess, he could deal with his—and they needed time away from each other as it was.

The possibilities of what could have followed his attempted confession swirled in her head. She desperately wanted to blame the alcohol for the close call, but a nagging voice in the back of her mind reminded her that his feelings had been clear long before he'd gotten drunk.

Soon enough, Valora found herself at the edge of the stream.

She stripped down to nothing and left her folded clothes and boots at the water's edge. The rush of its soft current filled her ears and she dipped her foot in to test its strength. Nothing she couldn't handle.

Valora stepped into the near-freezing water and instantly tensed. She slowly waded out to the deeper water in the middle of the stream, letting each inch of her bare skin get used to the temperature before she tested her tolerance any further. But as much as the chilling water bit, it did lessen the headache Valora had felt forming as soon as she woke.

She continued to bob up and down, dipping below the water when the air became too much to handle, and her body grew more accustomed to the water. The warmth it brought to her skin was a welcome contrast to the chill of the air at the stream's altitude.

Valora hadn't swum since her family's last visit to the lake just outside Norlyn. Once Bo had convinced her the fish swimming below the cloudy water wouldn't bite her toes, Valora had jumped in and swum for hours. She'd spent the rest of the day trying to catch the fish with a net and diving down to see if she could reach the bottom in one breath.

But even with her experience, Valora couldn't remember a time when the water had become so warm—even after her body adjusted to it. The only other time she remembered being submerged in water so warm was when, as a child, her mother would heat her bath water over the fire before—

Valora shot up, emerging above the surface with a gasp. She needed some fresh air, but her reaction came along with the realization of why *stream water* could heat to such a high temperature.

As soon as she ran her hands down her face and cleared the water from over her eyes, Valora saw Ryker sitting on the edge of the stream, his trousers rolled up to his knees and his feet hanging into the water. He kicked them back and forth, his typical grin plastered on his face when he realized he'd earned Valora's attention.

"Feels good," he said.

Valora scoffed and splashed him. When he turned away to avoid the water, she quickly wrapped an arm around her chest and sank far enough below the water's surface so only her head was visible. She double-checked the opacity of the water, wanting to make sure Ryker couldn't see anything she didn't intend to show him. The small current created whitecaps that helped her immensely.

"Do you *mind*?" she spat.

He didn't, clearly, based off the way he rested his weight back on his palms and continued to kick in the water. Every so often Ryker kicked hard enough that the splashes reached Valora. She had no choice but to take the water to the face unless she wished to expose herself to him. Again.

"Why yes—my injury is doing terrific. Thanks for asking, Val." Ryker smirked. "I can always count on you to worry about my well-being."

"I'm trying to bathe, Ryker. If you need help with your injury I can—"

"No, no," Ryker insisted. He moved his weight to one palm so the other hand could lift up his shirt. Valora couldn't help but stare, just as she did every time Ryker revealed his toned body to her.

"You should become a healer," he complimented her, though Valora didn't know why. The wound wasn't particularly pleasant to look at. In fact, she thought she saw some pus around the edges of one gash. "Truly, you're incredible."

Valora rolled her eyes and sank lower under the water, her chin dipping under the waves. Water splashed onto her lips every so often.

Though she refused to make any further eye contact, Valora knew Ryker never lifted his stare. She felt it—so much so that it almost made her uncomfortable.

Quickly, she submerged herself below the water again and remained as long as her lungs allowed. It probably would have lasted longer if the water wasn't so bloody hot.

Valora tried to ignore the temperature and concentrate on her breath-holding. Soon, she began to squirm under the water's surface—not because her lungs hurt, but because the water was *too* hot.

Air bubbles escaped from her as she squealed, rising until they burst. She could only imagine Ryker watching as the surface filled with the bubbles that released from her nose and mouth. Still, Valora tried to remain underwater as long as possible.

That time grew shorter with each unwanted, underwater shriek.

Valora surfaced, careful not to come too far out of the water, and wiped her face clear of the liquid droplets. The minute her head appeared, the temperature cooled significantly, either because the air assisted her body temperature or because Ryker had gotten what he wanted. She assumed the latter.

"That was impressive," Ryker complimented. Valora leveled a

glare at him. "You lasted much longer than I thought you would."

"You almost boiled me alive!"

Ryker removed his big toe from the water, his body shaking with silent laughter from his seat on the bank. Valora narrowed her eyes and hoped he felt the invisible daggers she aimed at him. If that wound on his abdomen wasn't giving him enough trouble, she would make sure he felt some pain by the time she finished with him.

"You're too easy to rile up." He smiled then lightly splashed some water in her direction. "Lighten up, Val. Oh—wait. I bet that's easier said than done for a shadow bender, isn't it?"

Valora rolled her eyes when she noticed his veins beginning to glow and turned her back to him. As soon as she looked at the water again, she screamed. Fish that had fallen victim to Ryker's heating floated in front of her, their little glassy eyes staring at nothing, their mouths hanging open.

Valora turned sharply over her shoulder to see Ryker stand.

"Hope you like fish." She didn't. "Those guys will feed us for the last few days we're up here together."

With the berries collected, Valora had hoped their time in the mountains had met its end. Valora wanted warmer air and an altitude that didn't hurt her head and occasionally her lungs. She also needed a real bath, not one shared by fish and invasive campmates.

But as Ryker walked away, Valora saw why they needed to stay. He could say he felt better all he wanted. His slowed pace and the hand he kept near the wound argued otherwise.

Valora swam back to the bank and grabbed her clothes. She wondered if Ryker would turn around when she hopped out of the stream, but he did no such thing, much to her delight. She dressed in peace and tied her wet hair up in a bun with a leather band.

Ryker hardly made up any ground while she dressed. He was just about to disappear down the path to their camp when Valora started to follow after him. Sure, he limped pretty bad, but after only a day he *was* walking. Valora remained bedridden for weeks after Ryker had rescued her from the forest. Besides, he had nearly boiled her like the fish. She couldn't let him walk away so easily after a stunt like that.

Just before she caught up to him, Valora opened her hands and flicked her wrists towards her companion. The few shadows available in the daylight crawled silently toward him until they wrapped around his torso. Ryker was none the wiser.

"Enjoy your swim." Valora grinned as she passed him.

She flicked her wrist backwards towards the stream before Ryker could question her. Valora continued on to the camp, laughing silently after she heard Ryker splash into the water.

**R**YKER SLOSHED INTO the camp not long after Valora returned, his clothes dripping and his normally messy hair matted down to his forehead. She couldn't help but snicker at how funny the new style made him appear. The clear dissatisfaction over being thrown into the stream helped.

At first, Valora thought the accompanying fishy smell came from her—despite the obsessive amounts of lavender oil she'd extracted from the plant then rubbed on her skin—or perhaps

Ryker's clothes, but then she saw the six fish, dangling by their tail fins, in his fist.

They locked eyes, then Valora's focus shifted back to what she assumed would be her dinner—whether she liked it or not.

"Do you know how to prepare them?" Ryker deadpanned.

Valora, shocked by the edge in his tone, only shook her head before she found the ability to speak. "I don't eat fish."

Ryker tossed three down in front of her. Valora flinched. She severely disliked fish; their scales freaked her out. It was one thing to swim in a lake where she couldn't see them below the water. It was another to have one in front of her, its glassy eyes watching.

"You do now."

When Valora looked back up at Ryker, he met her with a challenging brow. She could tell he did not want an argument, so she didn't give him one.

Tentatively, she reached out to grab the fish. She and Bo had fished with nets, so Valora never needed to touch them. Her brother, on the other hand, had grown skilled enough to reach in and grab the fish with his bare hands, claiming it took less time. Valora had never pointed out the time he spent teaching himself could have been used actually catching the fish the old-fashioned way.

Thankfully, the fish was not slimy at all. Still, Valora took caution when handling it. The shine of the creature's eyes made her wonder if it only played dead.

But when Ryker struck his knife through the fish's stomach, all Valora's worries vanished.

She jumped, fearing Ryker would go too far and put the blade through her thigh as well, but the fish came away clean. Well, as clean as it could anyway. Blood leaked from the puncture wound and soaked into her leggings.

"Just a reminder," he spat, "I'm afraid of water."

They didn't break eye contact until Ryker willed it. He turned on his heels and collected his fish.

Valora gazed down at her lap without the slightest idea of where to begin. She only managed to complete her task by stealing glances at the uncharacteristically silent Ryker, following him step by step until the fish looked like one her parents had brought home from the meat market. If he knew she watched him, he didn't let on.

When Ryker rose from his spot on the ground, Valora couldn't help but notice how slowly he moved. His face remained twisted in pain as he marched around the campsite, searching for sticks sturdy enough to impale his fish with.

With her experience in the recent months, Valora knew how long it actually took a wound as large as his to heal and thought Ryker would too, given he'd been the one to nurse her back to health.

Ryker clutched his wound as he crouched again, still on his mission to find the perfect stick.

Valora set her fish down on a blanket and went to join Ryker in the hunt. He hardly glanced at her when she joined him. Only when she started to move much quicker than he could manage, picking up sticks as well as extra kindling for the fire, did he argue.

"Let me help," he insisted, trying to match Valora's pace. "I'm fine."

"You are not *fine*, Ryker," Valora countered. "You were attacked by a *mountain lion*."

"So?"

Valora wanted to rip him apart and remove his tainted sense of well-being. She couldn't stand men and their insufferable habit of never admitting anything was wrong.

"*So*," she said as she picked a large stick out from under Ryker's hand before he could crouch low enough to grab it, "you go back over there and sit on your rock and brood some more."

Ryker looked down, and Valora swore she saw his lip jut out in a pout.

"I do not brood," he muttered then thrust the few sticks he had managed to collect into her arms. "I am a very cheerful person. Brooding is *your* specialty."

He didn't pull his arms away. She placed her hands atop his, making Ryker break eye contact only to look at where they touched, and tilted her face up to get a better view of him.

"It can be both our specialty while you heal." She nodded toward his rock seat. "Now go."

And so he went, grumbling to himself and lifting his shirt slightly to examine his wound before shoving it back down. Valora smiled to herself. She knew he saw how right she was the minute he glimpsed the mess running across the front of his body.

They went on that way for the remainder of their days in the mountains. Although Ryker insisted many times he could walk back down to his house in the forest, Valora knew otherwise. She'd spent enough time with wounds on her back to know he needed rest. Most of the time, she got him to shut up by throwing his own words regarding proper healing back at him.

As much as she had hated the forest when she first arrived, Valora felt a strange comfort at returning to the darkness, shrouded by trees. The mountains had been too open, and she had felt too much pressure to make sure she kept her shield up—not that she'd done a particularly brilliant job of that.

She watched as Ryker slung the two knapsacks he'd carried down the mountain onto the kitchen table then sank into one of the rickety wooden chairs. He looked exhausted.

Valora unhooked the four she carried and tossed them on the ground.

"You should rest," Valora suggested.

"I rested for four extra days in the mountains," Ryker argued, tilting his head to rest against the back of his chair, his eyes closed.

"You're doing a terrific job convincing me of your outstanding health, Mr. Falkov. Do continue. Or will you need a pillow and a nice fuzzy blanket?"

When he lifted his head, Valora expected Ryker to gift her with one of the icy stares he'd given her each time she tried to treat him on the mountain. Instead he met her with one of his grins. Her heart jumped at the sight, and she tried to hide the reaction. She never thought she'd actually miss seeing Ryker grin.

"Out of everything you could have taken from our trip, it's the memory of my surname?" he inquired.

Valora shrugged. "Kind of hard to forget when a drunk madman keeps repeating it."

She heard Ryker chuckle, and her heart leapt again. As much as she complained about his enthusiasm, that familiar rumble of his laughter comforted her.

"Please go rest, Ryker," she tried again, this time with her head turned so he couldn't see her blush. "You kept me confined to that bed for two rutting months. I'm asking for one more day."

Ryker stared at her back. She felt it—every inch his eyes raked over, burning as hot as his fire. He said nothing in return, though, before he pushed back his chair, the legs scraping against the wood floor.

"Can I expect you to come treat my wounds for one more day?" Valora turned over her shoulder with a raised brow. "I treated you for *two rutting months*—and then some."

Valora sighed deeply. "Go nap. I'll come see you in an hour or two."

Ryker tilted his head at the sacks Valora had tossed on the ground. "There should be enough supplies in there for tonight's treatment. If not, I always keep extra stores in the bins over there."

Valora already knew that, but she nodded anyway. She didn't want the conversation to continue. She wanted Ryker, whose eyelids were beginning to droop the longer he stood there, to go sleep.

Before he entered the shared bedroom, he called back, "Bellemore is a lovely surname. *Valora Bellemore*. Though, if you ask me, Valora Falkov has a nice ring as well."

Valora scoffed but felt her cheeks betraying her with a rising blush. Thankfully, Ryker didn't turn around again. He pointed his finger at the fireplace, set the logs blazing, then entered into the bedroom, shutting the door behind him.

SPLINTERS OF WOOD went flying from the log Valora was

targeting. She thought she had finally mastered the new trick she had spent the better part of an hour teaching herself.

Torches lined the perimeter of the clearing, providing her with enough light to find her targets in the growing darkness. Thus far, she'd managed to destroy most of the firewood and end the lives of a few unfortunate creatures that she and Ryker would later eat for dinner.

The shadow whips could still be enough to handle Juno. As a girl without power, Valora worried the least about facing her again and knew she likely would have to when she next returned to Norlyn. Juno had been one of her best friends—probably the closest to her out of any of them besides Aurelia.

She'd been lucky to survive the first time, but the second time around, Valora didn't plan to show as much mercy.

Days had passed since Valora had last surveyed Norlyn, and she wondered how much, if anything had changed. She and Ryker had left almost immediately after her failed attempt at killing Juno. Valora hardly knew the repercussions from that particular visit but couldn't help chuckling at the thought of what the villagers might think. A girl claiming she'd been harmed while having no physical proof and most of the baker's stock stolen? What kind of ruthless cook could Norlyn be dealing with?

One thing Valora could be sure of, though, was that Aurelia would be ready. Juno's near death solidified the pattern of victims—practically screamed that Aurelia would be the next target if Juno hadn't already warned Aurelia herself.

Facing Aurelia had not initially worried Valora. Her one-time friend held no powers and, for as much as Aurelia liked to brag, Valora knew even Juno outshone the group's leader in terms of physical endurance.

But as Valora stood there, slashing her shadow whips down on wood and wrapping them around the necks of the forest creatures, she grew more and more nervous. Aurelia didn't possess abilities like Valora or Ryker or the twins, but she held other powers. Manipulation, for one. It had not taken mind control to get the rest of the group to follow her plan. She'd managed that with the power of words—of promises that her remaining friends had never seen fulfilled before their demise.

Who could be sure what kind of verbal havoc Aurelia had wreaked in Valora's time away? For all she knew, the entire village could be prepared for her—even without Kent's confirming word—torches lit and pitchforks sharpened. Ryker reported that the Master had heightened warrior presence in the village. They could be waiting for her—she didn't need any additional trouble caused by Aurelia running her mouth.

But how could Aurelia manage to band them all together without admitting her sins in turn? It was why Juno couldn't admit how she'd been harmed the night Valora broke into her room. Now, with Kent gone, no one could speak to the girls' case.

That thought alone kept the little ember of hope Valora possessed burning as she sent another whip down on a log, shattering it to bits.

"Now, what did that poor log ever do to you—other than sacrifice its life to keep you warm and cook your food?"

Valora jumped and spun around to see Ryker leaning against the doorframe. Per usual, he was wearing no shirt, but neither was Valora. She had wrapped bandages around her chest to keep herself in place while she trained but had removed the worn-out cotton shirt she'd put on that morning.

Ryker pushed off the door and strode over to her. Valora couldn't help but glance at his injury as he walked. It looked better. Still brutal—but better.

He watched her too, taking in her sweat-slick skin and hair that refused to stay pulled back neat and tidy in her leather band. The chest bindings hid most of her scars, but Valora wanted to believe Ryker would stare at them just as intently as she stared at his wound.

"I was beginning to think I would need to rescue you again." He grinned. Apparently, all it took was a nap to rid him of a bad mood.

"Why?"

"Not that our lovely surroundings give us much daylight as it is, but I'm pretty sure I fell asleep sometime in the early afternoon." Ryker nodded up to the canopy. "It's definitely dark now."

Valora tilted her head up only to find out he was right. She hadn't noticed with the torches acting as her main source of light. The physical activity had kept her body temperature up as well, protecting her from the increasing chill of the spring night.

She swore under her breath and shook her head. With her body still rising and falling from the effects of what had accidentally turned into a few hours of activity, Valora met Ryker with apologetic eyes.

"I didn't realize," she said. "Do you still need help with the poultice?"

"I think I can manage, but I may need help preparing dinner. And chopping more logs."

Valora peered back at the splinters of wood left scattered around the clearing. She sighed and shook her head again. Ryker was right in front of her when she looked up again.

"What's wrong, Val?" She didn't respond immediately because, honestly, she didn't know why she felt the way she did. So, Ryker continued, "If it's something I did, I—"

He jumped when she hit his shoulder—on his uninjured side.

"Would you stop blaming yourself?" Valora reprimanded him. "Hell, if I was put in a bad mood every time you did something to annoy me, I'd go insane."

Ryker chuckled softly, and Valora moved her eyes away—first to his wound then to the small pile of dead creatures located not too far from where she stood.

He placed a gentle hand on her bare shoulder. Considering how much skin she was revealing to Ryker, Valora felt very self-conscious in that moment—her hair a mess, her body sticky and smelly from her sweat, her very not-flat midriff exposed. She couldn't do anything about her odor, but Valora desperately wanted to fix her hair and put her shirt back on to hide her insecurities.

"What's wrong, Val?" Ryker repeated, much gentler than before, his voice not much more than a breath.

She lifted her eyes to him once more. "I'm scared."

"About committing murder? I thought you would be a seasoned professional by now."

Valora's lips quirked up in the smallest of smiles, but it didn't last long.

"I came out here to train because I missed it," she informed. "I was going to kill an hour or two while you slept then come and help you. But…but I got to thinking and I got nervous. I'm not sure why, but something about facing Aurelia… it's terrifying."

"Aurelia organized the plot to kill you. I would be nervous to face her too."

"You would?"

"Hell yeah I would," Ryker confirmed with a huffed laugh. "And I don't suppose you'll let me talk you out of going against her at all? Two lives aren't enough?"

Valora shook her head. "No. You said it yourself: Aurelia organized the assassination. If anyone deserves to die, it's her. It's just…she has no abilities."

Ryker practically shoved Valora away.

"She has no abilities and you're *afraid* of her? That's not the Valora Bellemore I know. Hell, the Valora Bellemore I know fights mountain lions and *wins*."

"Not before it was too late," Valora muttered, glancing at Ryker's injury. "She became a warrior for a reason. The Master doesn't let anyone without powers join the ranks unless they prove themselves. Juno…her athleticism allows her to outrun anyone or wield a sword better than people twice her size. I never noticed any particular strengths with Aurelia. She tried hard, sure, but…Bo should have been considered for the warrior ranks before Aurelia, and the Master turned him away."

"So, you're nervous because there's something you feel you're missing and don't know what it is?"

Valora nodded. She had spent years as Aurelia's friend—as a friend to all of them. She'd thought she knew their weaknesses better than anything else. She had gotten past Mona and Myrcella by manipulating her thoughts because she knew they depended too heavily on their abilities. Valora had hit Juno right in the conscience. For as willingly as she sided with Aurelia, Valora knew Juno possessed the strongest morals—which apparently Valora possessed some of as well, seeing as Juno still lived.

She almost laughed at that thought. If Juno were the one with the best morals and she had still gone through with the assassination plan, Valora must look like a saint—even with the blood on her hands.

Anything beyond that, she saw as strength. Their determination, wits, confidence—everything worked in her old friends' favors.

Even so, Aurelia fell behind the others. While Valora knew she was in no way perfect, she also knew where she outshone the supposed leader of the pack. Aurelia knew it too. It had inspired the assassination attempt in the first place.

"Tomorrow we'll train," Ryker said, firmly enough that Valora didn't bother trying to argue. "I won't use my abilities for anything other than healing. That way we can simulate what it would be like going up against an opponent without a power."

It wasn't the worst idea Ryker had ever come up with. That title went to the trip to the mountains. Still, Valora saw some issues with it, the first and foremost being Ryker's physical strength that went above and beyond anything Valora knew Aurelia could achieve. She'd spent months seeing his muscles on display while he trained, usually without a shirt. Ryker never tried to hide his strength, even if he didn't always use it fully during their training sessions.

Though, going up against that full strength might prove beneficial. After training with a more challenging opponent, fighting Aurelia would feel like nothing.

"Fine," Valora agreed. She picked up her shirt from the ground and held it in her fist. "But if you burn me even once, I'll find another body of water to dunk you in."

"Then you'll find yourself waking up to a nice, big trout

sharing your pillow."

Valora jumped when Ryker grabbed the curves at her sides. His hands remained there for a moment as they walked back to the house before trailing down to her hips. She swatted him away with her shirt.

A wave of relief overcame Valora when she heard him chuckle. She smiled in return—but didn't dare let Ryker see.

## CHAPTER 23

**THE DARK AND** mysterious forest felt like home after all the time spent in the clearing. Valora had missed the safety of the confinement Ryker shared with her, but she needed to remember she was in no way protected from danger. Plenty of creatures waited to rip her to shreds just outside the covering of the brush surrounding Ryker's home.

It seemed as though Ryker had missed the forest during their time away too. He suggested they venture out into the open and train rather than remain by the house.

"Besides," he added as they walked out the door, "I'm far too injured and you're far too lazy to risk anymore decent firewood."

She hit his chest for that but instantly regretted it, knowing full well that she wouldn't have stood around with an axe chopping firewood for hours. Maybe once she mastered the new technique from the day before she would, but until then, wood-chopping remained Ryker's chore.

Hitting his chest seemed even more unnecessary when the training began.

Once they found a suitable training ground—in Ryker's opinion, anyway—he planted Valora where he wanted her then marched a few steps away. She watched him with a quizzical expression until he took up a defensive stance and unsheathed two daggers.

"Alright. Go," he commanded.

Valora cocked her head to the side. "Are you sure?" She couldn't help but smile just a little at how ridiculous he looked. She had never seen him use weapons.

"Yeah, I'm sure. Just make sure you—"

He didn't get the chance to finish his thought before the shadows Valora sent slithering along the forest floor grabbed Ryker's ankles and took his legs out from under him.

"Good," Ryker complimented through his coughing. "Surprise is good. Just…maybe a little gentler for the handsome, injured fire bender next time."

"Worried about your face?" Valora taunted as she wiggled her fingers, sending the shadows curling around Ryker. More hid behind his back.

"Without my abilities, it's all I have going for me to distract you." He brushed off his trousers then aimed a gorgeous, toothy grin at Valora. "Is it working?"

*Yes.* "Not a chance."

The shadows grabbed him from behind and tossed him to the side, though much gentler than they would have for any other opponent. If it had been Aurelia in her shadows' grasp, Valora couldn't have promised she wouldn't send her flying into the thickest tree trunk in sight. Ryker only ended up in a shrub.

The training went on as such. Ryker made it close enough to Valora to attack with the daggers when she allowed it. Only then did she resort to using physical combat—something she struggled to use against her taller, more muscular opponent, but knew she could succeed in against Aurelia. Though both girls were the same height, Valora had more strength, especially in her thicker legs. She used them to her advantage when facing Ryker, using her lower half to fend him off while her hands kept the daggers at bay.

Nearly a week had passed since the last time they had trained with each other, but Ryker still gave her the same harsh commands as before. This time, though, Valora listened rather than complained. The sooner she did what he wanted, the sooner he would stop his barking. And she would never improve if she argued with everything he told her.

Sometimes Valora forgot Ryker had once trained as a warrior in Norlyn. The way Ryker worked the sparring, guided it where he wanted her to go, showed just how he'd gained his favor with the Master. She wondered how much greater he could have been had he not run away.

"Harder, Val. Harder," Ryker commanded. Valora punched his palms and tried to dodge the random blows he decided to deliver in return. "You're not going to hurt me, but I want you strong enough to hurt that little bitch who gave you those scars on your back."

Valora punched left, right. She ducked under Ryker's swing then got back to it, punching his palms wherever he placed them. Her breath came out in heavy pants while her hair came loose from its tie, some of it matted down to her forehead by her sweat. Her shirt lay discarded by a tree, only this time she didn't care about her stomach or physical appearance. She cared only about improving, about not giving in to her fatigue, and continuing to succeed against Ryker.

When Ryker swung again, Valora acted quickly. She extended her arm and closed her fist. The shadow she summoned wrapped around the hilt of Ryker's dagger. She pulled her arm back and the dagger flew into her grip, guided by the shadow.

All that happened before Ryker finished swinging, while Valora ducked under his arm. When she rose, she put the dagger to his throat and he paused, breathing just as heavily as her. Despite the fatal position he found himself in, Ryker managed to summon a small smile, his eyes flitting to the dagger before they landed on Valora.

"You're going to have to teach me that trick."

Valora lowered the dagger and handed it back to him. "Sorry. It's reserved for warriors with abilities that won't melt the weapon."

Ryker chuckled and replaced the dagger in its sheath. Valora winked at him then went to find her canteen of water. The minute she swallowed her first sip, she froze.

She had learned the ways of the forest as well as any other animal that lived in it, and that included picking up even the faintest of noises. As far as she knew, no animal spoke in her language.

Ryker was at her side in seconds, both their shirts in one hand, the other used to usher Valora into the surrounding bushes. He didn't need to tell her to stay quiet. Valora's nerves prevented her from speaking.

They crouched in a bush, the branches poking uncomfortably

into her side. Valora felt a drop of blood running down her side from where one cut her and wondered how Ryker was faring. When she looked at him, his eyes were focused ahead, entirely concentrated on the approaching voices.

"How much further, Zeke?" a man called out.

"Not much now."

Valora's heart beat violently against her chest. She wondered if Ryker could hear it when he reached for her hand and laced their fingers together. He still didn't look at her, his mouth a straight line, his eyes serious, expectant.

The two men came into view. From what her position among the bushes allowed her to see, they looked like any of the men Valora would find walking around Norlyn. For all she knew, she could have talked to them at the tavern or sold them a candle at her parents' shop.

A wolf howled somewhere in the distance. The man named Zeke didn't seem bothered, but his companion stopped to examine their surroundings, knife drawn.

"Still think this was a good idea?" the scared man asked.

"Nothing like a bit of fright to strengthen our brotherly bonding," Zeke said.

They both stopped not more than a hundred feet from where Valora and Ryker hid. If Ryker had forgotten to pick anything up, they would know they weren't alone.

But Zeke appeared satisfied—more so than his brother who stood shaking with his knife, his nervous gaze darting about the forest.

"We should go, Zeke. There's a reason people don't come here, and I think those wolves are it."

Zeke chuckled. The malicious undertone of it clued Valora

into what was about to happen, but, unaware, Zeke's brother might have found it normal.

"It's not the wolves people have to fear in this forest, brother." He walked back to where the other man, who didn't pay any attention to his brother and certainly not to the knife now in his hand, stood. "In this forest, people only need to fear each other."

Valora gasped when Zeke thrust his knife up into his brother's stomach. Ryker quickly covered her mouth, and she bit down on his palm to keep from crying out in anguish for the man. And as much as she wanted to, Valora could not look away.

Had it been just as easy for her friends as it had been for Zeke? She remembered the feeling of the first knife going into her back and the searing pain that had followed. She remembered blacking out, her last memory being that of her friends walking away, their knives dripping red with her blood.

"Now it doesn't matter who Dad writes his fortune off to, does it?" Zeke hissed. He pulled the dagger from his brother and stuck it in the other side, making a twin mark to the first. "Hopefully he'll be dead before I return. I can't bear to watch him mourn you too. Not after Mom."

Zeke pulled the knife out again and stepped back. His brother crumpled to the ground, blood dripping from his mouth, eyes staring blankly ahead.

Ryker pulled Valora to him and forced her to avert her eyes by cradling her against his chest. Tears slipped silently down her cheeks.

Without another word, Zeke ran from the scene, back the way he and his brother had come from only minutes before.

Ryker waited until the silence returned to the forest before he shot out of the bush and rushed to the injured man. It took Valora a moment to realize what was happening before she ran to join him.

When she crouched beside Ryker, she found him clutching the dying man's hand. So much blood came from his mouth that the man couldn't speak.

"It's going to be okay," Ryker comforted. "Don't worry—it'll all be alright soon."

He moved his hands to rest atop each of the wounds. Valora didn't hold out much hope when she felt Ryker's heat radiating off his hands. The odds of survival would be slim, even with the immediate heat treatment.

A gurgled breath then silence confirmed that mere minutes later.

The heat subsided, and Ryker kneeled, defeated, beside the man he hadn't known, but tried to save.

They sat in silence, Valora holding the dead man's hand and Ryker staring at the wounds he had been unable to heal in time.

She didn't know what to say, so she kept staring at him, hoping the right words would come to her, but none did. All she could think of was the man lying beside her, betrayed in the same manner she had been—stabbed due to the greed of someone he trusted.

"We should bury him before the wolves smell the blood," Ryker whispered. Valora nodded. "You can go back to the house if you want. I've managed this plenty of times on my own."

The statement made Valora's heart break. Ryker had witnessed so much death—had sometimes been the cause of it. Something told her that was the reason he felt obligated to help those who died in the forest. Not only because he was a decent human being, but because he was still consumed by the guilt of an accident that had happened years before.

Valora reached out and grabbed his hand.

"I want to help," she said.

Ryker stared at her a moment before he nodded once.

They spent the next few hours of light silently burying the man they didn't know.

FUELED BY ANGER caused by the stranger's death, Valora set out early in the morning to train in the clearing. Ryker slept a few hours longer, but she didn't care. She wanted him to sleep, to heal, so that he would be stronger when she faced him. Valora was tired of him going easy on her. She wanted a fight.

She had slept very little the night before, her mind filled with the memory of the dying man, of watching Zeke so effortlessly shove his knife not once but twice into his brother's stomach. Valora could never imagine doing something so vile to Bo, and based off his steadfast dedication to defending her, Valora didn't fear Bo betraying her either.

Then she had woken up under warm blankets, the soothing comforts Ryker whispered surrounding her.

*It's going to be okay. Everything will be okay soon.*

Those were the words that had greeted her when she'd first woken afraid in his house. It was the same sentiment he had left the forest's latest victim with as well.

The shadow she wielded sliced cleanly through the log, chopping it directly in two, no splinters to be seen.

A low whistle sounded from behind her and Valora jumped. Ryker strolled across the clearing to examine the cuts of wood, feeling the smooth surface where the darkness had made its cut.

"Remind me never to get on your bad side."

"That's going to be hard."

Ryker chuckled and stood up. Valora noticed the knives already at his hips, and a knapsack slung over his shoulder, filled with what she assumed were canteens based off the sloshing she heard each time Ryker took a step.

"Ready to go?" he asked as he hiked the sack higher onto his shoulder.

"Go where?" Valora wasn't sure she felt safe traveling outside the confines of their clearing after the previous day's events.

"The forest border." Brilliant. "I thought we might do some scouting before our training today."

"And do you expect to climb a tree with that injury?" It had taken Valora months before she had healed enough to climb to her favorite perch.

Ryker smiled. "I was hoping those lovely whips you threw me around with yesterday could find an alternative purpose. You know—like a pulley and rope."

It wasn't his worst idea....

Valora needed to watch herself. She was beginning to think Ryker was smarter than he actually was.

She went along with it anyway. Soon enough—after some adjusting to make sure Ryker was secure in his journey up the tree—the two companions were settled on their branch, watching Norlyn with Valora's darkness shielding them.

Unable to help herself, Valora tried to find Zeke. She asked Ryker for confirmation when she thought she had located him, and when he gave it, she couldn't look away.

Just like her old friends, Zeke seemed to feel no guilt about his actions, though his timing did appear to be perfect. Two men carried a stretcher out of the house Zeke stood outside of, a white sheet laid atop it, covering what Valora could only assume was a body.

She let herself wonder if Zeke had gotten what he wanted—if his father had signed over his entire fortune after the news of the other brother's death. If the murder had been worth it.

A shiver ran down her spine, and she felt the desire to run her fingers along her scars. Before she could let the sudden burst of anger control her, though, Ryker shook Valora from her thoughts.

"There," he said.

Valora followed his intense gaze and found the target they had set out to watch in the first place.

Aurelia went about her normal training routine, except for the first time in her life, no one trained with her. None of the other warriors went near her aside from when the Master instructed them to pair up. Even Juno had distanced herself at the other end of the training ground, facing off against a warrior Valora didn't recognize.

Valora felt a small twinge of empathy. What did it feel like to be an outsider? To be seen as the next link in a line of mysterious nighttime attacks? The other warriors must have been worried sick to talk to Aurelia. Two of her friends had been killed, the other attacked in the night. What if merely associating with her made them the next target?

The feeling didn't remain long because Valora *did* know what it meant to be an outsider—the unwanted one. She knew that better than anyone.

Soon, Valora grew bored. She glanced sidelong at Ryker who scrutinized Aurelia with the utmost intensity, as if trying to pick out anything Valora should worry about when the girls finally faced off.

Valora tried to find something too but came up short. She watched the same old Aurelia—not strong enough, yet somehow the strongest person in the vicinity.

Her shoulders slouched, and she sighed. Maybe she was being irrational about the whole situation. Like Ryker said, she was a seasoned professional when it came to murder, aside from a few mishaps here and there. As terrible as that sounded, Valora knew she shouldn't worry about facing Aurelia. She would go at it the same way she had for the twins and Juno: sneak into the village at night, break into the house, murder without any trace. Or at least with less of a trace than she had left after Mona and Myrcella. The mishaps would only make this part of her mission easier, now that she knew what not to do.

"Don't give up now, shadow bender," Ryker taunted monotonously. His concentration remained on Aurelia. "You're almost done. All you need to do is find out what's worrying you."

"There's nothing different, though," Valora replied angrily. "She's the same warrior she has always been."

The Master called for the end of training, and the warriors dispersed, their professional demeanors replaced with those of normal young adults.

Aurelia sauntered over to a group of guys Valora knew her old friend had previously flirted with one time or another. None suited Valora's tastes but all held a lot of power. Aurelia focused most intently on the one with enhanced strength. Valora rolled her eyes. Leave it to Aurelia to still find time for flirting, despite everything that had happened to her friends.

"Is she always like that?"

Ryker's question surprised her. Valora turned to watch him only to find that he remained focused on Aurelia and her new friend.

"Looking for an easy hook-up?" Valora didn't enjoy the bitterness in her tone.

Ryker turned to her, finally, and looked her over from head to toe. When amber eyes met with hers again, he said, "Not my type." Ryker returned to surveying the village. "It's only that I know her current target. Dante—I…I don't want her using him."

Valora raised a brow and followed Ryker's gaze. Aurelia trailed her arm flirtatiously down the stronghold's arm. All this time she and Ryker had watched over her old friends, but Valora had forgotten Ryker had once lived in Norlyn too. He had a life, relationships aside from that with his ex-partner.

"You weren't the first one who *disappeared* in the forest," whispered Ryker after some time.

She turned slowly to look at him. "What's happened to all of them?" Valora wasn't sure she wanted to hear the answer.

"They die. I bury the ones I find—so, from wherever they watch in the afterlife, they know someone tried to save them." Ryker sighed and turned towards his companion. Valora's heart skipped a beat.

"You weren't the first to be betrayed, Valora. But you were the first with enough strength to keep living despite it."

Ignoring her idiotic stare following his comment, Ryker continued, "Have you found anything useful?"

Valora shook her head, partially in response and partially to clear away the invading thoughts.

"No," she replied. "It's driving me mad."

Ryker nodded slowly. "I noticed she struggles keeping her arms up during fights. It's almost like she isn't strong enough to do so."

"She's never been strong," Valora confirmed. "She's never been fast. She's never been agile. She's always been Aurelia—a smooth, witty talker who somehow manages to always get what she wants."

And with good reason. Valora had always hated being on the receiving end of arguments with Aurelia when she didn't get her way. She was rarely correct, but only Valora had challenged her—stubborn as a mule until Aurelia threw in the towel.

Stubbornness wouldn't be her friend in this fight, though. She couldn't kill Aurelia with a verbal face-off, as much as she wished she could. Although, sometimes Valora had thought her friend would drop dead from embarrassment after the others took Valora's side in an argument.

A snort fought to escape. As petty as they were, the arguments had probably created yet another reason why Aurelia wanted Valora out of the way.

Perhaps she had actually snorted because Ryker turned to her, brows furrowed, and asked, "What's so funny?"

Valora shook her head again, not wanting to explain the dark thoughts that had inspired her laughter. Ryker shrugged it off and went back to watching Aurelia. She soon strolled off in the direction of her favorite tavern with the boys, Dante on her arm.

"She doesn't know you can use whips," Ryker stated casually as he leaned back against the tree's trunk. Valora heard him wince.

She turned on the branch so she faced him, her legs dangling off either side and her hands braced in front to keep steady.

Ryker noticed her confusion immediately and conjured a small fire whip, keeping it a very cautious distance away when he flicked it. Even so, Valora strengthened her shields in order to protect herself from the flame as well as protect them from potential prying eyes.

But he was right. Ryker had mastered the tactic on his own while living in solitude—and he'd correctly assumed Valora could master it as well if she channeled her abilities a certain way. Aurelia would be none the wiser if she used them, and without abilities to use *against* them….

The image of Ryker being thrown into a bush the day before popped into Valora's head. She snorted again and covered her mouth to hide her growing smile.

Ryker's head shot in her direction again. Valora placed her other hand over the first as she fought against the laughter. Occasionally, she failed and a small sound escaped beyond her hands.

"Something *is* funny," Ryker said, pointing an accusatory finger at his companion. "I'm over here trying to help you find your enemy's weakness, and you're caught up daydreaming."

Valora removed her hands, her body shaking with silent laughter, random squeaks sneaking past her lips.

"You—you should have seen your face yesterday," she said between laughs. "When I threw you into the bush."

She broke down, trying to remain as silent as possible. Her shield would hide them from people's vision, but she could do nothing to impair anyone's hearing.

Much to her surprise, Ryker cracked a smile, and his body

shook with silent laughter. Eventually, neither one of them could look the other in the eye without letting some sort of sound escape.

"Shhhh," Ryker reprimanded through his laughter, grabbing Valora's hands and moving them to cover her mouth again. "We're going to be found out."

"And whose bright idea was it to come to the forest border in the first place, fire boy?"

Ryker rolled his eyes and shook his head. Valora still couldn't stop laughing, but it had subdued some. Her hands rested on the branch again, and Ryker moved one of his atop them. Still, she didn't stop laughing, if only to not let onto anything amiss—to her heart beating against her chest like a hammer.

"Let's go back to the house," he suggested. "We're not going to get anything else done today with you so giddy. Would you be opposed to finally baking those pies?"

His eyes were so gentle—for the first time in days. Valora felt Ryker's thumb brush softly over the back of her hand while they partook in their unofficial staring contest.

"It would be a shame to see all those berries and stolen supplies go to waste."

# CHAPTER 24

**AS MUCH AS** Ryker liked to believe he was perfect, Valora had noticed some faults, one of which being his inability to properly measure out the ingredients for his ma's pie recipe.

He failed miserably at it—mostly because he couldn't remember it very well after three years away—and it only made Valora's laughter continue from their time scouting in the tree. Not seeming to care much about making a mess of the delicacy, Ryker laughed with her, the two of them smiling as they argued about how much butter and sugar and salt and flour they needed to make the crust.

Once they decided their mixture would work well enough, Valora moved onto creating the berry filling while Ryker pressed out the too-sticky dough for the crust. When Valora went to get more berries and sugar, Ryker stuck his finger into the filling mix. Valora turned back around to find him with his index finger in his mouth, guilty eyes watching her. When he removed his finger he proclaimed, "Needs more sugar."

The next issue arose when Valora realized she had stolen all the necessities—except the pie tin.

They stared at each other, Valora smiling sheepishly and Ryker trying to keep a straight face. She watched the corners of his lips twitch up, watched his arms hang at his sides while he pretended to be mad until she suddenly found herself dodging a dusting of flour flung in her direction.

Valora shrieked and tried to defend herself only to make matters worse. When she unfolded herself, she found her entire side, clothes and all, covered in white. It clung to her hair, a stark contrast against the black.

Ryker laughed at his handiwork, and Valora scoffed. She flicked her hand through the flour on the table and sent it flying towards Ryker in retaliation. He was quick, though, and already had the bag of remaining flour in his arms.

He dipped his fingers into it and flicked more at his opponent while backing away to the other side of the table, putting distance between them.

No powers, no hostility—just two housemates that had been through far too much turmoil in recent months to care about the mess they made of their home. For the first time since the berry patch they were laughing—truly laughing—and managing more than a few minutes without firing back with sarcasm.

Ryker darted around the table so he appeared behind Valora. She turned quickly, knocking the bag of flour out of his hands and making a giant white cloud float up and coat them. She also fell victim to the sprinkle that Ryker dusted on her face.

She made to hit his chest, but Ryker grabbed her petite hands in his. Before Valora knew what was happening, he moved her arms around his neck, and his lips were on hers.

And she let them remain there.

Covered in flour, the two stayed there in the middle of the destroyed kitchen, kissing each other as hungrily as they had in the mountains. Ryker's arms snaked around Valora's back, pulling her tighter against his body, and she found hers tangled in his hair. It took but one brush of his tongue on her lower lip for Valora to open up for him.

Valora wanted this, she realized as they stood there, as he picked her up and set her on the flour-covered table, never once breaking away from her. Valora had wanted Ryker for months, and he'd made it very obvious he wanted her in return.

But wasn't that how it always began—with such happiness and reciprocated devotion—before Valora found herself pushed to the side? Left for new conquests? Left for dead?

The thoughts flooded into her head so fast. The memories of her friends, her lost love, countless others before them enveloped her so much so that she almost forgot where she was and whom she was kissing.

She wanted Ryker—yes—but he couldn't become another name on her list.

The hurt that swam in his eyes didn't surprise Valora when she pushed him away and hopped off the table. She forced herself to turn away, tired of seeing it so often but knowing she could do nothing to prevent it.

"Why do you always do that?" he inquired after a few moments of silence. Valora didn't miss the biting tone of his voice. "Why—when I think I've finally broken through—do you never fail to close yourself off again?"

"Ryker, I—"

"No, don't *Ryker* me, Val." He was angry. "I'm sick of hearing excuses. You want this. I *know* you want this. So, why are you so determined to close yourself off to me?"

Valora met his stare with tear-filled eyes. His veins glowed with his power, his hands in fists at his sides, and her chest instantly tightened while the rest of her body grew weak. Ryker had already had someone he cared about leave him in the most permanent way, and she was only throwing salt in that wound to avoid being hurt herself.

"It's never my choice—when people push me away," she explained in a soft voice, fighting against her tightening throat. "But they always do. I always end up alone, and I'm tired of it," Valora finished through a humorless chuckle.

The glowing faded, and Ryker's hands eased open. Valora stared into his sad, amber eyes and hoped that he would understand why she couldn't allow herself to get close to him, no matter how much she knew she wanted to.

"Valora," Ryker breathed. "Val, I'm not going to push you away. I…I would never do that."

"That's what they all say." The tears spilled over as the memories of all the people Valora had once cared about came flooding back to her. "They say I'm their friend—maybe that they love me, that we will be forever and always. It's the same every time, then they disappear. Again and again, they leave me."

A shuddered breath escaped her. "This time it's my choice. I'm not letting you come too close because I know I won't be able to handle it, Ryker. Not with you."

His face fell, and his shoulders slouched. Valora watched him struggle for what to say, small noises escaping every so often from his mouth that opened and closed like a fish out of water.

For once in his life Ryker had nothing to say.

And it was the one time Valora needed it, wanted to hear it.

She strode past him into the bedroom, slamming the door shut behind her.

**H**OURS LATER, THE tears began to subside, though the images of Ryker's sorrow wouldn't leave her mind's eye. They replaced those of all the people Valora had once loved. Unfortunately, they were just as brutal.

In an attempt to distract herself, Valora ran her knife against a slab of whetstone, trying to sharpen it. She had already finished three of her daggers and still had two to go. Still, she didn't think she would be settled when she finished.

She couldn't imagine continuing to live with Ryker after that argument, and that realization hit her the hardest. In the mountains, it had been different. She'd played it off as her lust getting the best of her. But the last kiss....

Valora couldn't look at him again, knowing Ryker knew how she felt, and pretend like things were the same. Like she hadn't just confessed her feelings for him.

So, she knew she needed to face Aurelia that night. She needed to kill the last of the traitors so she could return home to Norlyn and leave Ryker behind in the forest for good.

As if summoned by her thoughts, a soft knock sounded on the door. Ryker entered a few seconds later, after Valora neglected to invite him in. He shared the room with her, after all. He could come and go as he pleased. He had always just been too polite to do so.

She smelled the sweet, fruity scent of baked berries the moment the door opened. Valora fought the urge to look up but found she didn't need to when Ryker sat at the end of her bed. The wolf-pelt blanket upon which Valora sat cross-legged at the head of the bed pulled under the weight of its new occupant.

He pushed his gift towards her a moment later, and Valora was no longer left to wonder what Ryker had brought her.

The piecrust was molded around the bottom of the bowl and clung to the rim just as it would a proper tin. The rest of the bowl was filled with the berry mixture Valora had been in the middle of making. Golden-baked strips of the dough crisscrossed atop it—the final piece of the pie's presentation.

It was a makeshift mess so bad that Ryker had brought a spoon for Valora to eat it with, rather than a fork. And he'd made it specifically for her.

Her body shook with the tease of a fresh sob. She made her face go parallel to her lap, refusing to let her companion see the new tears welling in her eyes.

Silence filled the room until Ryker finally said, "The day you tossed me into the stream with those bloody shadow whips of yours, I told you I was afraid of water. I'm a fire bender, after all. Water is the one place I am absolutely powerless—where it's all up to whatever physical strength I have acquired over the years.

"After I...after *she* died, I contemplated only using my physical strength. The last thing I wanted was for anyone I cared about to...to fall victim to my abilities again. I wanted to say *screw it all* to my fear and never wield fire again because nothing—not even drowning or being without the one part of me that brings me the most joy—would hurt more than being without her.

"Then I met you, Valora. I can't say it was love at first sight, because it wasn't. Your attitude annoyed the hell out of me sometimes. But as time has passed…." Ryker sighed. "I feel like less of a monster when I'm with you. You know all my secrets—well, the big ones, anyway—and you still look at me like I'm human. And maybe it's because you're going around murdering people left and right"—Valora couldn't help the strangled laugh that escaped her—"but you never stopped treating me the way you always have. You didn't run or shy away like others would."

He paused, collecting his thoughts, then, "I've wanted you for a long time—just as any man who finds a woman attractive would. I wrestled with my feelings for you for a few weeks before we went into the mountains, then we shared that night where you finally let me hold you—touch you. I knew that night there was something more…more than just want.

"Then Kent came, and I killed him right before your eyes. I thought that would be the moment you ran because it's a hell of a lot different when people see something rather than just hear about it. You had just seen first-hand what my powers could do." Ryker released a shuddered breath.

"When you knelt down next to me and took me in your arms—when you told me I wasn't a monster—I knew I loved you, Valora. And I knew I would never be able to stop loving you."

He stayed quiet, his confession finished. The bowl of pie grew colder the longer Valora stared at it, letting Ryker's sincerity sink in. After she had so cold-heartedly rejected him—again—to find the courage to come to her and admit he loved her….

"Well, now that that's out in the open…."

Ryker sighed as he pushed himself off the bed. Valora still

couldn't meet his eyes but felt words at the back of her throat desperately trying to escape, trying to give back after Ryker had revealed so much.

It took up until the door was nearly shut behind him to finally get them out.

"I'm afraid of spiders," Valora blurted. It was the first and easiest fear she could think of.

Ryker peeked his head back into the room. Now, Valora refused to look anywhere but at his beautiful amber eyes.

"I'm afraid of spiders," she repeated, and he walked back into the room. "There was one the size of a raspberry in the bathtub with me once. I've been terrified of them ever since—and of baths."

Ryker situated himself at the end of the bed again. The way he looked at her—it was clear he expected something more than the revelation of her arachnophobia. She owed him as much.

"I'm afraid of the darkness that goes beyond my powers and…and consumes my mind. All my thoughts," Valora continued. She swallowed audibly. "I'm afraid of the days it gets so bad that I feel like I can't get out of bed."

Her eyes strayed to her lap again, but when she peered up, Valora found Ryker watching her intently.

She moved her knives, whetstone, and pie to her bedside table. When they were out of the way, she inched forward, closer to Ryker. He adjusted himself so he sat angled towards her and not so close to the edge of the mattress.

"I'm afraid of saying the wrong thing to you," Valora choked out, fresh tears falling silently down her cheeks, "and I'm afraid that on the days you get angry enough to stop talking to me…you won't start again."

She was crying again, silent streams running down her cheeks.

"I am so, so afraid of losing you, Ryker," she said. "I know I'm not an easy person to get along with. I'm stubborn and sassy. I always have to be right, and I can sometimes take things too far. And I suppose that's why so many people have pushed me aside—tried to be rid of me for good. I'm just… I'm so afraid you will become one of those people."

He reached for her, wrapping her in his warm embrace. Valora cried into Ryker's shoulder, clutching at his shirt while he caressed her ravaged back and placed gentle kisses on the top of her head.

Everything was out in the open. Everything stirring between them for months—it was out for the other to do what they pleased with the information.

When Valora's crying slowed, Ryker pushed her back so he could see her face. It was a tear-stained mess—her eyes red, her skin blotchy—but he still looked at her as though she were the most beautiful person in the world.

Ryker grabbed Valora's face in both his hands and wiped away the tears not previously soaked up by his shirt.

"You listen to me, Valora Bellemore," Ryker began in a stern, yet soothing, tone. "I will never—*never*—be one of those people that pushes you away, do you understand? The only way you will ever be rid of me is because you can't deal with my constant blabbering anymore and you kick me out on my ass. But it might be better to just keep me around because then I'll be forced to follow you around, begging for you to take me back. As a roommate, as a friend, as a lover—I don't care. Just as long as I have you with me."

Valora couldn't help but crack a smile at the typical Ryker

response. She looked down, embarrassed for whatever reason, and let out a huffed laugh. The sound of it made Ryker smile too.

Watching him from under her lashes, she saw it fade. His hands dropped over hers, and Valora twisted them so their palms connected. Ryker's focus settled on the freshly sharpened daggers on the bedside table.

"You're going to kill her tonight." It wasn't a question.

"I was planning to—yes."

Ryker laced his fingers with hers. "And you think you're ready?"

Valora nodded. Even if her original intentions had included leaving Ryker that night, she still felt ready to fight her one-time friend. The time spent in the tree that afternoon had confirmed her suspicions that there was nothing to fear. She was worrying for nothing.

Ryker pulled her hands onto his lap. "I can't lose you, Val," he whispered before bringing both of her hands up to his lips to kiss them. "I…I can't go through that again—losing someone I love."

Valora sniffled and gently pulled her hands free of Ryker's hold. At first, he appeared worried—as she supposed he naturally would. She had rejected him so often after they'd shared intimate moments that he probably expected it every time. But then she moved onto his lap, straddling him as she had that night in the mountains, her arms around his neck and his snaking their way around her lower back.

"I'm ready, Ryker. I need to finish this."

"And then you will return to Norlyn permanently."

Valora shrugged. "Perhaps. Or…." She ran a hand back through his shaggy brown hair, a grin appearing on her lips.

"You've saved me twice. I have saved you once. Have you heard of that old warrior tradition? About life debts?"

Ryker grinned too. "Are you proposing I call in the debt now?"

"I'm proposing," Valora drawled as she leaned forward, her lips centimeters from his, "that if I live beyond tonight, you can decide what you want to do with that little bit of information."

Ryker chuckled as Valora closed the distance between them.

His arms tightened around her, holding Valora tight against his muscular body while they kissed, picking up exactly where they left off in the kitchen.

Ryker grabbed at the hem of Valora's shirt, and she lifted her arms, only removing her lips from his long enough for the fabric to pass over her head.

He crawled across the bed, carrying Valora the short distance before he placed her on her back. She wanted to complain when he pulled his lips away again only to find herself silenced by him removing his shirt and revealing the muscles below, his skin glowing orange from the fire in his veins, the fire she would never fear.

She stared at the remains of the gashes running across Ryker's front. Valora reached up, running her fingers gently over the raised skin of the nearly healed wounds. His abs tightened in response to the touch, making them more defined.

Valora peered up at him with narrowed eyes and a playful smile, expecting him to grin back at her, but she found his eyes glazed over, looking everywhere but her face. While he kneeled over her, Ryker took in what she'd chosen to expose to him. The same feeling of self-consciousness that had overcome her a few days prior returned, and Valora shrank back, pulling her hand away.

Ryker noticed, leaned back down, and, placing a gentle hand on the side of her face, said, "You're perfect."

And even though she thought of herself as far from such, Valora knew Ryker meant it. For him, she was perfect.

She pulled his head down with the hand she'd placed at the back of his neck. Valora savored the taste of him while she could before he moved to trail kisses down the rest of her body. The memories from the night on the mountain came back to her, and she moaned at the sheer thought of the sensations she knew Ryker could make her feel.

Valora wondered if the heat she felt pulsing through her body in that moment was what Ryker always felt with his power. If so, it was no wonder he always acted so indestructible.

For once, Valora felt none of the darkness that usually overpowered her. She felt only the warmth and protection and security that Ryker promised her with each kiss, each touch, each gentle caress of his fingers and lips on her scars, and eventually each inch where they joined.

She hoped she would never feel the darkness again after that night.

**V**ALORA DID NOT know the time she woke. She only knew that enough had passed for darkness to invade.

She felt Ryker's naked body rising and falling behind her, his breathing relaxed during his slumber. His arm was wrapped around her, holding her against him as if even in his unconscious state he wanted to keep her from going to Norlyn.

Valora swallowed the lump in her throat. She would give anything to stay there with him, to wake in the morning to his cheeky grin, and repeat the night's activities over and over and over....

But she had come too far in her mission to turn back at the end. Falling for Ryker had not been a part of the plan she'd begun formulating the second she opened her eyes alive and in his care. She couldn't let it stop her now.

Careful not to wake him, Valora slowly removed his arm and slithered out from under the blankets.

As she dressed, she realized she would miss not only the man sleeping in her bed, but the house as well. She had gotten used to the simplicity of it, the hunting, the uncomfortable beds, the broken glass Ryker called a mirror.

The forest, no matter how terrifying, had become her home too.

Placing the last of her knives in the belt at her waist, Valora took one final glimpse around the room. Perhaps she wouldn't leave permanently the next day. Perhaps she would wait a few weeks—a month—until Aurelia and Juno's deaths became old news among the Norlynians.

"Val?"

Valora turned over her shoulder to find Ryker sitting up in bed, propped up by his elbow. The glow he had possessed earlier no longer presented itself. Even his amber eyes looked more brown than gold.

He was nervous.

"Good luck," was all he said.

Valora walked back over to the small bed and leaned down, placing a kiss on his lips. She let it linger longer than necessary, if only to memorize the feel of him.

She brushed back his sleep-ruffled hair and replied, "I'll be back before you can miss me."

Valora tried not to take offense to the skepticism in his expression before she walked away, ready to complete the final piece of her mission.

# CHAPTER 25

**W**ITH THE CURFEW in place, Norlyn felt like even more of a ghost town than the last time Valora had visited.

All the village's inhabitants were tucked away in their beds, doors locked, fires burning in their fireplaces causing plumes of thick smoke to rise from every chimney in sight. Temptation got the best of her, and Valora looked to her family's home. No smoke rose from the chimney.

Whatever threat roamed the village at night didn't scare them. Perhaps because the young woman who had once lived under their roof had died long before Valora's targets.

Soon. Soon Valora would live under that roof again, as much as it now hurt to know she would abandon her new home in order to do so.

Before her heart got the better of her, Valora continued silently through the village center, shrouded in her summoned darkness. She made sure to keep it as strong as possible so as not to draw the attention of the warriors on patrol that evening. She didn't want to learn the fate the Master had instructed them to inflict upon the murderous beast terrorizing their village.

The night wind howled around her as she made her way past her family home, past Mona and Myrcella's family home. She peeked inside the window she had broken through nearly two months before. The beds were empty, untouched for weeks, and the floor still wore a faint stain from Mona and Myrcella's blood—the result of a clear attempt to clean it away, but having waited just a little too long, due to the investigation of the human and animal footprints.

Valora didn't linger much longer after she remembered Ash.

It was strange to recall that night when everything had begun. She still remembered the way her lungs had burned as she ran from Norlyn into the forest, relishing its sanctuary. Knowing so many vicious creatures surrounded her had made her actions seem lesser somehow. Just like the wolves and the mountain lions and whatever else lingered in the darkness, Valora did what she needed to survive—eliminating the threats.

She could not return to Norlyn and expect a normal life if the biggest threat still prowled, still plotted, still posed a danger to Valora's well-being.

That would change soon.

Valora saw Aurelia's home in the distance. With only Aurelia and her mother living under the roof, the possibility of getting caught was slimmer than that of the previous victims. Valora need not worry about siblings or family pets.

But there was something different about Aurelia's home—something off.

No smoke billowed out of the chimney.

Valora didn't know what to make of it. Were neither Aurelia nor her mother threatened by the possibility of a killer? Or did Aurelia think she could fend off whatever danger would inevitably come for her in the night—

Her thoughts were cut off by panic when someone grabbed Valora in a tight hold, a hand over her mouth.

Valora wanted to scream, but couldn't. If she did, she would give away her position to the villagers and patrolling warriors. And she doubted her captor would release her when they all came to investigate.

Then, a thought struck her.

Her shields surrounded her, stronger than usual. She should have been invisible—a part of the night.

How had anyone found her? Unless….

Valora's head whipped around and, sure enough, she found the Master—the only man in Norlyn capable of negating others' abilities—staring back at her.

He released her, and Valora took a step back. Knowing he could see past them, she made sure her shields remained fully intact. If the villagers thought the Master had gone mad for speaking to thin air, that would be his problem. She had her own she needed to deal with.

"I knew it was you," the Master whispered.

Valora stayed silent, her chest rising and falling heavily with nervous breaths. Then finally, "How?"

The Master aimed a wolfish grin at her. "I favored you for a reason, Miss Bellemore."

Not exactly the answer she wanted, but Valora would take it. The Master had never been a man of many words—or proper explanations.

"Why didn't you search for me if you were so sure?"

"I may be the most powerful man in Norlyn, but I am still a man. I can be wrong from time to time." He shrugged. His smile faded. "What did they do to you, Miss Bellemore?"

Valora swallowed, the scars on her back stinging, as though they were trying to send her a message. Like they wanted her to reveal everything that had been done to her during that first trip to the forest.

The Master had favored her before, and it appeared as though he still did. He could help her when it came to time to face Aurelia. Her foe would very likely come with back-up as well in the form of Juno. Bringing the Master would be a means of evening the odds.

If that were the case, though, Valora could have asked Ryker to join her.

Just as she'd intended when she first planned her mission, Valora knew she needed to do this on her own, no matter what odds were stacked against her.

She straightened her posture before telling the Master, "They didn't do anything to me that I couldn't handle."

The Master appeared to appreciate that response. "And are you prepared now?"

Valora nodded once. "Yes, Master."

The Master watched Valora with intense, narrowed eyes. Before, she would have shrunk away under that contemplative stare. Now she stared back at him, no longer afraid.

He nodded once in return. "Do not let her deceive you."

He didn't plan to stop her, Valora realized. The Master wouldn't stand in her way of defeating the last of her friends—

the traitors.

She stood erect for the leader of the Norlynian warriors, attempting to show respect, before she turned her back on him, ready to complete her mission.

"Valora." She stopped at the unfamiliar sound of her given name coming from the Master's lips. "He is alive, isn't he?"

Valora didn't need to ask whom he spoke of. She knew that before he'd favored her, the Master had favored a fire bender.

"Yes," was all she said before she continued on her journey through the village.

Her legs refused to stop shaking the whole way. It took only a few minutes after Valora left the Master to arrive at Aurelia's house, yet it felt like she had walked miles.

It would all be finished soon. Aurelia would be dead, she'd find Juno and finish her too, and Valora could return home, see her parents, see Bo. She could return to training with the Master—granted he kept their little run-in a secret from the rest of Norlyn. It would not bode well to return with *everyone* knowing she was the monster that killed the girls.

*You are not a monster.*

But not even those thoughts could stop her from worrying—just a little. The lack of smoke concerned her, and the Master's parting words sent irrational fears poking at her senses—enticing them to listen to the nonsense.

*Do not let her deceive you.*

Aurelia and the others had deceived her for years, making her believe she belonged in their group, before they all finally mustered up the courage to do something about her. The deception had started long ago, and Valora intended to end it that night.

Figuring she had already survived the worst of Aurelia's tricks, despite what the Master had warned, Valora reached for the front door of the house. Her fingers barely grazed the knob before it squeaked open, the haunting sound echoing in the quiet night.

Strange, but it didn't stop Valora from tiptoeing through the entrance—her easiest break-in yet.

After scaling the chimney to get into Juno's home or even after having to run who-knew-how-many miles to escape Mona and Myrcella's dog, Valora would take whatever she got. If that meant entering through an unlocked door, so be it. Add that to Aurelia's lack of powers and Valora figured she actually would return home far before Ryker could miss her—or before he got out of bed.

She smiled to herself at the thought of surprising him, her body full of adrenaline and excitement for having completed her self-assigned mission, as she made her way to Aurelia's bedroom. The door across the hall was closed, Aurelia's mother sound asleep behind it and none the wiser that her daughter would be the next victim of the village attacks.

Damn fools. They were damn fools for not taking precautions. Leaving the door unlocked, no fire in the fireplace—Valora wanted to laugh at their stupidity. She only refrained for fear of giving herself away.

Her mom would have been beside herself with fear, had her dad put a deadbolt on the door, made her and Bo sleep with knives under their pillows, maybe even sleep on the floor of Valora's bedroom if she for even a second thought her daughter would become a victim in a string of crimes.

Aurelia's mother must not have had such qualms.

She reached for Aurelia's bedroom door and turned the knob. Having been shut properly, it let out a soft *click* when opened.

But when Valora pushed the door open, she found the bed empty, the blankets left undisturbed.

Aurelia was nowhere to be seen.

Valora backed away from the room, ready to turn and run from the house when something hard crashed into the back of her head.

# CHAPTER 26

Valora struggled to get up, her head throbbing and vision blurred from the impact of whatever had hit her. When the fog finally cleared, she found Aurelia standing in front of her, holding a thin wooden plank. A smaller figure stepped out from her hiding place behind Aurelia.

Juno.

The former took a few more steps forward, her movements appearing in slow motion while Valora's vision continued to fade in and out from the impact of the blow.

"I was wondering how long it would take for you to show up," Aurelia taunted, hitting the plank against her palm.

A little bit of red streaked the flat side of the wood. Valora hoped it was paint, but when she reached her hand up to touch her head, it came away stained with blood.

Aurelia let loose a dark chuckle, any sign of the girl Valora had once considered her friend vanishing. Only the sadistic killer that had lured Valora into the forest remained. Juno, so far as Valora could tell, stood weaponless and silent while she waited for what Valora was sure to be some sort of cue. They'd likely starting planning this attack the day after she'd fled from Juno's home, preparing in case Valora decided she wanted to finish her mission.

She'd never been more determined to do that than she was in that moment, her head spinning, her legs trembling with the desire to get moving—to end it all.

"You have perfect timing, actually. Mom was excited to visit her brother at first, but I think she's getting restless in Black Hallows—especially knowing her only child is home alone while a murderer is on the loose." Aurelia stalked towards where Valora struggled to get off the ground. "You took longer to visit me than you did the others. Distracted? Or frightened?"

Healing was more like it, but Valora didn't say anything. She leveled the iciest glare she could muster at her opponent—who had unfortunately managed to take an early lead.

"Are you sure it was only healing?" Aurelia continued, answering Valora's unspoken thoughts. "I could have sworn I was catching another scent *all over you*."

Valora's head still spun, but she didn't think it had been a strong enough hit to make her lose her sanity—up until Aurelia made that comment. She inhaled deeply through her nose, trying her best to pick up the scent of alcohol that usually lingered around Aurelia. She came up with nothing.

An evil laugh rumbled in Aurelia's throat. She shook her head and took a step towards Valora. "You're so predictable, Val. So, so predictable."

She swung the plank again, but Valora rolled out of the way, pulling a dagger from her belt at the same time she lifted herself onto her feet. Her vision was still coming back to her—or at least she hoped there weren't truly three Aurelias and Junos in front of her.

With so much concentration needed to remain steady, Valora knew she couldn't use her abilities yet, not if she wanted to stay on her feet.

She angled her knife at Aurelia, ready to partake in physical combat if her opponent got too close.

The three Aurelias slowly faded back into one smirking girl holding her plank, knives at her hips, as if she had been as ready for the fight as Valora. Juno, likewise, materialized into one figure once more but wearing far less weaponry than Valora would have expected.

Before Valora could think much on it, Aurelia came fast—too fast—and knocked Valora back with one devastatingly strong, backhanded blow. She crashed into the wall of Aurelia's bedroom and toppled to the floor in a heap.

That hit—Aurelia couldn't have delivered something so strong. And the speed—when had Aurelia gotten so fast? Valora would've missed the movement if she had blinked.

No—those were qualities of speedsters and strongholds. But no one person ever held both abilities. No one in Norlyn held more than one ability, and if anyone did, Valora would know. Although not every citizen with an ability became a warrior, they all knew of one another. After so many years of training, Valora had imagined she knew or heard of all the Norlynians with any sort of power.

But it didn't stop at the enhanced strength or speed. No—

Aurelia had read her thoughts. She had *known* Valora thought about her time spent healing, then countered with a remark about *scenting* someone on her.

"Keep going, Val," Aurelia taunted, stalking across the room with her usual air of confidence. "You're almost there."

Again. She had read her thoughts again.

Now Valora knew it was not the blow to her head making her hallucinate.

Enhanced strength and speed and smell. Telepathy. The first three surprised Valora but she understood the correlation. The telepathy…it threw off her intuition.

Valora thought back to everything she had learned with the Master—everything about all the abilities of Norlyn and beyond. Her education had taught her it was near impossible for a child to be born with more than one ability. Rare cases occurred when a child's parents each possessed powers, but even then, some hybrid version of the abilities was passed down.

Valora had never known Aurelia's father, but Aurelia's mom held no power. Aurelia's genetic makeup held no chance of a hybrid ability. The possibilities of other powers though…without knowing if or what Aurelia's dad had possessed, the possibilities were truly endless.

Strength. Telepathy. Speed. Scent.

Valora wracked her brain for the next option. If Aurelia's father possessed powers, perhaps they had gone undetected—like Kent. Aurelia could have similar powers—Valora had to piece them together just as Ryker had when they dealt with Mona and Myrcella's uncle.

The twins stuck in her head. Had they known Aurelia had shared their ability, among others? Did *anyone* who shared similar abilities know Aurelia was an equal match? Valora knew of two speedsters in Norlyn. Then there was the boy, Dante, with enhanced strength that Aurelia had gone home with earlier that afternoon—

Valora's eyes popped open, and the Master's warning ran through her brain on repeat. *Do not let her deceive you. Do not let her deceive you. Do not let her deceive you.*

Because Aurelia had deceived her for years. Not only with their friendship but with her abilities. She had deceived *everyone* for years. No wonder the Master had let her join the warriors. It didn't matter that Aurelia was not as physically strong as the others—he'd seen right through her abilities. He saw Aurelia for what she was and knew he had one of the most coveted abilities in his ranks. He had an—

"Energy vampire," Valora breathed.

And not just any kind of energy vampire—a *residual* energy vampire. Aurelia could hold an infinite amount of abilities within her being after only coming in contact with the original owner once. The originator would never know what happened, but Aurelia, should she choose to take a bit of their power for herself, would hold that power forever.

Aurelia's smirk proved Valora's conclusion correct. With a quick glance in Juno's direction, it was clear the secret had been kept from her as well.

The energy vampire dove for Valora again, but this time she reacted to the speed. She jumped out of the way before Aurelia laid so much as a finger on her, two daggers now in her hands. The Master had often paired her with speedsters as opponents in training, so Valora knew somewhat how she might defend herself against that particular ability. But paired with the others....

Valora willed her thoughts into nothing, repeating the same bland statement or thinking nothing at all, just as the Master had trained her to do when facing off against Mona and Myrcella—just as she had when she'd killed them. But it was harder said than done, especially when tasked with trying to figure out how to escape.

*I favored you for a reason.*

Valora kept that thought in her head as motivation and as a reminder that she knew how to fight each of the abilities Aurelia possessed—or at least the ones she had displayed thus far. There was no telling how many abilities Valora would find herself fighting against that night.

"I thought, with all your analyzing all the time, you would piece everything together sooner. I can't believe the Master never gave it away, either. He always told me he valued my ability, but he thought others might be scared of me if they found out what I was capable of. That I would drain them—which I have, of course, but never in full. Besides, there are other reasons they should be afraid of me. You know all about that, don't you, Val?

"Yet you still came into this fight thinking you would kill me in a matter of seconds." Aurelia put her arms out, bent at the elbows and palms upraised. "That might have worked for Mona and Myrcella—almost for Juno"—her grin became sinister—"but never for me."

Valora prepared herself for what would come next from Aurelia, and to her great horror, her ex-friend presented the one ability that had never betrayed her.

Her own.

# CHAPTER 27

THE SHADOWS ADVANCED at an almost embarrassing pace, indicating that perhaps Aurelia had not mastered them in their entirety. But it still took Valora a moment to remember that she could shield against this attack even more easily than she could any of the others.

She whipped her hand out in front of her, sending the shadows away from her, then clenched her fist, willing them into her control.

They moved back towards Aurelia, shifting from the loose, mist-like form they had previously traveled in, into the sturdy whips Ryker taught her to summon.

Juno must have remembered her last encounter with the whips and tucked herself into the corner, while the energy vampire used her speed to dodge them just before Valora willed them to ensnare Aurelia's limbs. The next attempt proved just as unsuccessful with Aurelia using the stolen power to fight against the shadows, trying to pull them back under her command. Valora felt the wall pushing back against her summoning as Aurelia tried to steal the power from her, both of them vying for control.

Suddenly, Valora was knocked to the side again, her breath leaving her in a *whoosh* as Aurelia ran past, quick as lightning. The blow, though only delivered by Aurelia's palm, caused a much greater reaction than it should have, given the stronghold abilities in play. Valora's body, still not recovered from the first few hits with the plank and working mostly on adrenaline, struggled to find the strength to get back up—and keep control of the shadows.

"Come on, Val," Aurelia taunted. "Juno told me all about your fun new tricks. I was expecting to be more impressed, considering you almost killed her with them."

Valora dared a glance to the corner where Juno resided, her hand trembling as it clutched the one knife she kept on her person.

A foot connected with her side, and Valora was forced to look away, her breath stolen from her once more. Wheezing coughs escaped her while she tried to get back to her feet, to gain control of her shadows.

She would not fall to these girls. Not like this. Not again.

"The weakest link in the group and you couldn't even kill her, huh, Val?" Aurelia continued, standing over Valora. "Maybe you aren't as strong as the Master thought, after all."

The next kick prevented Valora from arguing that she *was* strong. She'd survived—and she'd do it again, as soon as she beat out Aurelia for the control of the shadows.

Valora dared another glance at Juno. This time, their eyes met, each of them having their own reasons for the tears brimming within them.

"C'mon, Val—get up," Aurelia goaded. "I want a proper fight this time."

Valora continued to summon the shadows while she took great heaving breaths. Aurelia attempted mastery of them too, but her distress over not being able to do so showed plain as day across her face. She might have used other abilities to get Valora down, but in that moment, she was still only second best to Valora when it came to controlling the shadows.

Aurelia's lip curled in a sinister smile.

"This will be even more satisfying the second time around," she whispered before reaching into her belt and removing a knife.

Valora stared at the weapon, brought back to that day in the forest, when she'd been kicked and shoved and stabbed in just the same way she had that evening. She couldn't fail again. She *refused* to fail.

But maybe…maybe she wasn't meant to succeed, no matter what others told her about her power and her skill. Maybe Aurelia was meant to finish everything that evening instead.

The wall that pushed against Valora as she tried to gain full control crumbled at the same time Aurelia did. The energy vampire fell to the ground, unprepared for the blow to her head that came from the same wooden plank she'd used on Valora not long before.

Valora pulled all the shadows towards her as she stared wide-eyed at Juno, the bloodied plank clutched in the girl's hands.

Juno might have been the only one in the group without abilities, but that didn't make her the weakest link. The girl didn't need the strength of a stronghold or enhanced speed to win at sparring.

Just like she'd underestimated Valora, Aurelia had also underestimated Juno. And just like Valora, Juno was done being the victim of slander.

The girl's attention shifted from her victim, still moaning and struggling on the floor, to Valora.

"Go!" she shouted. Juno moved to the window, and with a great heave, shattered it with the plank. "Get out now!"

Wasting no time, Valora pulled the shadows around her, shrouding herself in complete darkness, utterly invisible to anyone else, before she hopped out the window. She felt the sting of a fresh gash on her leg, then the blood running from it. She hoped her leather leggings prevented the glass from going as deep as it could have, but as she ran through the village, the amount of pain left her unsure.

She hardly made up any ground before she heard a shriek and a crash from the house she just escaped. Then came the sound of a door being ripped off its hinges. There was no way for her opponent to know her location—except through her enhanced sense of smell. Valora didn't think Aurelia would steal power from the Master to negate her shadow-induced invisibility entirely, but then again....

They needed to get outside of Norlyn. They needed to go where Valora held the upper hand, where Aurelia would struggle to use some of her powers and Valora would find hers at full strength.

She needed the darkness of the forest.

Valora tried not to pant as she continued sprinting for the comforting sight of the forest edge. She felt a rush of wind go past her every so often, but refused to unveil herself, even if Aurelia already knew her position.

The forest edge grew closer, closer, and Valora pushed through the pain in her leg. She wondered how terribly it was bleeding—if the scent of it was allowing Aurelia to track her. But she could not stop. She had to make it through each painful step, as she propelled herself forward. Faster, faster, faster—

Something hard slammed into her, and Valora lost her footing. She fell to the side, tumbling in the half-dead grass just outside of the forest's edge, her shield fading, giving Aurelia full exposure of her location.

The energy vampire stopped running and watched Valora on the ground, a low, sinister chuckle rumbling in her throat.

"Not fast enough, Val," Aurelia taunted. "Now to finish what I—"

Valora's eyes flew wide open when Aurelia went flying backwards, the smell of the burning leather of her jacket filling Valora's nostrils.

Her head whipped around to find Ryker stalking out of the forest, his arms ablaze up to his elbows, and his eyes gleaming with wrath.

Suddenly, all the stories Valora heard of fire benders in the past made sense. The rage that joined their fire existed, but Ryker had managed to push it aside—conceal it out of his fear for harming anyone he cared about.

That no longer rang true.

Ryker looked ready to kill.

"What are you doing here?" Valora asked as Ryker helped her to her feet, his flames temporarily doused.

Aurelia struggled to fight against the fire as it ate away at the fabric of her white shirt and smoldered on her brown leather jacket. Valora wondered how she had withstood the fire at all. When Ryker set his target…well, Valora was just thankful she would never be the target. If Aurelia was still alive, Ryker must have intended it.

"You told me you'd be back before I could miss you," Ryker replied. Despite the situation they found themselves in, he managed one of his grins. "Seeing as that happened the minute I heard the door shut, I thought I showed a lot of restraint waiting as long as I did before chasing after you."

He would have gone all the way to Norlyn, Valora realized. Ryker would have stepped foot in the village that had haunted him for the first time in three years to make sure she was safe. The thought made the corners of her lips curl with a smile, until her leg began to throb, and Aurelia groaned on the ground.

Both Valora's and Ryker's eyes shot to the girl. He removed his arms from around Valora, whom he'd been trying to hold upright, and they immediately caught fire. She threw her shadows around him, making the blaze invisible to those awoken by the noisy escape from Aurelia's home.

The fireball Ryker had shot at Aurelia had burned through enough of her shirt that they could clearly see the burns that marred her skin. Ryker appeared proud of his work for a moment—before Aurelia's skin began to heal itself. His face dropped immediately.

"Terrific," he said. "She's a regenerator."

"She's a residual energy vampire, actually."

Ryker looked down at Valora with wide eyes then back at Aurelia. He nodded once. "Even better."

Aurelia made it back to her feet, glowering at the pair in front of her, while her body continued to heal itself.

"You found yourself a fire bender, huh, Val?" Aurelia inhaled deeply through her nose then smirked. "The one whose scent is *all over you.*"

Each step Aurelia took towards them, Valora and Ryker took one back, making sure the distance separating them remained.

"So she has regeneration and enhanced smell," Ryker said, analyzing whatever details he could. "Anything else I should be aware of?"

"Enhanced speed, strength, telepathy, and shadow bending," Valora informed him. Saying everything aloud made Aurelia even more threatening.

"So she's an ability whore."

"Yup."

"Got any idea how to fight her, sunshine?"

"Not even a little. You got anything, fire boy?"

Aurelia growled—the sound more terrifying than an angry wolf—and looked ready to pounce again, her burns entirely healed.

"I think I might have something." Ryker nodded.

"And that is?"

Aurelia charged and Ryker reacted, casting out a wall of fire over the dry, dying grass.

"Run. Very fast."

He doused one of his arms and pulled Valora with him as they ran away from the spot where his wall remained to trap

Aurelia.

Valora glanced back over her shoulder to find Aurelia struggling to find a way through the wall of fire. It seemed no matter where she went—no matter how fast—the fire obstructed her path.

Ryker tugged at her shoulder while they ran.

"Haven't you learned not to look back by now?" But he did the same and swore under his breath.

Valora followed his gaze just in time to see Aurelia run through the fire. Her clothes caught a few small flames that sputtered out quickly, her skin healing immediately where the daring move had caused it to burn.

Repeating the same vulgar word as Ryker, then turning to face forward again, Valora pushed on, willing her injured leg not to give out. In an attempt to help it, she summoned a shadow whip and wrapped it around the injury like a brace.

They crossed over the forest's edge just before Aurelia rushed in after them. Neither Valora nor Ryker slowed their pace, running further and further into the complete darkness of the dense trees.

This would be the second time Valora had gone into the forest with Aurelia, but unlike the first time, Valora vowed to make sure Aurelia knew who held the upper hand. Unlike the first time, only one of them would walk away with their life.

**VALORA FELT THE** rush of wind with each pass—each taunt from Aurelia that she would catch them. She found it miraculous that, at such a speed, the energy vampire could navigate the forest with such skill. Even at an average human pace, Valora found herself stumbling over roots and low bushes, hidden from her in the dark of the night.

Ryker caught her arm just before she toppled, tripping over yet another fallen branch, and pulled her along. If either one of them fell behind it would mean stopping to fight. Valora knew, with the way her leg throbbed, she wouldn't be able to start running again.

Suddenly, Ryker was no longer beside her. It took Valora a moment to register what had happened before she saw Ryker slam into the side of a tree. He clutched his side from his spot on the ground, groaning in pain.

Aurelia stopped running and stalked over to him.

"I've never been with a fire bender before," Aurelia drawled. She turned her head halfway over her shoulder so Valora could hear clearly as she said, "Is he good in bed, Val?"

Before Valora could think of an intelligent retort—or any words at all—Ryker sent another fireball at Aurelia.

She yelped, and it turned into a full scream when Ryker dove for her, tackling the energy vampire to the ground. Valora ran towards them, wanting to help, but wasn't fast enough. Aurelia grabbed Ryker's shoulders and flung him to the side as if he weighed no more than a feather.

Valora watched him tumble back over a large, upraised root before she set her focus on Aurelia. The energy vampire waited, a confident grin on her lips.

"C'mon, Val. Show me why you're the Master's favorite."

It would always come down to that. Aurelia wouldn't rest until she fell into as much favor as Valora. The Master *knew*

Aurelia's secret and still neglected to favor her.

Without any indication of her plan, Valora summoned the darkness, hardly moving her fingers at all. In the night, only Valora knew where the shadows moved—felt them as they traveled towards Aurelia in silence.

Ever so casually, they wrapped themselves around Aurelia's ankles and tossed the energy vampire against a tree. It was just as satisfying as Valora had thought it would be to watch Aurelia connect with the trunk. Even more satisfying to hear the accompanying crack of bone.

The regeneration allowed Aurelia to rise far quicker than she should have under normal circumstances, but it still gave Ryker enough time to find Valora again. His arms were ablaze, his deadly stare leveled at Aurelia. Valora fought the urge to wipe away the blood that dripped down his face from a wound hidden by his hair.

Aurelia graced them with another animalistic growl, then charged to fight.

It became easier, despite the many abilities used against them, when Valora and Ryker worked as a team, their abilities utilized in tandem. One fireball followed by the whips holding Aurelia back, preventing her from using her speed and strength. When she managed to dodge both, Valora and Ryker were ready, meeting Aurelia with physical combat, albeit much weaker physical combat than she delivered to them.

Valora could see the anger in Aurelia's eyes when she came close enough. It killed her to remain second best, to continue to fall short to the girl she thought she had managed to kill—and to see that same girl had found a powerful, fire-bending ally.

Ryker looked ready to pull Aurelia off Valora when suddenly

Valora fell victim to one of Aurelia's powerful blows. She flew backwards, luckily not into a tree. When she sat up again, Aurelia was breathing heavily, as was Ryker.

Valora made to get to her feet but stumbled. The blows and the blood loss were getting to her.

Aurelia noticed the hesitation and smirked. She said nothing before she took off, running around Ryker in a circle.

At first, he tried to defend himself, throwing fireballs at where he thought he could catch Aurelia. But the longer Aurelia ran, the smaller his ammo became until it faded to nothing at all.

Valora watched in horror as the flames that covered Ryker's arms shrank and sputtered out, then as he began coughing, clutching at his throat in desperation.

Aurelia was stealing his air.

Valora panicked and tried to run towards them, but stumbled again, barely managing to stay even slightly upright before she found herself on the ground again.

"Stop," she rasped. "Stop."

But Aurelia did no such thing. She continued to create her vortex around Ryker, cutting him off from any hope of summoning his fire—and of breathing.

Valora crawled forward, using whatever dwindling strength she still possessed to try to get closer to where Ryker kneeled, gasping for air.

She threw out her shadow whips hoping one would catch Aurelia to no avail.

Ryker was dying right before her eyes, and she couldn't muster up enough strength to do anything about it. The man who had saved her—who had given her another chance at life—could not be saved in return.

He fell to his side, no longer grabbing at his throat, his body rising in heaving attempts to collect whatever air he could. Aurelia still did not stop running.

Valora's eyes and throat burned as she watched the life sputter out of Ryker. He had done nothing—*nothing*—but save her and protect her and train her and love her, and now he was dying at the hands of what should've been Valora's problem because of it.

If only she hadn't set out on her stupid mission. If only she had listened to him when he'd warned her to leave well enough alone.

Anger surged through her body and Valora fell to the ground, her forehead touching the cold floor of the forest she called her home. She couldn't watch Ryker die. She wouldn't let him die.

*It's going to be okay.*

*Everything will be okay soon.*

She didn't know where the power came from, only that she felt it surging through every inch of her being, filling her veins the same way Ryker's fire filled his.

Darkness erupted.

The wave of shadows that came from Valora knocked Aurelia to the side. It engulfed the energy vampire, trapping her inside the darkness the same way Valora had always been entrapped by it. Now, she let it free. Letting all that had once confined her—controlled her—be controlled in return. The darkness had always been her strength, and it had taken Valora too long to realize what everyone had always known.

She glanced at Ryker, lying on the ground, unconscious. She couldn't tell if he was breathing.

The shadows came from her, flowing out of her skin,

transforming her obsidian hair into flowing wisps of smoky darkness, turning her already dark eyes pitch black. Only when Aurelia sat up and got her first real look at the monster Valora had become did the shadow bender know how much power truly coursed through her. Pure fear shone on the energy vampire's face at witnessing what she'd tried, and failed, to put an end to.

Valora had become a nightmare of true, unconstrained power that Aurelia would never escape from.

Valora lashed out, sending more than just whips out to grab Aurelia. As fast and as strong as the energy vampire was, Valora's shadows were faster, stronger.

Aurelia struggled in the hold, her once-confident eyes filled only with terror.

On the ground nearby, Ryker coughed as his lungs refilled with air, but Valora didn't let it distract her. She continued letting her shadows consume Aurelia.

They went down her throat, choking her, while others wrapped in coils around each of her limbs and neck. They flowed from Valora like water in a river, ready to do as their master bid them.

Ready to kill.

Valora closed her fists and heard Aurelia gasp when the hold tightened. Her fingers twitched helplessly, trying to take control of the shadows, but not even the little bit of stolen power could overthrow Valora's utter authority over the darkness.

The shadows lifted Aurelia into the air and Valora felt no remorse as she conjured new, stronger whips and sent them clear through Aurelia's body like spears. Like the knives that had once similarly pierced Valora's body.

Aurelia's body shook as the impaling continued, through her

sides, her stomach, and her back. With each new jab, Aurelia's body moved accordingly, flung left, right, up, down, as the shadows attacked her. Valora sneered as she sent a series of whips into the exact spots where she knew she wore scars on her back, feeling as little remorse as she imagined Aurelia had felt. Crimson waterfalls cascaded onto the forest floor from each new wound, soaking into the ground the same way Valora's blood had.

Ryker sat up, watching as Valora finished, once and for all, the task she had set for herself.

With eyes as dark as her shadows, Valora stared at Aurelia, suspended in the air, her mouth gaping like a fish out of water, the life not yet sucked from her completely.

Valora bared her teeth. "No hard feelings, right?"

One final shadow spear went through Aurelia's back, and when it emerged from her front, it held her heart.

# CHAPTER 28

AURELIA'S HEART DROPPED to the ground, released by the grasp of the shadow whip. Valora watched it with her darkened eyes until the bloody organ came to a rolling stop, then she dropped Aurelia's body atop it. Regenerator or not, no one could come back from having their heart removed.

The darkness receded back into Valora's body, seeping back into her pores and disappearing wherever it normally resided beneath her skin. Her hair recovered its natural texture and sheen, falling gracefully down her back. And when the last of the shadows disappeared—when the whites of her eyes appeared once more—Valora sucked in a deep gasp of air.

She was exhausted, she realized, and teetered on her feet, the pain from before her power surge hitting her like a club to the head.

Valora felt herself beginning to fall.

"Whoa there," Ryker said as he took one large step forward, catching her just in time. Valora had been unaware he'd even made it to his feet again.

"Ryker?" she rasped.

A small smile spread across his lips. "You say that like you've forgotten me, and we both know that's impossible."

Slowly, he lowered them both down to the ground, allowing Valora to take the weight off her injured leg. He crouched with his legs spread in a vee while Valora sat up, her back resting against his inner thigh.

She reached up tentatively and placed a hand on his cheek. It was warm and flushed with life.

"You're alive," she whispered.

Ryker brushed some hair back from her face. "Thanks to you." He placed a kiss on her forehead. "Consider your debt paid."

Valora chuckled and shut her eyes, resting her head back on Ryker's leg. She desperately wanted to sleep, but knew neither she nor Ryker had enough strength to get back to the house quite yet.

"You did it, Val," Ryker whispered while he brushed a soothing thumb back and forth on Valora's cheek. "You did it."

She sat up slightly to look at the form of Aurelia's body, silhouetted in the darkness, before she lay back down with a groan. Ryker chuckled.

"What do we...what happens to the body?" Valora asked.

She knew Mona and Myrcella would have received proper burial from their families. Not that Aurelia necessarily deserved any special treatment after the hell she had just given Valora and Ryker, but....

Ryker stroked her cheek again. "I hear there are some

wonderfully vicious creatures in this forest that can take care of it for us."

Valora couldn't believe she laughed at something so dark, even if it was probably the weakest laugh she'd ever emitted.

It faded into a sigh, and Valora laid her head against Ryker's leg again. Sleep…she needed so much sleep.

"I want to go home," she whispered.

Ryker asked no questions about which home she spoke of before he scooped Valora into his arms. She felt his legs shaking under her weight, his own strength not quite at its peak, but knew she couldn't make it back to the house without his help.

The first few steps felt like they were difficult, but soon Ryker found his rhythm. Neither one of them looked back at Aurelia's body as they departed. Hopefully Ryker was right and some creature would make a nice meal of it.

They enjoyed a comfortable silence for the beginning of the trip, both of them too tired to muster the energy for even the simplest conversation. Every so often Valora peered up at her companion, at the eyes that stared straight ahead, focusing on where they needed to go. She guessed Ryker would collapse if he didn't set his target.

Then he caught her and grinned. Valora's cheeks flushed, and she felt the rumble of his chuckle.

"I've gotta admit, Val," he began. "That whole queen of darkness thing you did back there? Kind of turned me on."

If she weren't so weak, she would have smacked his chest. Instead, while Ryker beamed and laughed, knowing full well he could only get away with a comment like that while Valora was out of commission, she shook her head and shut her eyes, letting herself fall asleep in his arms.

**V**ALORA WOKE SAFE in bed, covered by wolf pelt blankets, to the comforting sounds of the forest leaking through the walls of the small house. They had greeted her every morning in the two months since Aurelia's death.

As sincere as her intentions to leave had originally been, she'd found the idea difficult the day following the battle—and not only because she'd woken up wrapped in Ryker's arms, curled against his body while he slept peacefully behind her. Valora truly didn't have the strength to walk more than the distance to the outhouse. Even then, she felt as though she had pushed her limits.

Ryker wasn't much better. He found out the next morning—after sleeping on his side, his body curved around Valora's all night—that the pain he'd decided to ignore turned out to be two broken ribs. Valora assumed he would have dealt with the pain, passing it off as nothing more than a bruise, if she hadn't called him out for shuffling slowly across the kitchen.

So, while he remained bedridden, Ryker treated Valora's leg. Just as she had hoped, the leather leggings had provided decent protection from the glass. Compared to the other injuries she'd received recently, the one she'd obtained while hopping out of the broken window looked like nothing more than a papercut.

When she felt she had regained enough strength, Valora took over the chores that Ryker usually handled. He tried relentlessly to get out of bed and help her, but until the bones set, Valora didn't want him moving. The heat therapy wouldn't work on his ribs the way it worked to clot his blood and heal open wounds.

Still, Ryker did sometimes manage to convince her to allow

him a little bit of freedom, most often in the form of sitting at the kitchen table watching her skin squirrels and rabbits for meals. Valora hadn't tried to hunt for a deer yet, not sure if her weak leg would allow her the speed necessary to do so.

On one of her hunting trips, though, Valora did venture to where she and Ryker had battled Aurelia. At the time, only a week had passed. No signs of the fight remained—not even a body.

With the image of bloodthirsty forest creatures in mind, she'd quickly left that particular part of the forest and never returned.

After two weeks, Ryker began to question her about her plans to return to Norlyn. The pain in his gaze only subsided when she assured him it wouldn't be until she knew he could take care of himself again. Oddly enough, the injury got *worse* after that. At least until Valora's constant nursing began to annoy Ryker, and he worked up the nerve to tell her to leave him alone. After the *months* she'd put up with him telling her this and that about proper healing, Ryker ended up refusing the same kind of coddling.

The next week, Ryker seemed to forget his desire to be left alone—Valora didn't feel like arguing that he actually forgot about it five minutes after he initially made the request—and suggested Valora, with her recovered strength, push their two beds together.

Valora, having missed the feeling of Ryker lying next to her at night, obliged.

It took some getting used to, partially because she had never shared a bed with someone night after night and partially because she was afraid she might accidentally elbow Ryker in the ribs while she slept. If she did, he never said anything about it.

With Ryker sleeping on his back, she escaped easily in the mornings. Valora often snuck out of the house before dawn to start her chores, but when her leg regained its full strength, she took some detours.

Norlynian life went on as usual, though she did see a lot of locksmiths adding extra security to many of the front doors and windows. It looked like some households even installed thicker, sturdier glass. Not that it really mattered. As far as Valora was concerned, the break-ins and silent nighttime murders were finished.

She sat on her favorite perch, hugging her knees to her chest, as she watched the villagers go about their days. Aurelia's mother had returned from Black Hallows and wore the same sad expression as Valora's family after her disappearance. All of the family members of the dead girls did.

Valora wondered if any of them knew the kinds of girls that had lived under their roofs, eaten at the same dinner tables, slept in the next bedroom over. Had they known their daughters and sisters had such sinister intentions before their untimely and mysterious deaths?

She didn't let herself dwell on it. Valora had seen the sorrow that losing a daughter and sister had placed on her own family. The only difference was that she would return. Mona, Myrcella, Aurelia—they were gone forever. And Juno…she continued to go about her daily life, the lucky, lone survivor of the attacks.

But, two months later, Valora still didn't know exactly when she would make the triumphant and miraculous return to Norlyn.

Ryker was healed—or very close to it. He went back to his normal life in the forest, joining her to chop firewood, hunt, clean. Yet neither of them mentioned the improvements. Neither of them wanted to admit Valora could leave should she wish.

She sat up, clutching the blankets to her chest to cover herself. Ryker had left her alone in the room, having already gone out for the day, so Valora didn't have a reason to hide the sad stare she gave her already-packed bag. It had sat in the corner for weeks, packed and repacked again and again as Valora continued to extend her stay at the house in the forest.

But how much longer could she and Ryker keep pretending there was a reason for her to remain there? The last thing she wanted was to leave him, but she could still visit, couldn't she? Valora could go back to Norlyn, live with her family, work at the candle shop, and sometimes disappear for a few hours to return to the forest—to Ryker.

Only if her family allowed her out of their sights, of course. Something told her that after almost nine months of being believed dead, going anywhere without a chaperone or without having to check in every hour seemed unlikely.

Valora groaned and let the blankets drop so she could run her hands down her face. She could think of no way to return and continue her relationship with Ryker. She needed to choose—the family she had been dying to return to or the man she had been willing to kill for?

**V**ALORA FOUND RYKER at the kitchen table when she finally emerged from the bedroom, the bag with her few belongings slung over her shoulder. He looked up when he heard the door open, grinning like a fool, but lost all interest in her when he noticed the second knapsack she carried at her side.

His face fell, and he focused on nothing but the second bag as Valora stood in the doorway to their bedroom. She refused to speak first, but it appeared Ryker had the same idea.

Seeing as neither of them felt inclined to say anything, Valora made the first move and walked around the table. Ryker pushed back his chair to make room for her, and Valora took a seat in his lap. His arm snaked around her waist and hers draped around his neck.

They stared at each other in silence before Valora leaned down and placed a loving kiss on his lips. She let herself linger for a moment before she pulled away.

Ryker's free hand slid up to cup her cheek at the same time that Valora whispered, "Come with me."

His throat bobbed. "Valora…" he whispered back. "Are you sure that's what you want?"

Valora paused, then nodded. "I don't want you to be another name on my list."

"Not the kill list, I hope."

The corners of her mouth twitched with the tease of a smile. "No, not the kill list. Never the kill list."

The darkness of her eyes stared into the fire of his while Valora waited for Ryker to give his answer. She knew her request had a high chance of being denied. He'd trapped himself in the forest for a reason, and leaving wouldn't be easy for him. It wouldn't be easy for either of them. But Valora wanted to see if he would do it—if he'd keep the promise he'd made the night of Aurelia's death. Valora wanted him in her life, as a friend or lover or roommate—she didn't care. Ryker just needed to be there.

However, that couldn't happen if he remained in the forest

while she went back to her family.

Tears started to brim in Valora's eyes the longer she waited, until one finally spilled over. Ryker's thumb caressed her cheek as he wiped it away.

"You want me to come with that bad, huh, sunshine?"

Her lip trembling, Valora nodded.

"Well," Ryker said, then leaned in to kiss away another tear, "it's a good thing you already have my bag packed."

Valora sat back in his lap. "Wh-what?"

"I just really wasn't in the mood to pack everything up. It will probably take a few trips to get *everything*, but—"

"No, Ryker," Valora interjected. "Y-you're coming with me?"

Ryker chuckled, the grin he'd worn when she had first entered the kitchen returning. Valora stared at him in awe, unable to tear her eyes away, even as he leaned down to kiss her.

"I told you once I needed an extremely good reason to return to Norlyn after all these years," he said when he pulled away. "I've found it."

Valora was glad she was sitting, because she wasn't sure her legs would be able to support her. Ryker was going to return to Norlyn. He…he was going to return to the village and face whatever horrors he had been running from, face his parents, face the speculation of where he had been for the past three years *for her*.

Whatever dread awaited them in the aftermath of the murders and disappearances, they would face it together.

She pressed her lips firmly against Ryker's. Valora felt him chuckle as he pulled her to him—felt his smile as well as her own fighting to break through.

"Let's go home."

# CHAPTER 29

So MUCH TIME had passed since Valora had seen Norlyn in the daylight—at least from level ground. She could only see the tops of houses and buildings, most with smoke billowing from their chimneys. The wind carried the sounds of children playing, warriors training, the daily life of Norlyn to her ears, and Valora's heart began to race.

She was going home. She was really going home.

Ryker's hand wrapped around hers, and she pulled her eyes away from the looming sight of the village to look at where they touched.

"You ready for this?" he asked.

Valora gazed up at him. Per usual, Ryker didn't appear outwardly nervous. She figured his heart was beating at a speed similar to her own, but nothing of his physical appearance let his nerves show.

She smiled softly and nodded. Ryker smiled back and gave her hand two reassuring squeezes before saying, "Then let's go."

At first, no one noticed the two faces that strolled into the village, as if they hadn't spent a significant amount of time away, living in the forest that sent chills down the spines of any intelligent Norlynian.

They walked casually, hand-in-hand, bags slung over their shoulders, doing nothing to draw attention.

No, what drew the attention was the way the Master suddenly halted his training when they passed, a smile spreading across his lips, and his students followed his gaze. Disbelieving whispers and gasps rushed through the warrior ranks like a tidal wave.

Valora tried not to focus on any of the awestruck faces of her fellow warriors as she locked eyes with the Master. She returned his smile and he offered his approval with a single nod before refocusing his attention to the other warriors.

It was no use.

They rushed to Ryker and Valora, enveloping them in hugs and a flurry of excitement. The two were forced to separate if they intended to return the sentiment with just as much fervor.

She had missed these people, Valora realized. As more and more warriors came to greet her, she understood that while they may not have been her best friends, these people cared about her. And when she caught sight of Ryker embracing the strongman, Dante, a few others surrounding them, it brought a tear to her eye.

No matter how outcasted they had felt, Norlyn would always

hold a place for Valora and Ryker.

"Val?"

Valora turned from her current conversation to find a small figure emerging from the warriors surrounding her. Everyone fell silent at the sight of Juno.

The small girl's eyes brimmed with tears, and on her forehead, Valora noticed the scarred remnants of a trauma injury. It matched those which she had also sustained from Aurelia.

Valora opened her arms in truce, and Juno rushed into them, her tears immediately soaking into Valora's shirt.

"Your secret is safe with me," Juno whispered as they embraced.

"So is yours," Valora assured her.

It was for the better that they—and Ryker—would be the only ones that knew the details of what had happened all those months ago. The other girls would be forgotten in time, and so would the terror of their actions.

"Valora?"

She pulled away from Juno at the sound of the familiar voice. Just outside the training grounds, Bo stood with his friends. All the boys wore their shock, plain as day, on their faces. All except for her little brother who looked ready to weep.

Valora left Juno and pushed through the crowd to get to her brother. The minute they embraced, they both allowed themselves to cry.

"I thought you were—I thought they—"

"Shhhh," Valora soothed, running her hand down the back of his hair. "I'm alright. Everything is alright."

And she knew, as she said it, everything truly would be.

A warm hand found her shoulder, and Valora pulled away

from the embrace to find Ryker standing behind her.

"This is the infamous Bo?" he asked, and Valora nodded.

Ryker extended his hand to Bo. "I hope we can talk more later," he said. "I have to go find my parents. Are you okay on your own, sunshine?"

Upon looking around the group of warriors surrounding them, her brother, and the Master, Valora knew she was more than okay. She nodded.

"I'll be taking him, then," said the stronghold, Dante, popping up behind Ryker. A few other young men joined, all beaming with joy at the reappearance of their long-lost friend. "But can I be the first to say, we all cannot wait to get to know Ryker's new—"

"Not now, Dante," Ryker interrupted. "Just…let's go find my parents."

"Oh, we're going to make sure that happens."

Valora, her face stiff from crying, broke into a massive smile as the stronghold picked Ryker up like a sack of potatoes, flung him over his shoulder, then took off running through Norlyn with the other boys, shouting, "Mr. and Mrs. Falkov! We have a surprise for you!" at the top of their lungs.

Valora didn't realize how intensely she was watching the show until Bo elbowed her in the side.

"That your boyfriend?" he teased.

Nine months without knowing where she was and Bo still had the audacity to tease her about such frivolous things.

She missed it more than she'd thought she would.

Valora laughed and wrapped her arm around her brother's shoulders. He smiled at her as he returned the gesture.

She was finally safe. She was finally home.

# EPILOGUE

"Mama B, has anyone ever told you you make the most delicious roast chicken in all of Norlyn?"

Valora chuckled as Ryker helped her mom clean off the dinner plates. He had decided to stay for dinner—again. Not that her family minded. Ryker sticking around happened so regularly that the Bellemore family found it strange when the fifth chair at the table sat empty.

"Cut the crap, Ryker," Imogen retorted, making Ryker burst into laughter. "Besides, it's Papa B you should be sucking up to."

Jeffrey Bellemore grumbled from his seat at the table. Valora's eyes slid to her dad just in time to see him steal a glance at the small diamond ring on her left hand. The decreased length of time that he stared at it before returning to the newspaper indicated he was adjusting to the idea of his little girl's engagement.

"Dad's pissed," Bo piped up from where he continued to push his dinner around his plate.

"I am not," Jeffrey defended himself, suddenly uninterested in whatever new taxes were due to plague Norlyn. "There is no one I trust more to take care of your sister than Mr. Falkov."

Valora felt two hands on the back of her chair. She tilted her head back to find Ryker grinning down at her.

"I'm honored, Papa B."

Valora waited for some kind of response, but none came. When she looked at her dad again, she found him indulging in the paper once more. She shook her head and laughed silently at the normalcy of it all.

She had found it challenging to adjust back into the day-to-day life of Norlyn at first. Valora had forgotten what it was like to have stores, to have restaurants, to have more than one person around her at any given time. And if *she* felt the need to kill and eat every squirrel that ran through the village, she only imagined what kind of adjustments Ryker had dealt with.

But after the first week, he'd seemed perfectly fine—spending time with his parents, with old friends, at warrior training where he and Valora often got yelled at for sneaking away to steal kisses.

It had shocked no one—except Valora—when he had proposed a month after they returned. Apparently saving each other's lives on multiple occasions and falling hopelessly more in love each time was solid grounds for such a rushed engagement—or so Ryker said during his proposal.

Valora agreed.

Aside from Ryker's companionship, coming back from what everyone had thought was certain death made Valora the most popular girl in the village. She found a new group of friends to spend her time with, even though she knew the possibility of some of them fading away existed. Juno attempted to speak with Valora from time to time, but Valora couldn't quite bring herself to trust Juno fully. They remained cordial and they kept the secrets they had promised they would, but Valora knew that friendship would never be the same. Besides, she enjoyed the company of her new friends far more than her previous ones.

No one spoke of those girls. The moment Valora had returned, it had been clear they had all lied about what happened. And from what she and Ryker picked up as they passed by the village gossips, it seemed everyone in Norlyn agreed those girls had had it coming.

"Trying to get rid of that sweet girl and telling her family she was dead! What a nasty thing to do!"

Valora and Ryker's upstanding reputations kept them from any lingering suspicions, as did Juno's miraculous survival. It was hard to pin the deaths on Valora when not all the girls who had wronged her had died. Only the families of her old friends disagreed. Not that Valora particularly blamed them. She wouldn't want to believe she shared the same blood as a murderer either.

Even so, Valora made special care to avoid those families. When she did have the misfortune of running into them, it usually took a casual, friendly comment from Ryker to get her out of the potentially problematic situation.

"Would Harmony like any more candles?" Imogen asked as she continued to clean up from dinner.

"I'm sure she would love them," confirmed Ryker.

"Lavender?"

"Yes. Those are her favorite."

"They're Val's favorite too."

Ryker peered down at Valora again from his spot behind her chair. "You don't say...."

Valora rolled her eyes. Ryker chuckled and bent down to kiss her forehead before he returned to his seat beside her.

"Mom, are we still going dress shopping this weekend?" Valora asked.

"That's all that's left. Are you two sure you want such a small ceremony?"

"Oh, yeah, we're sure," Ryker assured her. Imogen never argued against what Ryker said.

"Does that mean you have your honeymoon planned?" Jeffrey asked without looking up from the paper.

Bo made insinuating noises and wiggled his eyebrows. Jeffrey set his paper down and lightly hit his son's shoulder with the back of his hand, but Bo didn't seem to care.

"We have," Ryker confirmed and grabbed hold of Valora's hand under the table.

"Well, are you gonna tell us about it?" Imogen pressed.

Valora and Ryker continued to look at each other adoringly, their hands clasped, small smiles tugging at the corners of their lips.

"It's a secret."

Because only the two of them were crazy enough to visit such a place for their honeymoon. Only they would make the first adventure of their marriage one that so many people feared. Only they would want to spend their first days as husband and wife in the darkness, surrounded by bloodthirsty creatures in a small house in a clearing.

Only they would dare to return to the forest.

# ACKNOWLEDGEMENTS

So much time has passed since I wrote the first draft of *From the Shadows*. I let this manuscript sit on my computer for almost four years, and I never thought I would make it to this day, where I'm writing the acknowledgements for a story that means so much to me. A story that is now out for the world to read.

I have to start with the obvious: Mom and Dad. Thank you both so much for always being there for me, for giving me advice even though you guys admitted you didn't know much of anything about publishing, for trying to learn as much as you could along the way, for supporting me throughout this whole process, for getting just as excited as me when I showed you the proof copies of this book, and for just all-around helping me achieve my biggest dream.

Thank you to my little brother, Jimmy, for always having my back and for promoting this book to everyone he ever came across on the University of Dayton campus, even though it was not even close to being released yet. Maybe you'll actually read this book, Bubs? Probably wishful thinking….

Thank you to my wonderful, beautiful friends: Marie, Meghan, Ellie, Cassie, and Emily. You are all the best friends I could have asked for, and I am thankful every day to have you in my life. You guys have taught me no matter the distance or where life takes us, true friendship will last.

Thank you to my beta readers: Lang, Chloe, Meghan, and Marie. Your feedback helped me shape this story into what it is today, and I am forever grateful. Also, I'm sorry, but Ryker is only one person and cannot possibly date you all at once.

Thank you, Carolyn, for your advice, guidance, and support while I decided what I wanted to do with this story. I cannot thank you enough.

Thank you to Ashley at Green Thumb Editing for turning this book into a work of art. You helped me realize just what this book needed to improve, and you understood my characters even better than I did sometimes. Thank you for taking your time to have Zoom calls with me to go over feedback, and for turning my messy writing into something people can enjoy. Also, thank you for gushing about my characters with me before anyone else really could!

Thank you to my proofreaders, Emma and Camilla, for helping me put the finishing touches on this book.

Thank you to family and friends who left me encouraging messages and/or helped me spread the word about this book each time I shared an update. All your support always brought the biggest smile to my face!

Thank you to my colleagues at work for checking up on me and my writing journey, and for showing so much enthusiasm for my projects. You all made me feel like I was doing something really cool, when in reality I was just staring at a computer screen and drinking a lot of coffee by myself.

Thank you to the Instagram writing and bookish communities, especially Maggie, Lang, Chloe, Kim, Emilie, Jennie, Emily, Jessica, Vivian, Gee and so, so many more (literally, I could go on forever) for pushing me to keep going and providing endless support. Each like, comment, share, and message meant the world to me throughout this entire writing and publication process, from first draft to actually receiving a physical copy of this book. Whether you joined me at the beginning of the journey or you just joined recently, I appreciate you so very much.

Thank you, Anna, for bringing Valora and Ryker to life with your beautiful art—on more than one occasion!

And, finally, the biggest thank you to anyone who read this story. As an indie author, having you take a chance on my little book baby means the world to me. Readers like you are the reason I am able to fulfill my dream, and whether or not you actually enjoyed what you read, know that I appreciate you taking that chance.

## STAY CONNECTED

Want to be the first to hear about new releases from McKenzie Burns? You can follow her on Instagram (@kenzie_writes) and Twitter (@kenzieeburns).

Printed in Great Britain
by Amazon